BEARSKIN DIARY

BEARSKIN DIARY

A NOVEL

CAROL DANIELS

 NIGHTWOOD EDITIONS

Nightwood Editions
P.O. Box 1779, Gibsons, BC, V0N 1V0, Canada
www.nightwoodeditions.com

COVER DESIGN: Carleton Wilson
TEXT DESIGN: Mary White
COVER IMAGE: "Stealing the Light" by Carol Daniels

Printed and bound in Canada

Canada Council   Conseil des Arts
for the Arts   du Canada

BRITISH COLUMBIA
ARTS COUNCIL
An agency of the Province of British Columbia

Canadä

Nightwood Editions acknowledges the support of the Canada
Council for the Arts, which last year invested $157 million to bring
the arts to Canadians throughout the country. We also gratefully
acknowledge financial support from the Government of Canada
through the Canada Book Fund and from the Province of British
Columbia through the BC Arts Council and
the Book Publishing Tax Credit.

Cataloguing data available from Library and Archives Canada
ISBN 978-0-88971-311-6 (trade paper)
ISBN 978-0-88971-077-1 (ebook)

This book is dedicated
to the memory of
Lilly Daniels – Wapimaskwa Iskwew (White Bear Woman)

REMINISCE (AWARD SPEECH—OCTOBER, 2015)

Everyone in this grand ballroom has come to hear her speak. She appears elegant and filled with pride. She appears to have always been strong and self-assured, a woman who has never misstepped along her pathway. She speaks:

People are always asking me to tell them my story. All I know for sure, is that time passes so very quickly. It's hard to believe I officially retire this week. Some ask whether there was a turning point in my life. That one is easy to answer. I stumbled across my old diary this week, but I don't need it to look anything up. Every detail is still fresh in my mind, like it all happened days ago. Mine is a story about falling from grace, finding grace and learning the value of gratitude and humility. I have faltered many times. It is the things we cannot see that have given me strength. My story begins in a place with so few redeeming qualities.

—I-Maskwayanakohp-Iskwiw (Bearskin Robe Woman)

REMNANTS, 1984

Twice a month Sandy and Ellen meet up for girls' night, a night to themselves to celebrate being young and beautiful and free. Girls' night usually starts with a nice, spicy meal at Meeka's, their favourite Greek restaurant. But not tonight. Plans have changed because of Ellen's overactive libido. Sandy feels compelled to hold her breath, hold her nose and hold her purse tight to her body. She's embarrassed to be making her way into a sleazy cowboy bar, still in disbelief that she let Ellen talk her into coming here.

A couple days back, Ellen mentioned that she'd met a gorgeous saddle-bronc rider from Wainwright, Alberta. He was visiting Regina for Agribition and the championship rodeo. That's what brought him swaggering into the tourism office where Ellen works. "Where's the best place to go for line dancing in this town?" he asked, winking and smirking at the same time.

It made Ellen blush, accentuating the colour of her long red hair and amber-coloured eyes. Ellen was eating lunch at her desk and had just taken a bite from her tuna fish sandwich when she looked up to see his eyes, as black as frying pans, and his smile, dancing like aurora borealis. Her nerves caused her to wipe the sides of her lips in case some mayonnaise had squished out. She stuttered an answer to him: "The Den"—a downtown bar with a dubious reputation, but that's what came to her mind.

It's also why Sandy stands here now, wondering how to describe the Dancin' Den. Every city has one, a place where anything goes on a Saturday night. Drunks shout loudly at every table, and drug dealers sit quietly in the corners waiting to pounce on potential customers. They are also waiting to pounce on anyone who might pay attention to them or spot them a free drink. Each table has a terrycloth topper with an elastic bottom that quickly snaps off to be washed at the end of the night, a wise housekeeping decision. Sandy doesn't want to think about what's been on them.

Like its brethren across the country, the Den attracts all kinds.

Bikers.

Suits.

Horny married men who tell you they're single.

Affluent people.

Street people.

Nice girls.

Bad boys.

Sometimes the lines are blurred.

Upon entering, Sandy notices her reflection in the mirror that is hanging at the entryway. The glass surface is covered with smudges and dirty fingerprints. Still, it reflects her soft, brown skin and long hair pulled back in an elaborate braid. A few tendrils outline the shape of her small oval face. She's wearing a navy-coloured sweater dress, which is the fashion rage this season.

But it is a violent rage greeting Sandy in the Den foyer. An over-weight and greasy-looking man in his mid-forties is bleeding from the nose. Two bouncers push him out the door into a waiting cab. If he wasn't so drunk, he'd surely be swearing.

Sandy has heard about the Den. Some say it's a fun place to go. In the next breath they admit there are other times you hope not to get stabbed there. It has a personality all its own. Sandy figures it's probably female and subject to mood swings. Maybe it's a personality influenced under the sign of Gemini—the twins can be either sacred or profane, or a combination of both. Tonight Sandy hopes for the sacred. She gets the profane, feeling assaulted the moment she passes the threshold: the bass guitar is turned up too loud, its thumping taking her breath away like somebody is sitting on her chest.

She remembers stories of the Old Hag. Sandy's Baba used to scare her into staying in bed at night by telling her about the mythical spirit. "If you don't obey your parents, the Old Hag will show up while you're sleeping. She'll sit on your chest and draw out the life force. So always be good and do as you're told."

Grandmotherly advice—now Baba rests in peace. Of all the people in her adopted family, Sandy was closest to her Baba. The comforting memory makes Sandy think she should turn around right now and go home, but she can't. She'll feel guilty. She promised her Ellen that she'd be here by 11 P.M. The unwritten girl code—you can stand up a guy but never a friend. Sandy skitters toward the bar, averting her dark eyes. She doesn't want to catch anyone's attention and give the impression she might be interested.

The skinny guys with tight jeans and oversized belt buckles size her up anyway. They're out hunting tonight. That's what they call it, wanting and willing to fuck just for fun. But to Sandy it's empty. Intimate touch with no intimacy. What's the point? They all look ridiculous to her. Besides, she's wary of anyone who wears an over-sized buckle. Empty men raised on powdered milk. Her disinterest doesn't stop them from brashly approaching her; Sandy can only guess it's because she's an Indian girl. "A couple of beers and you girls always put out," someone actually says. She can't stop herself from asking if he wears his huge cowboy hat to cover up his bald spot. He calls her a bitch and staggers over to where another Indian girl is sitting. She dances with him.

It's already five minutes past eleven. *If I don't see Ellen in the next ten minutes, I'm gone*, she promises herself. Clutching her small beaded purse, Sandy finds a seat at the bar, noticing that the tip jar contains only pennies. An indication of tonight's clientele? She thinks it's a sign to just get the hell out. But she orders a glass of wine instead. The bartender seems okay, kind. She wonders whether he has a regular day job. He looks out of place here and has rough calloused hands like a farm worker. He gives her the wine, calling her "Miss" and hurriedly turns to pour a pint for some other thirsty patron.

Just as she reaches for the stem of her $2.50 red wine, someone's smoke ring drifts into her eye. It prompts a craving for a cigarette, even though she's been trying to quit. She pulls a piece of gum from her purse, popping it into her mouth and checking her watch. *Where the hell is Ellen?* She taps her fingers, glancing toward the newly introduced shooter bar. Ellen likes tequila, so she could be over there. Finally Sandy notices her, looking awkward and stumbling in her direction. Ellen resembles a flamingo tentatively avoiding reptiles in the swamp. The colour of her lipstick matches her fluorescent pink sweater. Her large hoop earrings are fuchsia too.

Ellen gives a quick wave, trying not to spill the beer she's carrying—but that task is impossible. Tiptoeing at the edge of the polished hardwood dance floor, a short, well-groomed couple bump into her. Maybe it's because Ellen is so tall, almost six feet, that the couple can't miss. A bit of the brew splashes onto Ellen's left breast. She's too embarrassed to wipe it off her sweater, leaving a stain for the remainder of the evening like a breastfeeding mother suffering leakage.

Once she arrives where Sandy is seated, Ellen smiles and makes an announcement: "I just met this really cute guy over there and I asked him to come sit with us. I hope you don't mind." But Sandy does mind. It's girls' night out and she is only interested in the company of her friend. She'd rather stick pins in her nipples than do the small-talk thing with some stranger. Grimacing, Sandy's memory races back in time to a similar bar scene a year ago.

Some guy had come over to strike up a conversation, but really he was just annoying, his comments intrusive. "You must be a parking ticket, because you have *fine* written all over you."

She'd heard the line before and always responded the same: "And you are like a warm cup of milk on a cold winter's night. Too bad I'm lactose intolerant."

It was obvious he wasn't smart enough to realize she'd just told him to fuck off. He kept hanging around so she tried another skill, using her body language to get the message across. She put her hand over her forehead, rubbing her temples, and closed her eyes as if suffering a bad headache.

He still didn't get it, telling her, "For a quarter you can get a couple of Tylenol out of those dispensers they have in the bathroom. You know, the same place where you buy the condoms." He smiled, revealing yellow teeth, and proceeded to tell her how he knows about the Tylenol in the girls' washroom, as if she cared. "My last girlfriend used to get migraines all the time," he said. *Smart girl*, Sandy thought, adding aloud, "I gotta pee." She left him quickly and without hope.

Memories of guys like that don't make her keen to meet a new one tonight. That is until she sees the guy Ellen has invited over. He's impossible not to notice. Sandy would remember every small detail upon meeting Blue Greyeyes. It's an odd name and Sandy wonders if he's from a big family—maybe his parents didn't want to spend too much time choosing a name.

Blue. His name reminds Sandy of someone she knew as a child, growing up in her small town. From a local farm family with ten children, his name was Seven because he was the seventh child born. Maybe Blue is named after the colour of the sky the day he arrived. Maybe something else. Maybe Blue's mother was sad, in a blue mood, when he was born. As Blue comes closer to where she is sitting, her melancholy is replaced by intrigue.

Confident. It's the first word that Sandy thinks of as a way to describe Blue. He reminds her of a deer exuding both grace and strength, a rare combination for a man. Blue is tall and lanky with broad shoulders. Sandy wonders what he does for a living to be so impeccably groomed. He flashes her a broad, white smile, lighting up as their eyes meet.

"Hi, I'm Blue and this is my friend James," he says gesturing toward his friend. Such a contrast. James is the opposite of Blue. His look is hard and mean, a deep frown line accentuating one eyebrow. His skin is like rice paper, so white and thin it appears he might be suffering an iron or vitamin D deficiency. James' dirty blond hair is wiry and misshapen like he slept on it and neglected to use a comb.

"Thanks for letting us join you," Blue says, sliding onto the seat next to Sandy. His leg brushes up against hers. Is it an accident? She doesn't know. But she isn't inclined to move, hoping the physical contact, albeit innocent, is an unspoken gesture that Blue finds her attractive.

He leaves nothing to guesswork, making a joke that clearly indicates his interest. "So I hear you like sex on the beach? Gotta love these new shooter bars. Such names." He laughs. "Sex on the Beach is the name of the shooter your friend told me to get for you," he says, handing Sandy a small glass filled with a silky-white liquid that makes her think of semen.

"Ellen... That information is supposed to be private." Sandy winks.

Blue smiles, raising his glass. "Here's to new friends. Would you like to dance?"

Normally, Sandy would shoot out a terse and flat "No" at having just met someone new who is obviously intent on picking her up, the same dismissive and aloof way she did with the skinny yellow-toothed guy. Tonight, though, is different. Blue is different. She nods her head and smiles. "Yes, I'd love to dance."

He takes Sandy's hand. When they get to the dance floor Blue sparks her delight. He does not lightly cup her hand. Instead, his long, brown fingers deliciously intertwine with hers. "You like country music?" he asks, sliding his arms around her thin waist.

She lies. "It's all right, I guess. But I don't know how to two-step."

Blue moves his hands slowly toward the small of her back, touching just the tip of her long black braid. "That's okay. Neither do I."

The music begins and Sandy puts her head on his broad, muscular chest. The perfect comfort as she nestles her face in reminds her of a pillow that she could get used to sleeping with every night. He wears a scent that smells of spice. It suits him. She closes her eyes and breathes him in.

But the tired waitress stops serving drinks. The band stops playing. Closing time comes too soon. "It's time to head back to the dorm. We should go," James spits out, more like a command than a suggestion. His surliness is expected. Even Ellen had commented that James acted like a jerk all night long.

"Rude prick," Ellen whispers. "Only capable of delivering insufferable discussion about nothing. Or worse—negative conversation about everything."

Sandy nods in agreement. She doesn't like James either, especially after overhearing a comment he made to Blue that she was not meant to hear: "Hey Blue, these brethren of yours here are likely to be our future clients. Best you get to know their faces now in case they've lost their ID next time you see them." James puked out a cackle, toasting toward a group of Native men sitting in the corner.

Sandy is inclined to confront such attitudes, but has held back. She doesn't know if he and Blue are close friends or just colleagues. Besides, being combative at the start rarely makes a good impression. "For God's sake, is he blind or just plain stupid?" Sandy whispers to Ellen. "He's sitting here with two other people who are clearly Aboriginal. My lord, the man's got no forehead!"

Ellen grunts, agreeing that James has not evolved from the Neanderthal era.

James aside, Sandy doesn't want to say good night to Blue. "You can come over for tea, if you like. I'm not tired." She invites everyone at the table, though her comment is directed toward Blue.

He seems to know that. Ellen does too, and she knows her cue. "Hey Sandy, thanks. But I'm kind of tired so I'm heading home. Give me a call later in the week." Ellen winks. Her saddle-bronc rider never did show.

"Hey James," Blue says. "You head back. I'll catch up with you tomorrow." James scowls and heads toward the door. Sandy is relieved to see him go.

EARLY WORRY SYSTEM

Sometimes Mother Nature has a twisted sense of humour. Tonight she cracks a half-moon smile and scatters a light skiff of snow on the ground. It covers up icy spots on the sidewalk and Sandy slips, most ungracefully at a time grace is the only thing she wants to exhibit. She might have chipped a tooth, bruised her chin or even broken her nose if she continued to fall. Instead she feels the softness of a down-filled sleeve—Blue's parka crinkles as he reaches out to grab her.

"Whoa. Just about took a nose dive," he says. "Here, you may as well hold my arm for the rest of the walk home." Arm in arm with Blue feels blissful until a memory sneaks in, intent on causing harm.

How old was Sandy when her mom first allowed her to visit the city by herself? Fifteen? Her older foster-sister Mollie had just started a job as a Safeway cashier. The store wasn't far from Mollie's small apartment, just a short six-block walk. During those walks, Sandy wondered why people didn't buy paint. Their homes sure needed some—so did their paint-chipped fences. Some of the houses had plastic instead of glass on their veranda windows. Rusted ten-speed bikes, many missing a tire, littered front yards.

Still, the sun was welcoming and warm on those autumn after-noons. Sandy loved listening to the sound of crunching leaves on the hard sidewalk. She even enjoyed the smell of exhaust fumes as cars drove by. The bustle of city life was so markedly different from what she was used to. In her small hometown, autumn was harvest time, the smell of burning stubble hanging in the air as the dull roar of slow-moving combines provided ambient sound. It was pleasant and familiar, a simple life that was safe. So a walk in the inner city was an adventure for Sandy—until the harassment started.

"Hey hot pants!" a well-dressed, middle-aged man with a handlebar moustache and deep blue eyes yelled out from his passen-ger-side window. A thick, gold wedding band with an impressive diamond was on the hand holding out some money. "How much?" he asked. He was driving a light blue Lincoln Continental Town Car and wearing a dark blue suit. Bad timing for bad memories.

It's not too late, she thinks. *There's still time to say, "Thanks for walking me home, Blue. Goodnight."* But does she really want to play it safe? By the time Sandy stops second-guessing herself, they are already standing at the front door of the old brownstone where she lives. Sandy puts her key in the dark wooden door with the large bevelled windows. "Gotta love old architecture," she states nervously, inviting the stranger in. Blue tries to take off his gloves as they enter the building, fidgeting with them and causing Sandy to fidget and fumble too. She drops her keys. When they both go to pick them up Blue touches her hand, smiles and holds the door.

Good, he's a gentleman. Please not another empty one night stand. Sandy crosses her fingers. They make the climb up the old wooden staircase. The hallways, which often have smells of cooking, are quiet now but for their footsteps leading to Sandy's apartment door, #333.

"Nice place. How long you been livin' here?" Blue clears his throat as they walk inside. It makes Sandy wonder if she should offer him a glass of water.

"About two months," she answers. Blue walks across the living room to look out the big bay window. The noisy echo of the hardwood floor may as well be a drum roll signalling that Act One of some drama, romance or comedy is about to begin.

The opening scene? The view. It is early November but already the trees outside her third-floor window are covered in hoarfrost. Forty-eight hours ago it was unseasonably cold, going down to minus-thirty degrees for one night only. It was frigid enough that the thick evergreen outside the alcove looked to be wearing a spectacular white fur coat. Tonight's temperature hovers around minus-twenty and the air hangs thick with ice crystals; their sparkle glints off city street lamps.

"You have a great view from here," Blue announces, his cadence reminiscent of a realtor. It is their only small talk all evening, providing for a delicious, awkward moment. Sandy looks at Blue standing by the window. With the haze of the bar now gone, replaced by moonlight, she finds herself glad she invited him in.

A cold draft seeps through the heavy push-up window, reminding Sandy she hasn't made the time to buy a sheet of plastic to cover the window before winter storms set in. She starts picking at a bit of ice that has formed near the base of the frame.

Blue plays out his own nervous behaviour by glancing around to figure out where he is and what he may have gotten himself into. A sense of relief comes as he notices one of the many prints hanging on her walls, a reprint of Van Gogh's *Sunflowers*. He's seen the image before and asks Sandy why she's attracted to it. He likes her answer: "Because it is optimistic and filled with the promise of growth. Like everyone's life should be." Blue wonders if she is talking about the print or what she hopes might happen that night.

"Someday I want to be able to buy original art instead of prints. The colours and textures are so much more vibrant. But for now I can only afford prints, so there you go." Sandy hesitates for a second before adding, "But better than the Kiss and Frampton posters some of my friends have hanging on his walls." She laughs.

Blue continues his survey of the room, noticing several pottery pieces displayed atop old wooden Coke cases. Sandy tells him she collected most of the pieces at local garage sales. "I don't like mass-produced art. So when I'm able to afford original work, I buy it." Above her brown couch, though, is the masterpiece, an elaborate quilt made by Sandy's Baba.

Sandy explains that the quilt tells of a Ukrainian family history, pieced together with bits of thread. "Baba told me their lives were pieced together too when they arrived in Canada years ago. Each piece of the quilt tells a story of rebuilding and rejoicing in the start of something new." Sandy shows him one of her favourites telling of family pride with images of children playing. "Baba said that every culture wants the best for their kids, no matter where they might come from or what they've been through. That was the day Baba told me something else about family history—she said the stories on the quilt are similar to stories in rock. I didn't understand, so she brought out a book about Native petroglyphs. It was the first time I'd seen anything like that, and the first time I heard about Aboriginal people. Baba was always trying to find information on Aboriginal people. She told me it was important for me to learn."

Any discussion about Sandy's Aboriginality usually made her uncomfortable—it seemed too heavy or too intimate—but she hopes Blue will understand. She doesn't bring up the fact that she was adopted, but expects Blue may know that *Baba* is the Ukrainian word for grandmother.

She changes the subject. "Hey listen, I asked you over for tea. Better make some." She laughs, heading toward the kitchen. *Oh my Christ, he's going to think I'm a slob*, is Sandy's silent lament at realizing she hasn't done her dishes all week. The shameful display of sloth heckles. Every dirty plate is piled high on the counter; bits of dried spaghetti sauce and wilted lettuce seem to snicker at her. After all, they've been demanding her attention all week and now there is no room to manoeuvre.

Hide the dishes. She hopes Blue won't notice. But he does, smiling as though he's seen it before. Without being asked, he helps Sandy neatly stack the dirty dishes in the oven then quietly closes the door. Out of sight, out of mind.

Sandy looks through her tea collection. "So what kind of tea do you want? I have regular and this herbal, fruity stuff." Blue checks the label and goes for the raspberry. The euphoria of possibilities causes Sandy to forget that her feet are killing her. She's wearing a pair of fashionable granny boots with black leather and stiletto heels. She scowls, taking the weight off her feet as she plants her butt on her soft brown leatherette sofa. Blue sits on the floor beside her.

"Those shoes are really nice, but don't look very comfortable," he guesses correctly. "Would you like me to rub your feet?" No one has given Sandy a foot massage before, so the offer intrigues her. Soon, his touch captivates her. Sandy's skin prickles with excitement. He may as well be lathering her back in a claw-foot bathtub, the perfect moment for a first kiss...

The kettle on the stove thinks not and begins to whistle. Sandy hesitates for a second then gets up. In a daze, she goes to the kitchen to slowly pour hot water into the teapot. She finds the last two clean mugs in the cupboard and puts everything on a tray before heading back into the living room.

After getting seated Sandy plays with her hair, taking out her braid and twisting strands around her index finger as they talk about their mutual love of jazz. She takes it as a suggestion, popping a Billie Holiday cassette into the stereo—*Lady in Satin*. She pours the tea, totally unprepared for what happens next.

Blue's body language is awkward. "I'm glad we met tonight. Even though we won't get to know each other better, I'm glad we got to know each other at all." Blue pauses. "You are a beautiful and amazing woman. I wish we could have more time together—I'm leaving soon."

REVELATION

Why are you leaving? Where are you going?" Sandy spits out the words so quickly Blue scarcely manages to finish his sentence.

He explains that he and James are in Regina for a short time only, training at the police academy before returning to their home detachment in Saskatoon.

"You're a cop? What made you want to do that?"

"I want to make a difference in people's lives. I've seen so much shit, especially with single mothers. They don't have to live like that." Even Blue is surprised he's so candid; maybe it's the lack of sleep during his training that's left him vulnerable, or maybe it's the alcohol. Sandy wants to retract her question, watching as Blue's eyes go from endearing to as lifeless as a shark's. "I don't know how you grew up, Sandy, but me? I was pretty much left by myself most of the time. I know my mom cared about me. She just wasn't home much. Why am I telling you all this negative stuff?"

Sandy shifts her body on the couch to make herself more comfortable, encouraging Blue to continue. "I don't know, maybe you need to say these things. I don't mind." Sandy wonders if her story about the quilt unearthed this cascade of bitter personal truths.

His thoughts drift momentarily. He starts talking about someone he spotted at the bar earlier in the evening—a young Aboriginal lady he recognized as a client at the local women's shelter that some of the new recruits had visited earlier that week. In her early twenties, she already had three children living with her at the shelter. And there she was at the bar, quite drunk, letting men touch her in public and carrying on as though she had no care in the world other than tasting another glass of cheap beer. It took Blue back to his childhood, when some nights his mother wouldn't come home.

Why do I keep telling her all this stuff? Blue asks himself, already knowing the answer. He recalls something else from his child- hood—advice. His mom once told him that whenever people have a sensation like déjà vu—like they have done this or been here before, or they know something is going to happen before it does—then it is the truth. His mom claimed it was angels giving him instructions and he should always follow. He's dreamed of this conversation with Sandy unfolding just as it is, which is why he continues to talk...

"One memory in particular has always stayed with me." Blue clears his throat before recalling, "I was out playing with my friends. It was late fall—I remember because the chill that hung in the air was enough to bite, but not enough to *kill* the way it might do in the winter. It had been hours that we were hanging around outside, walking with sticks and looking underneath pieces of old, wet card- board to see if there were mice. But I started to get hungry. I think I was about six. So I went home. When I got there, the house inside was just as cold as outside. No one was there. I just sat there terri- fied, by myself for hours more, as the old house rattled and shook in the wind. It was dark by the time Mom came home. I kept thinking about ghosts."

Sandy realizes the ghosts are now a part of him, and hopes he makes no connection to the fact they've met in the winter. He continues: "I don't remember ever owning a proper pair of boots, and my coat was too thin, so I was always cold. Memories, eh? Mine are stale bread and hand-me-down clothing." He says it dispassionately, but not accusatorily toward his mother. "She did the best she could, I know. Even though I knew we were poor, there were so many times she would go out of her way to try to make me forget that."

A happy memory emerges. "Sometimes we packed up bologna sandwiches and Tang, headed out into the woods for a picnic. Just me and Mom. She'd pin her long, brown hair into one of those tight buns at the top of her head, and put pink lipstick on—the same colour she wore to go to church. She always looked pretty, and on those days she wore a hand-knit green sweater two sizes too big for her, a denim skirt and a fluffy scarf. We'd find a clearing and Mom would sit on an old blanket, wrapping another blanket around me. It was one of those scratchy woollen blankets, the tartan kind, tattered and worn. But on those days I never noticed the itchiness. Mom held me in her arms and would tell me stories about her own childhood. I loved those moments."

Blue's thoughts drift back to the young woman at the bar. "How could her pain be stronger than the love for her children? Is it the alcohol that allows her to forget?" He realizes his own glasses of beer have had their effect on loosening his tongue, but continues to purge, sharing his mother's financial struggles as a waitress who also cleaned houses to make ends meet. He doesn't talk about close friends, and his only mention of a father is to say he basically didn't have one.

"There was no one to play that role in my life. Mom said Dad was a drifter, a Cree musician. One look at each other and it was love at first sight—that's what Mom said. They were together for a couple years, but really only a few months that could be considered good. Dad drank too much and often didn't come home after his set was finished at the club. He wrote his own music too, you know. *Poetry*, Mom called it. But in the kinds of places he played, people wanted to hear stuff like 'Smoke on the Water.' Kind of like the place we were at tonight."

He stops for a moment to glance out the window. It's snowing heavy flakes that look like white feathers falling from the sky. Sandy figures Blue needs the time to clear the knot in his throat causing his voice to crack. "Mom said it tortured him, not being heard. But the way she tells it, one night it was all just too much. The drinking. The secrecy. She confronted him." Blue checks his watch—a diversionary tactic giving him time to regain composure again. "He just walked away. He knew Mom was carrying me at the time. I was born four months later. I never met him." Blue slumps on the couch, quiet and empty for a moment.

Sandy wonders what that must be like, growing up without a dad. Then she wonders if Blue blames himself for his dad leaving. If he does, she can't even imagine the weight of that burden.

Blue has more to share. "But one day she started smiling again. I remember it was during the fall," he says. "I just came home from school and Mom was there, in the bathroom doing her hair, taking out some foam rollers. She was dressed in a fancy black dress and told me I was supposed to go over to the old lady's house next door for a few hours. I'd get supper there, she said. Then she paused, smiled and told me that she met someone named Hank and he was taking her out. Mom said she'd be home in time to tuck me in. She was, and Hank came with her. He was also there the next morning when I got up for school. Eventually, he was always there. It was good for a while... Hank was new in town, working as a mechanic. That's how Mom met him. Her old car always seemed to have something wrong with it."

Blue recalled that Hank wasn't much taller than his mom— five foot eight at most. His hands seemed permanently soiled, with grease peeking out from under his fingernails. He pulled his light brown hair back into a small ponytail, which didn't suit him. He wore thick sideburns that made Blue snicker, reminding him of the low-quality shag carpet on his bedroom floor. Blue tells Sandy that Hank accepted him like a son "until that day when he went looking for some spare change. Mom always kept some coins in her miscellaneous drawer in the bedroom. It was there Hank came across an old photo of my dad. He went crazy."

Blue's voice gets low. "Hank stormed out of the house. He got drunk and came back mean and ugly. We'd never seen this side of him before and it was scary. He started calling my mom names to try to make her feel ashamed. I can still hear his slurring rants: 'You sick slut. You kept his picture! That's what you get for fucking an Indian! That little bastard is a no good troublemaker. Bitch!' His words were horrible." Blue stops speaking.

From there, Hank's furor over the old photo evolved into abuse. It went unreported. Tears begin to well in Sandy's eyes as Blue recalls another memory, the horror of a separate afternoon when he was ten years old. Hank's drinking had become more frequent. "He visited Jack Daniels all afternoon. When he came home, there was dry foam from spit at the corners of his mouth. I was in the living room watching TV, holding a pillow and laughing as Danny Partridge got into trouble once again." Blue says he used the pillow to muffle his ears. He did whatever he could to stop hearing the sounds coming from the kitchen, of Hank hitting his mother—hard. "When it was over, my mom's eyes were black and blue. Her dress was torn and her nose was bloodied and swollen. I remember her just sitting there on the cold kitchen linoleum and crying. I remember a wet tea towel. It stayed draped over her shoulder as Hank staggered out the back door."

Blue sidetracks momentarily, telling her the back door always squeaked and the screen was always torn. After regaining control of his emotions, he goes back to finish the story. "And then Hank yelled at Mom, 'I'm going back to Charlie's, you bitch!' Charlie's was a bar." Blue half-chuckles while explaining that Hank came back the next morning as though nothing had happened. "Through beer farts and a swollen face he actually asked my mom for a strong cup of coffee.

He called her *dear*," Blue huffs. "The bastard wasn't there when I got home from school later in the day. No one missed him either."

Blue tells Sandy he didn't sleep properly for weeks afterward. It was that incident that eventually made him decide to become a cop. "Now, I have the opportunity to make a difference. To be there for single moms, like mine was, who have nowhere else to turn." Blue takes a sip of his now-cold tea. "I hope you don't mind me telling you all this. And I don't know why I am, but you're so easy to talk to." It is Sandy's cue to start remembering her own childhood.

FILTHY CLOAK

lue had mentioned he was Metis but didn't grow up on the rez. Neither did Sandy. In her small town, she was the only Cree for miles, not that anyone there knew the difference between a Cree and anyone else who was brown. All Sandy remembers is being the only brown-skinned child standing alone amidst a sea of grain and white faces on the flat prairie landscape. She remembers being viewed as an oddity or even a freak, and isn't about to share those memories with Blue, despite his own honest confessions. One painful memory takes her back in time. It sits just below the surface, but is her deepest source of shame.

Sandy was five years old. She remembers sitting in a metal tub filled with warm tap water by a lovely Ukrainian woman who would eventually become her mom. The woman placed the old tub on the kitchen floor, to keep an eye on little Sandy while still going about her chores. The woman loved to hum, making it easy to get caught up in happy thoughts. Maybe her humming distracted her from those few seconds that the little girl started hurting herself with a rough scrub brush that may as well have been made of steel wool. The little girl scrubbed, scrubbed, scrubbed her skin, so hard her forearms turned raw and started to bleed. But there was no crying. Sandy's physical pain was nothing compared to the emotional trauma of being so different. Brown. There was only one solution: scrub, scrub, scrub away the brown.

As she comes back to the present, Sandy realizes she's been scratching red marks into her hand with her long fingernails, signalling the time has come for her to unearth some bones now, some with rot and sinew still hanging. "Have you ever heard about the Scoop?" Sandy was hoping Blue might offer some empathy, or at least some knowledge of the up to twenty thousand Aboriginal children taken from their homes between the 1960s and 1980s. It wasn't widely talked about; still, she thought he might know.

He didn't. She tried to explain but the words got caught in her throat before coming out. "The Scoop happened to single Aboriginal mothers who were deemed unfit, for no reason other than being single mothers." Often, Sandy had imagined how painful it must have been for her own mother. Carrying a child for nine months, bonding during that time, only to have Sandy ripped from her bosom at the moment of birth.

Was Sandy ever breastfed? She guessed not, though her fantasy was that there may have been a sympathetic nurse or two who were mothers themselves, who let Sandy's mom hold her even if it was against policy. Had her biological mom felt her soft skin and listened to Sandy's first sweet breaths of innocence? She hoped they had a few precious moments of tenderness before Sandy was stolen to be a ward of the Department of Social Services, to a place where she never fit in.

Her memories jump to another dark place, a place of hatred and intolerance that she faced on a daily basis during her elementary and high school years. "Every little Indian kid is a thief and a liar," twelve-year-old Sandy overheard someone's voice bellowing from the school office. Classes were finished for the day and she was heading home.

Her dog greeted her at the school door, like he did every day, happy to see her. "Hey Andy." Sandy patted the dog's head. Once home, she grabbed an apple from the refrigerator then headed to her bedroom. Her mom never let her go out and play until homework was finished. That particular day she was almost finished her math assignment when her mom knocked on the bedroom door.

"Honey, there's someone here to see you." Sandy responded enthusiastically, thinking one of her friends had come to visit. Her zeal quickly turned to apprehension on being met by a well-groomed RCMP officer standing beside the kitchen table.

Sandy's mom spoke up. "Sweetie, some money went missing at school today, so this gentleman is here to ask you some questions."

The young constable smiled uncomfortably and asked Sandy to roll up her sleeves and show him her hands. She started shaking a bit, unnerved by his presence, but held out her hands as requested.

The constable checked them carefully. "Looks like you haven't recently hurt your hands or arms anywhere?"

"No. Why?" Sandy responded.

"Some fundraising money went missing from your school today. Whoever stole it pried open the cash box and got a bad cut while doing so, left a fair bit of blood behind. I'm sorry to have bothered you, ma'am. Obviously your daughter wasn't involved." The officer left, leaving Sandy feeling violated.

"Why was I even suspected?" She started crying. There was no need to explain what had happened. Sandy knew she'd been accused of stealing money. "For what reason?" She knew the answer but didn't dare say it out loud. She kept hearing the voices she'd overheard from the school office. *Indians steal. They can't be trusted.* It's what everyone in her white community thought in general. It's what they thought about her.

Sandy fumbles with her teacup, remembering the scrubbing event again. The scar from it and other incidents, like being falsely accused of stealing, are internalized. She can admit to no one that as a child, she often stared in the mirror with self-loathing. Even today, it embarrasses her that she harboured such destructive thoughts. She used to tell herself, *I hate the fullness of my lips... I hate the darkness of my skin and the colour of my hair... Why are my eyes so dark?* All of Sandy's friends in her small town had thin lips, light brown or blonde hair, white skin and often blue eyes.

She has often wondered if her patchy blotches of eczema are brought on by genes or by God taunting her with just a few white patches of skin, surrounded by what has become an armour of brown. She knows little about her own culture and heritage, admitting that anything she does know comes from a book—which bothers her more than anyone knows. *What are my roots? Where is it that I truly belong?* Her solitary sorrows present themselves as insecurity, the real reason she looks at other Indians on the street as greasy bums, echoing the same words she heard used to describe her during childhood.

It is ironic that Sandy grew up in a town with a Cree name, *Okema*. Even the name of the province where she lives is derived from a Cree word. *Kisisaskatchewan* means "the river that flows swiftly." She must be the only Cree to have grown up in a place with two Cree names but only one Cree resident, her residency more by default than anything.

Sandy was kidnapped from the hospital, destined to be an orphan until a Ukrainian couple agreed to take her in. They didn't see her as a Native child, only as a child needing comfort. As the little girl grew, so did their bond. Love is colour blind and eventually Sandy's foster family legally adopted her, rescuing her from wandering the system like some stray. She counted herself lucky for that; there were too many others who never belonged anywhere. With thousands of Aboriginal children in foster care as a result of the Scoop, the Department of Social Services became overwhelmed.

Workers didn't consider or even care that many homes were substandard. Aboriginal children were taken and used as slave labour. Some children were sent to farms where the drudgery began: rising at the crack of dawn to do chores, being forced to sleep in barns and eating slimy, green bologna and stale bread while the foster family dined on fresh vegetables and steak. The foster kids were regarded as subhuman and neglected as such. How can anything good possibly *grow* in an environment like that? To answer that question, she now only has to look out the window: the downtown landscape is littered with human debris from the Scoop. Those lost ones are the real portraits of Scoop children. They show their scars on the outside; Sandy wears hers within.

It makes her wonder about Blue. Did he ever try to wash off the brown? She senses Blue doesn't have a problem saying he is Metis. But is he proud of it? She recalls a stat that 95 percent of police officers are white males. She figures he is probably treated just as badly in his workplace as she was at school. Maybe worse. She silently questions if his white gene instead of his Cree gene had been dominant, if he had white skin, would he identify as Cree at all? Those Metis. So many of them are ashamed to be part-Indian, so the light-coloured ones lie. They pretend to be white because their skin is that colour. *If Blue were lighter-toned, I wonder if he would be sitting here with me tonight?*

It is as though he reads her thoughts, even though Sandy hadn't spoken them aloud. "I've never gone out with a Native girl before."

"Why's that?" Sandy asks.

"I don't know," Blue says. Then he drops the type of news that crushes hopes just as they are beginning: "My girlfriend is white."

Sandy can't react, other than to turn ashen. She mutters the words "Oh boy," but nothing else. After a few moments of awkward silence, Blue mumbles something about needing to be up early and shuffles out the door.

Sandy sits, stung and alone, on the cold hardwood. She quickly wipes away one salty tear that has welled up so heavily it needs to come out, smudging her mascara. It makes her angry to see the black stain on the back of her hand, realizing it has also left a black stain on her heart. She goes to the fridge, needing something more substantial than raspberry tea. There is some beer in there, but wine tastes better. She remembers a half bottle of Pinot Noir in the cupboard. She pours it into her teacup, drinking it as freely as she wished to drink in Blue, but couldn't.

Sandy goes to her freezer, where her emergency pack of smokes is hidden. She feels no guilt in lighting up tonight, waiting to experience the subsequent light-headedness the nicotine brings. The wine disappears within seconds and Sandy vaguely remembers the number to Dial-a-Bottle, a service to deliver alcohol right to her doorstep. She begins to recite the words to a poem she'd written in her journal the last time she felt left out and unimportant.

Dulling

Hand me another glass of wine.
An old and melancholy friend, Pinot Noir.
Full-bodied conversations with him
are the only way to stop thoughts of you.

Temporarily tuning out
life's most precious emotions.

Love and desire.
Kindness and compassion.

In the morning
the preoccupation will begin anew.

It always does.

SPIRITS

It's a hell of a way to wake up: red eyes, empty bottles strewn about on her bedroom floor. And still clutching one half-empty bottle of beer in her left hand. A pronounced feeling of nausea strikes at the precise moment she slowly and shakily places the bottle atop her side table. It isn't even 10 A.M. and already a beer is welded to her hand. She hears phantom voices mock, *Take another swig, you loser, then wipe the foam off your lips with the back of your hand.* And why wouldn't she be hearing voices? She's spent a lot of time with beer and wine last night; it doesn't surprise her that the state she's in includes voices.

Booze has become her lover when no one else can or will—last night and again this morning. Hair of the dog, she justifies, popping the cap on her second bottle before even making coffee. *But,* she thinks, *who wants coffee today?* Caffeine might wake something up. It's safer to stay numb. She longs to laze around in bed and figure out what to do with the rest of the day and rest of her life. For the hundredth time, she makes a promise to the gods to never drink, ever again.

Sandy cringes as she puts her other hand between her legs. She wants to feel the skin there, hoping it won't remind her of a "glazed donut," how her girlfriends describe dried semen the morning after a "hit and run." She hates it when she can't remember. Bits of her memory roll in her brain like dust bunnies, trapped and forgotten in some lonely corner. She remembers flirting with that Metis guy at the bar last night. What was his name? Oh, yes, Blue. Very handsome. She can't remember if she did anything with him.

At least I'm home and alone and safe, she thinks. But safe is all relative. Her reaching hands feel something foreign in the folds of flesh where life begins. But what is it? Sandy throws on an oversized sweatshirt and stumbles to the bathroom to find out. *Shit, the floor is cold. Where are those damn socks?* She decides she is numb enough that the cold hardwood won't bother her and walks barefoot, all the while thinking about Polyfilla, Band-Aids and elastic bands. They are the tenuous things that Sandy relies upon lately to hold herself together. *But why am I falling apart?* She checks her panties. Blood.

There was a time that it meant something. Something important. In her quest for a place to belong, she started reading, going to the library and sneaking around the Canadian literature section. She'd find books on Aboriginal culture then quickly hide them under her arm on the way to the checkout, feeling like she was doing something forbidden. A couple years ago she picked up a book on spirituality. In it, she learned that Aboriginal teachings say a woman's "Moon Time" is sacred, a time when woman holds the most power. It's a time for ceremony and prayer, to cleanse the spirit while the body cleanses itself. Moon Time. It is a time for abstinence and a time to be good to yourself. No drinking, smoking or negative thinking. "Guess I blew it again this month," she mutters in disgust.

Sandy takes another swig of beer, wondering when it was that the teaching, and her ability to cope, began to erode. She used to follow the teaching; it made her feel special to celebrate her womanhood. She read that it's important to make an offering at this time of the month. She wasn't sure exactly what it meant, but every month when her menstrual cycle began Sandy diligently purchased extra tins of soup, tomatoes and beans to deliver to the Salvation Army. It was her way of giving thanks. *When did I stop listening to those spirits and start following these ones?* She reads the words on the label. "Fine brewers since 1847. Spirits." That's what they call booze. Such horseshit!

She wonders if making a food offering again today might cancel out her bad behaviour from last night, until another thought creeps in. She feels shame to even be thinking about Aboriginal teachings at a time when she has entirely dishonoured the spirit of those teachings. "Why do I drink so much?" she asks the bathroom mirror. There is something hiding under her smudged mascara. She studies her reflection. As she watches, a single tear, perhaps a cleansing one, slowly rolls down her right cheek. Seconds later she uses her index finger to wipe away some snot coming out of her right nostril. She knows the grey film that covers her face and soul this morning can be rinsed away. She will stop slowly destroying herself. She will stop asking questions and start looking for answers.

Sandy takes a look at the cold, brown beer bottle that is still in her hand, remembering all the times beer has helped her forget a problem by cancelling it out as a memory. Beer and wine used to soothe the pain of disappointment and heartbreak, the way a mother's kiss would for a bruised finger. Except this morning it disgusts her. She pours it down the drain. "Get the hell out," she demands, condemning the liquid to the sewer.

He has brothers who need to go too. They are in the fridge, nestled in a six-pack. Sandy grabs the box and takes it outside. She pays no attention to the fact she is barefoot in the snow. One by one, she violently smashes the bottles against the rusting walls of the metal dumpster. A bag lady, halfway up the alley, stands to watch as Sandy's bloodshot eyes once more fill with tears.

"Fuckers! Fuck you. Fuck you!" she yells as each bottle bursts against the side of the bin. Condemned to the trash. When all the bottles are smashed, Sandy yanks on the heavy steel door at the back of her building. She notices her bare feet have turned red, but the coldness of the snow doesn't bother her. She considers herself lucky for not having stepped on anything sharp.

Returning upstairs, she muses about how interesting words are, especially those with a double meaning. Kind of like the way some people are. Take "refuse" for example. As a verb, it means to say no. But as a noun it means trash. Both apply, as Sandy realizes she is refusing to let refuse influence her anymore. She feels exhilarated and stupid at the same time for having smashed the bottles when someone was watching. Poor old woman probably thought she was a nutcase. Actually, she probably wanted one of the beers.

Once back in her own apartment, Sandy checks herself again in the bathroom mirror. *Do I look any different?* But the question she really wants to ask is, *Will I be any different?* The smashing frenzy has been her affirmation to change. Sandy reaches for the tap to splash cold water on her face. To wash away the grey.

TRYZUB

On Monday morning any webs of disappointment from the weekend must be masked. For Sandy, makeup and hairspray always do the trick. It's going to be a busy week again. Sandy is still preoccupied with thoughts of Blue as she carefully applies a lip liner called "Rouge Pulp" while still in her Jeep. What better way to mask pain than by covering it with another mask? In this case, her lipstick. It is veritable artistry as she manipulates the gloss to accentuate the fullness of her lovely mouth. Next, she picks a colour called "Carnal," which is billed as a non-smudge, long-lasting lipstick.

At this point, she finds herself wondering if the people who think up these names like their jobs. A magazine article explained that adding a dash of shine to the lower lip offers a pouty look. In the large scheme of life, magazine advice is superficial and unimportant, but "pouty" is the look of choice in Sandy's industry. Sandy has started her career as a television news journalist. She's on TV every night.

Finishing up with the rear-view mirror and Rouge Pulp, she steps out of her Jeep and heads toward the front door of the station. As she walks, she prays it will not be another day where co-workers pretend to be deaf, where she says good morning and they look the other way—or where she asks a question and they ignore her. Harsh behaviour—except they don't realize Sandy is used to being ostracized; it happened all throughout her school years. Every time her new co-workers treat her badly, it gives her the strength in some twisted way to carry on and prove them wrong. She refuses to be broken. Sandy remembers her first day on the job in this newsroom.

She can still feel how elated she was walking toward the reception desk that first day. The secretary smiled, then phoned someone named Lilly Thiele. Lilly was tall and thin with shoulder-length auburn hair pulled back in a tight ponytail. Lilly wore very little makeup, an orange sweatshirt over a cotton print skirt, and runners. The casual attire made Sandy wonder what sort of executive she was. Lilly extended her hand and a smile. "Hi, I'm the production assistant for the supper-hour news. Follow me. You're just in time for the morning meeting."

Sandy followed Lilly down a long hall covered with old photos, mostly of sports heroes standing beside the local broadcasters. As Lilly pushed open the swivel-hitched door to the newsroom, Sandy was struck by the rank smell of too many people smoking cigarettes. She longed to be one of those smokers, craving a cigarette out of nervous habit. The thick, putrid and blue air reminded her of a bingo hall. She stepped over the threshold to see a dozen or so people seated around a large table in the middle of the room. The table was covered with newspapers, reports and coffee cups.

"It's our morning meeting," Lilly explained. "Every day we all sit down to figure out which stories will be covered. Hope you came with some ideas." Lilly motioned toward an empty chair, indicating that Sandy should be seated. She did sit, but not before smoothing out her lavender-coloured silk skirt.

Sandy was excited to be there, but something seemed off, like the joke was on her. That's when she heard it. *Whoo-whoo-whoo-whoo-whoo.* A man had actually cupped his hand over his mouth to make that old, Hollywood-movie Indian whoop. Sandy couldn't see who it was. The newsroom was cordoned off and split up by wall partitions that were covered in orange carpeting. A few people snickered at hearing the sound, as though in agreement, while others lowered their eyes in embarrassment.

Lilly gasped and quietly said, "Oh my God." She may have wanted to say more but the moment came to an abrupt end when Frank Furstrow walked into the room. He was wearing a taupe-coloured sport coat and plain navy tie. His denim jeans and beat-up sneakers seemed to work as a suitable ensemble because Frank could get away with partnering up things that didn't necessarily go together—like hiring Sandy, a brown-skinned rookie reporter amongst veteran journalists who were primarily white, middle-aged men. It was clear that Frank had got a haircut over the weekend because the greying at his temple was pronounced.

With a damp cigarette dangling from his lips, he held a notebook in one hand and a coffee mug in the other. Some of the hot liquid spilled onto the front page of *The Western Producer*, a magazine sitting at the edge of the main news desk. Frank smoothed his hair, took a quick sip then smiled at Sandy. "Hey everyone. We'll start today's meeting by saying hello to Sandy Pelly. She's our newest reporter and she'll be covering general assignment. Welcome aboard, Sandy."

Most of the staffers around the table smiled politely. Lilly gave a small but enthusiastic clap, and a couple of others joined in the applause. But not everyone extended a welcome. Dick Sauer signalled his disinterest by checking his fingernails, not knowing that he was being mocked in a silent way as well. Sandy had always giggled at the pronunciation of his last name "sour." She thought it reflected Dick's personality. Watching him on-air, he seemed like a pompous asshole. Now having met the surly bastard, she realized her opinion was correct and decided to secretly give him the nickname "General Sour Dick." Sauer was the station's political reporter, assigned to cover the Saskatchewan legislature, and looked the part—tall and handsome like a model, but ultimately unattractive because of his obnoxious personality.

"Let's get this meeting started," Frank barked. "Sauer, what's on your plate today?" One by one, reporters gave their ideas on what they thought should be covered, ranging from how inner-city kids will cope now that a local pool has closed for a week to how farmers are dealing with fluctuating wheat prices.

Frank nodded with each angle pitched, then checked with another member of the news team, Sean Waters, about how to co-ordinate the cameras to ensure each story received coverage that day. Waters could've been a caricature: his mannerisms nervous, always chewing on a blue ballpoint pen. The sleeves of his dress shirt were rolled up past his elbows and it was obvious he never combed his thick mane of brown hair.

On her turn to speak, Sandy proudly suggested a story she stumbled across days before at a downtown community centre. She described a new craft class program designed to keep Aboriginal culture and traditions alive among Native women. What made the story new is that there was a daycare on-site to ensure young mothers were able to take part in reclaiming culture.

"One Old Woman who is there certainly doesn't need the instruction." Sandy explained to her colleagues that the terms "Old Woman" and "Old Man" are titles showing respect within Aboriginal culture. As always, she'd learned this information from a book. It made her feel a bit guilty, like a phony, to be talking about Aboriginal customs as though they were something she'd grown up with, but she kept talking anyway. These people would never know the difference. "It is clear the Old Woman in this class is there just for the company. And maybe to act as a cultural ambassador or a mentor of sorts. Whatever the case, she's an interesting woman and we should do a story."

Sandy was talking about Bertha Bare Shin Bone, originally from Alberta. Her beadwork was exquisite. Sandy had seen beadwork in museums and in photography, but Bertha's was by far more beautiful and more elaborate in design. Her floral patterns were as vibrant and varied in colour as any prize-winning garden, but stitched on soft leather. Sandy talked about how the Old Woman's frail and arthritic hands would deftly handle beads appearing to be only a tad bigger than a grain of sand. She guessed Bertha was probably in her seventies, but Bertha's deep smile lines, clear eyes and sheer determination gave the Old Woman an ageless mystique.

Bertha had noticed Sandy's attention when she'd stopped by. "Come join, my girl." Tentatively, Sandy tried her hand at beadwork, only to be soon embarrassed. She couldn't even thread the needle, let alone start with the process of creating patterns. "You have the wrong thread," Bertha kindly pointed out. "Sometimes you young people can't figure it out. You give up, and then you leave and you don't come back. That makes me sad." Then she smiled and said, "You can keep it, my girl," offering Sandy a new spool of thread that was thinner.

Sandy explained to her news colleagues that the story she wanted to file was about keeping youth involved in learning traditions, in the inner city, as a way of keeping the culture alive. "It is one way of keeping them occupied with something positive so they aren't prone to getting caught up with life on the street."

But General Sour Dick obviously felt the need to shit all over her proposal. "Too sappy! Who fucking cares what some old Indian thinks anyway? Just give us the facts. No one is interested in this emotional bullshit," he snarled. Sandy didn't know how to react, so upset and feeling as though her voice had been amputated with antiquated, poisonous ideas. Sauer smirked in satisfaction at having derailed her.

Sean Waters shook his head in disbelief at Sauer's brash comment, taking over the discussion. "Good suggestion, Sandy," he uttered uncomfortably after several moments of awkward silence, "but I already marked you down for a ribbon cutting. There's a new seniors' care centre being built in the west end. That's what I'll assign to you today. We'll try to get to the culture story some other day."

Sandy gave a conciliatory nod, not being able to respond in any other way. She choked back tears and felt like a flake. She was also feeling betrayed by Frank, who chose to say nothing when Sauer spat out his bile. After all, when he hired her Frank commented, "You are being hired because the station wants to increase our community perspective. Bring in fresh stories that we've never covered before. There are all sorts of things happening in the Native community that we don't even know about. You can help make that connection."

Sandy's recollection of those first days on the job make her realize that rarely does she feel fresh—more like some cheap token. A cigar-store Indian, here for show but expected to keep silent. A hard thing to admit. The day-to-day shunning has continued with ugly under-tones suggesting she doesn't belong in this job, this industry. Her memory again spirals back to those first days:

Day One: On her new desk Sandy found a record from the 1970s: Cher's *Half-Breed*. She knew what people like Sauer were trying to convey by leaving it there. In response, her chest tightened. She escaped to the bathroom, not wanting anyone to know how upset she was.

Day Two: She overheard whispers and spotted Dick Sauer putting his hand to his mouth, making that awful sound again. *Whoo-whoo-whoo.* It was followed by maniacal laughter, childish and mean. Sandy felt like punching him in the face. She glanced around the newsroom to see if anyone might offer support. They heard it too. *Whoo-whoo-whoo.* But they offered nothing. In their silence, they condoned the behaviour.

Day Three: Sandy caught a glimpse of a secret pool being passed around. She thought it might be a sports pool since the local football team had a game coming up. But this pool reeked of ignorance and exclusion, asking the question, "How long will the Indian last?" The paper was quickly hidden when people like Sauer realized she'd entered the room.

Day Four: Someone from accounting, an old guy with a greying goatee and a bald head, actually asked her, "So, you think you got the job because you're an Indian?" Sandy had gone to his office to sign some papers, which would entitle her to things like dental and medical benefits now that she was a full-time employee. But that comment? The downside of employment equity, she lamented. The issue of employment equity was currently being discussed as part of labour law reform. It had been a story in the news for the past few months but now was being played out for real, proving only that this type of legislation was definitely needed.

Sandy has been doing this dance all her life, constantly having to prove that she is worthy. Even her application for getting into broadcast school was criticized and belittled. Her memory goes back to that day.

Sandy was so young, only seventeen, but smart and ambitious— so much so that the technical school invited her for an interview. As part of her application for study, she had sent some articles she'd written for her school newspaper. Prospective students needed more than just high marks to be accepted into the journalism program; they had to show initiative. While all the prospective students were lined up in the hallway outside a lecture room, a couple of young male applicants whispered in the corner, not overly concerned if she could hear them or not.

"She'll never get in. Who the hell will trust an Indian to tell them the news?"

Assholes. Sandy didn't understand. In her small town, she could account for small-mindedness. But in the city, and especially at an institution of higher learning, she had expected to find free thinkers open to change. But her disappointment didn't stop her. She was accepted, and graduated two years later at the top of her class.

It has brought her here today. Sandy unconsciously runs her fingers over an unusually shaped brooch that she wears on her lapel most of the time. It is a gift from her Baba, given as a high school graduation present and a prayer for protection. The ancient Ukrainian symbol on the brooch is that of a tryzub, a trident and weapon used in battle. "My beautiful granddaughter, you are smart and capable, and filled with promise. Take this tryzub. Wear it and use it," Baba said on graduation day. "And anytime anyone tries to put you in your place, you put them in theirs." The old lady smiled, handing it over and kissing Sandy on the forehead.

Baba knew Sandy would need the reminder. Baba had lived through intolerance herself. At six years old she had arrived in Canada with her family only to be placed in an internment camp as enemy aliens of their new country. The First World War had broken out and the Canadian government had implemented the War Measures Act. People of Ukrainian descent were ostracized and subjected to bigotry, stripped of their rights and placed in camps. Baba had told the story when Sandy was a teenager. Sandy remembers thinking it absurd that something like that could happen in Canada, and wondering why nothing about it was taught in school. But her grandmother assured her it indeed was real. Ukrainian traditions were spat upon, as was their language and way of life—the same as what had happened to the indigenous peoples of Canada.

Baba gave Sandy the tryzub because she knew the struggles her granddaughter was facing as a young Native girl in a white community. She understood Sandy was often excluded and regarded with disdain. Baba told Sandy the tryzub would act as her good luck charm. "Someday you will learn about your other family, but until then you are always a part of mine. I am so proud to call you my beautiful granddaughter." It was around that same time that Baba started buying books for Sandy, mostly literature about Native culture, and encouraging Sandy to learn more about herself.

Sandy silently gives thanks for her grandmother's wisdom. She would need the magic of the tryzub again for another week at the office.

BLANKET STATEMENTS

Where is that little bitch today?" Dick Sauer is pointing to a photo in the newspaper. The TV station had placed an ad announcing Sandy's hiring.

"Who cares? If we're lucky, she'll quit. I'm doing my best to let her know she's not welcome here," Lee McMillan answers. "Maybe the Little Indian Princess is hungover." Lee is nasty and conniving, a skinny blonde reporter who always smells sweet and foul at the same time, like the scent of expensive perfume masking the rancid stench of vomit. There's a whisper campaign saying that Lee's bulimic, which is how she stays so thin. McMillan is Sauer's closest ally in the newsroom.

The two of them happen to be standing at the water cooler in the main hallway of the station as they have their conversation. Seconds after Sauer and McMillan spat out their hostilities, Sandy appears from around the corner. It is clear by her look that she's overheard their words. Most people would react with embarrassment at realizing their faux pas. But not these two. They want to pick at Sandy's confidence right before the morning meeting, with words as their weapons.

"Just because you work here now, don't *ever* consider yourself one of us. You will always be inferior. It's the way you were born,"

McMillan sneers at Sandy then giggles toward Sauer. "Besides, no one wants to watch an Indian on TV. What the fuck was Frank thinking?"

McMillan's comment prompts Sandy to give her the finger. It's the proper response. Sandy has begun to refer to the duo as Shark and Remora, wondering if the two might be lovers (she finds the thought repulsive).

In spite of their badgering, or maybe because of it, Sandy is determined to file some solid stories this week. She knows that her hiring is some type of experiment that people like Sauer want to see fail. "I told you so" is surely what Sauer longs to say to Frank. But that isn't about to happen. She is programmed to succeed, having overcome a lifetime of challenges already. She is driven to debunk the blanket statements—blankets others have wrapped around her saying Indians are lazy and unreliable. Blanket statements like Indians are uneducated and inept—things that are disrespectful and untrue. Still it bothers her that Sauer constantly tries to trip her up, like he does again today.

Sandy has made some phone calls, trying to piece together a story about the need for another homeless shelter downtown. Over the winter, one homeless man was found dead in an alley. The cause? Hypothermia. If the man had had a place to go, it wouldn't have happened. Now, the topic of homelessness is being discussed again. Politicians will decide within days if a plan addressing the issue might be included in the budget for the coming year. It will need capital funding and require an operating grant. Sandy needs to score an interview with the coroner as the only missing element before filing the story for broadcast. So Sandy waits to hear back from the coroner before pulling it all together.

Two o'clock. No word.

Three o'clock. She's finished writing her script, except for the missing interview.

Four o'clock. It's getting very close to news time, and if the coroner doesn't respond soon, she'll have to shelve the story until tomorrow. Not good.

Four-fifteen. She goes to the bathroom.

When she returns to her desk, there is a yellow slip of paper near her telephone. Her phone call had been returned. It was from Maxwell Stiles, the coroner. Stiles had returned her call at ten o'clock that morning. That is the time the receptionist, who'd taken the call, had written on the note.

"Where did this come from?" Sandy's tone makes it clear that she is angry.

"Oh. I grabbed it from reception earlier in the day. Sorry, I forgot to pass it on," Sauer answers shrilly. He is clearly proud of himself for pulling off another practical joke. Sandy doesn't have time to argue. The newscast is going on air in less than two hours. She dials the number.

"Oh. Hi Sandy. I was wondering when you'd call back." Maxwell Stiles admits that he stayed close to his desk that day because he knew she wanted to talk to him. In addition to being the coroner, Stiles serves as a volunteer on an inner-city committee with a mission to revitalize the downtown area by addressing social issues. Stiles has a personal interest in wanting to speak with Sandy. He is in favour of seeing a shelter built and knows publicity is needed to sway public opinion. The kind Old Lady named Fate also brings the news that Stiles is just getting ready to leave the office for the day. "I drive right past your broadcast centre on the way home. How about I just stop in? I can be there in just a few minutes." He arrives within ten minutes and Sandy's story leads the news that night.

"What an asshole," is Sandy's only thought as Sauer walks past her desk later on his way home. He looks a little deflated. Despite his efforts to derail Sandy, she succeeded anyway, which has hurt his ego. Too bad.

Sandy's boss Frank never wanders into workplace skirmishes like this, even though he may want to. Frank just observes and grins. He loves Sandy's go-to-hell attitude. He works that way too. Frank has been with the TV station since it began broadcasting in the 1960s. There's been a lot of change over these twenty years: changes like the medium going from black and white to colour, technology evolving from film production to videotape, and from having only men working in newsrooms to now having women reporters as the norm.

He seems to be proud to have hired Sandy. She is the first Aboriginal person to work in the mainstream of broadcasting, and he discovered her. Frank doesn't care who you are or where you come from. He cares only about getting the job done well. "Don't let the bastards get you down" is his response to just about everything. It works, and it is good advice for Sandy. He smiles and waves good-night as he, too, heads home for the day.

PRESS CLUB

We're heading out for drinks after the show, Sandy. Meet you at the Press Club?" Lilly Thiele extends the invitation at the end of the workweek. "Social drinking" is what they call it. It makes Sandy wonder if there is an invisible and unspoken line between social drinking and addiction. Is there some sanitization in calling it a social event? Sandy isn't sure but whatever the case, it beats drinking alone.

Newsroom staff from all the city's media outlets converge every Friday evening on the Press Club, located in the old warehouse district. The newly revitalized area has developed a unique charm all its own. Some street art was commissioned, and elaborate murals of Prairie landscapes now grace the sides of otherwise-tired old buildings. Planters filled with colourful marigolds, daisies and shrubs have been placed on corners, and birch trees have been planted to brighten the whole area.

Tonight the freshly fallen snow covers the shrubs, now adorned with Christmas lights, and Sandy decides to join her television colleagues. But her reason for doing so is not to hang out with the crew from her newsroom. After all, that idiot Sauer will be showing up along with his remora Lee. Sandy has no interest in listening to them brag about how great they think they are. No, she will go to the

Press Club to network, wanting to meet with the other broadcasters as well as writers from the local daily newspaper. Those reporters intrigue Sandy. They are smarter, with more substance and humour, than people like Sauer and McMillan. And the newspaper types never assume that she is an authority only on Aboriginal issues. They openly include her in their discussions about politics, art, farming—any topic. It makes Sandy feel good to be accepted as an equal. But sometimes these forays into fitting in mean she has to leave her Jeep parked overnight. These people tend to drink too much.

Sandy discovered their lush factor on her first night at the club. Her intention that evening had been to go out for just a couple of drinks. It turned into an all-nighter but it was worth it. It was already past midnight when Sandy found herself drunk as a skunk, still sitting with the newspaper crowd toasting—one for the road.

She intended to drive home, but one stogie-smokin' columnist named John Kremshaw warned against it. "Sit down, kid, let's talk a bit." He ordered them each another Scotch. He was a short man with badly cut grey hair, and a friend of Frank's. "Way back when," Kremshaw was proud to say, those two codgers started their careers at the same small-town daily. "You have good energy, kid," he had told Sandy while holding out his smoke-stained hand to shake hers. His index and middle fingers were a dull shade of yellow from smoking unfiltered Player's cigarettes over a long period of time. It didn't matter: his unique "dumb as a fox" persona made up for any sins, like the yellowed fingers or drinking too much.

Sandy wondered if John's hair had always been grey. The wrinkles on his face seemed to be a map of a long, hard and fascinating road travelled. Considering John had been writing about politics for as long as she could remember, Sandy felt honoured in the interest he took in her career and her development as a journalist.

"It's good you're there," he growled after they downed the Scotch. It was probably his eleventh, maybe even twelfth shot. It was

Sandy's first time drinking the hard liquor and she found it harsh, clinging to the sides of her throat and leaving a burning feeling in its wake. It was then she figured out why early Indians called this stuff "firewater." But Scotch suited John's personality perfectly.

"You know, it won't be long before your people are a political force in this province, Sandy. They're just getting started. And you and I might be the only ones in this room who know it." John pointed across the dimly lit Press Club toward Sandy's television co-workers. "Most of those bozos in your newsroom likely can't even spell the word *inclusion* for Christ's sake. And they certainly can't see beyond the mirror, Sandy. Damn teeth and hair is all there is to them. So don't let the bastards get you down. You do good work."

Having voiced his barb, John ordered another Scotch before admitting he had not been passive in following Sandy's career. "They weren't going to hire you, you know. Some of those assholes in management didn't even look at your resume—they just looked at your brown skin. But Frank wanted you and he asked my opinion before you were hired. I told him to go for it. Best damn advice I've given this year." John smiled and toasted again, raising a stubby glass that contained no ice.

He and Sandy became fast friends. Sandy knew why; John and Frank were similar, speaking the same language and coming from the old school. Sandy imagined that as young reporters both could be found sneaking around in the bushes, rooting through trash bins and wearing fedoras. Sandy doubted that either one was ever truly off the job. Even today. The Old School teaches that journalism is about exploring people's lives and what is important to them; it has nothing to do with Rouge Pulp–coloured lipstick and hairspray. "You just remember that, Sandy. You're a good kid," he said again.

John also proved to be a wealth of knowledge on provincial politics and the history of the area. Away from the Press Club he had a reputation for being a "gruff old son of a bitch" but that's not how Sandy saw him. In the months since that first meeting, John always had the time to patiently explain any issue to her. He would never be patronizing, though he did lecture her that first night: "Put those car keys away, pumpkin." He talked about public image and how scandalous it would be if Sandy Pelly, the Native reporter, were ever caught drinking and driving. "Don't feed the stereotype. Never give them reason to say 'See, I told you so.' Always take a cab, honey. It's safer."

Sandy nodded in agreement, putting her keys back in her purse just before the bartender nudged John's shoulder. "Time to go, John. We're closing."

"Okay, Hop Sing. You did a great job tonight. Here." Kremshaw left a five-dollar tip on the table next to several empty glasses. "Do us a favour would you?" he said to the bartender. "Call us two cabs. One for me, the other for pumpkin here." Then Kremshaw kissed her hand the way royalty might be greeted. "My lady. It's been a pleasure chatting. You hang in there. Don't let the bastards get you down." That was months ago, but the Press Club scene played out pretty much the same at the end of each week.

IN THE OVEN TOO LONG

While yet another night at the Press Club may have been fun, Saturday morning was not. Sandy's head was pounding again. Her beautiful brown eyes were tinged with red and she was dehydrated. "Why did I drink that Scotch again?" Sandy curses, reaching for a glass of water by her bedside. She smiles, remembering drinking with John Kremshaw again last night. The guy must live at that place. She likes him and is thankful for his encouragement—she needs to balance out the treachery at the office.

General Sour Dick pops into her head. Sandy finds herself hating the fact that Sauer is on her mind again. She thinks about him often, mostly because she sees him on a daily basis, and on a daily basis he is a source of conflict. She heard him make that *Whoo-whoo-whoo* sound again last night at the Press Club, except no one laughed. Thankfully, one newspaper reporter even told him, "Stop acting like a redneck hillbilly and grow up."

Fuck off, you jerk. It's my day off. I don't need to deal with you today, she says to Sauer's image in her head, and pulls on the flannel robe at the edge of her bed. What to do today? She is itching to light up a cigarette again this morning, maybe even go out and buy a pack. She bummed a couple smokes last night, which is always dangerous. For someone trying to quit, having just one can mean restarting the regular habit. She brushes her teeth instead and heads for the kitchen.

Crumpets. There is a bag of them in Sandy's pantry and she decides to toast one while waiting for coffee. No matter how drunk she is, she usually remembers to prepare the coffee machine so she can just turn it on in the morning and wait for the glorious brew. The aroma of freshly brewed coffee is a warm memory of home. It is a habit her father has—drinking a big mug of strong, black coffee first thing in the morning—and a habit she seems to have developed too, now that she is on her own.

As she begins to relax, her thoughts turn to Blue. She wonders what he is up to today, whether he's thought of her since the night they met, whether he'll ever call. She shakes her head and decides that after coffee and a crumpet she'll take a walk around the park.

A crisp and beautiful morning greets her as soon as she makes her way outdoors. The trees are wrapped in a coat of snow and frost. Sandy loves the sound of freshly crunching snow under her boots, and the feeling of starting anew. The university campus is within eyesight, and Sandy finds herself walking in that direction, knowing it is where the police college is housed. Blue told her that the recruits often go out for driver training on weekend mornings, so she keeps an eye on passing traffic just in case. Just then, words from Sandy's Baba enter her head: "Better to have a bad husband than no husband at all." *Why does my family say such things?* Even though she'd only just met him, and found he's unavailable, Sandy wildly wonders if her preoccupation with Blue may mean there could still be a future for them.

If so, she dreams of a union as perfect as her grandparents'. Since she was a little girl, Sandy has marvelled at how wonderfully they treated each other. Baba is blessed that way, proving that the greatest love stories are those that are lived—not just written about.

Why does Blue keep popping into my head? The series of uncomfortable memories Blue had incited during their early-morning conversation continues, going back to when she was just four years old. It was the first time she remembers being upset because she wasn't white like everyone else in her family.

"Mommy, why am I so brown?"

"God left you in the oven too long." It probably sounded reasonable, even whimsical, when her mom said it back then. It didn't sound so nice when a neighbour later came to visit, pointing at her like some sort of freak. "Wow, is she ever dark. Hey, she's a little Indian!"

"I used to be but not no more." Already Sandy was adamant she wasn't different, yet felt so isolated that someone had pointed out her skin colour. She started to cry.

Sandy also remembers ugly words from an uncle when she was seven years old. "You don't want to adopt no stinkin' Indian. She'll only cause you trouble!" Sandy recalls her dad yelling at him. "She's my daughter and I love her. You get the hell out of my house!" Her dad. Her hero. The racist uncle never visited again.

By the time she was seventeen, she'd renounced her heritage altogether and started dating only white guys, making up stories about the colour of her skin. *I'm no Cree. No siree. I'm Polynesian, Asian, Italian, anything but Indian. It's just easier to fit in that way.* Her dates would buy in because she did well in school, had a good part-time job, but the parents never felt the same. They would always be disappointed when their precious son brought Sandy home. "Oh son, how could you lower yourself to dating one of *them*?" It made her feel ashamed. They always broke up. One date was blunt: "Hey you know Sandy, you are quite beautiful. But no one is ever actually going to want to *be* with you. Because you're an Indian. I'll sleep with you, though." *Fucker—by the way, if people ever try to tell you there is no such thing as bad sex, they're lying.*

These hurtful memories of alienation spiral around in her mind. Why is she so attracted to Blue? She hardly knows him. But he is Metis, and because of this, Sandy thinks it is likely he'll understand the lonely feeling of not really belonging anywhere and the tremendous need to belong somewhere. Maybe with him? By chance, a group of young recruits drives by. Sandy catches a glimpse of Blue in a patrol car. He isn't looking her way and doesn't see her. She wants to wave and get his attention, but lowers her eyes instead. Her heart follows.

PITCH

Work continues. Closing in on Christmas Day, but Sauer has no holiday spirit. This morning he's livid and confides the source of his ire to Lee McMillan. "Can you believe it? The network called to say it's interested in broadcasting one of the stories Pelly pitched to them."

The newsroom is operating on a shoestring staff this week. With the usual assignment producer, Sean Waters, booked off until the new year, Sauer has taken over the role of assigning stories. An ugly wrinkle forms over Lee McMillan's eyebrows. "The network called for Pelly? What the hell? What did she ever do that's worth talking about?"

Sauer sneers. "Yes, can you believe it? As if I'd do any favours for that little wagon-burner. So I lied. I told them she's not here today but I'm sure I could produce the story instead."

"Bravo," McMillan responds. "Did they go for it?"

"They did, considering I also told them Pelly was booked off on vacation and won't be returning until late next month. They want the story right away—you know how hard it is to dig up news so close to Christmas. So they say, 'Sure Dick, if you're able to piece it together, go ahead.' I'd love to have a story on the network. So I checked the notebook that Pelly left on her desk and called her contacts. They all said, 'No, we're not talking to anyone but Sandy.' Damn Indians, now they think they can tell us what to do!"

"So, what are you going to do?" Lee is willing to support Sauer's deception no matter what his plan includes.

"He's going to tell Sandy, that's what."

Both Sauer and McMillan just about shit their pants when they unexpectedly hear Lilly's voice and see her walk around the corner. Sauer and McMillan hadn't realized anyone else was in early today, because Lilly was in the washroom straightening her hair when their diatribe began. Sauer turns a caustic shade of red as though his head might explode. Lilly isn't sure if it's because he's angry at being caught or because he is embarrassed. "Of course we're going to assign Pelly," Sauer stutters. "She in yet? I was just joking you know."

Lilly snickers then checks her watch. "She's not scheduled to be in for another half hour. As for your joke, I'll let Frank know what you said. We'll see if he thinks it's funny too."

It took mere minutes for Sauer to make a call to the network to straighten things out. "Yes hello, it's Dick Sauer. That Pelly story you wanted? Looks like she is booked in today after all. There was a bit of a scheduling mix-up so I will assign her to this today. You can put it in your lineup."

An early Christmas present for sure. Sandy is elated to hear the news when she comes into the office. Lilly decides not to tell Sandy what Sauer and McMillan had attempted to do, wanting Sandy's focus to be on nothing but producing a superb story. "Hey listen, if you need any help producing this, just ask. But while I'm at it— do you mind if I read the memo you sent pitching the story to the network?" Without hesitation, Sandy hands it over. Lilly smiles while reading, easily understanding why the network is interested in broadcasting it across the country.

MEMO

To: Toronto Office

Story Pitch and Treatment by Sandy Pelly

The old Kresge's Store downtown is one of the only spots left where an unpretentious lunch counter can be found. It's complete with an overworked waitress who pulls her hair back into a tight ponytail and wears dark red lipstick.

I raced in there one noon hour to grab a ham sandwich and a Coke. While waiting in line to pay, I overheard the words of a distraught Native woman. She was speaking to a friend. Their conversation went something like this:

"I can't believe it! I leave town for two days and come back to this!" The young lady's voice trailed off. She had to stop for a moment to compose herself—otherwise tears instead of words might have come out. It piqued my interest.

I sat down with the young ladies and introduced myself.

The young mom is named Julia. She's Saulteaux and living common-law with the father of their young son, Anthony.

Julia tells me she had gone back to her reserve for a couple days to pick up a dance bustle for Anthony. A bustle is an arrangement of feathers that powwow dancers use when dancing. Julia's grandmother handmade the dance bustle as a surprise gift for Christmas. Naturally, because it was a surprise, little Anthony stayed home, back in the city with his dad.

When Julia came home, she was horrified.

Anthony's beautiful long black braid, which he'd been growing since the age of three, was gone. The dad says he cut it off because he didn't want the other kids at school making fun of him.

Julia tells me that within Aboriginal culture, a braid is important. She says that the three strands signify love, kindness and humility. When Native people wear braids, they are making a promise to live with those qualities.

She also says that since the haircut, little Anthony is depressed. He says he feels naked and no longer wants to dance at the powwow. Julia has left her common-law spouse and has gone to the police with the story. She wants to know whether the common-law spouse can be charged with assault.

It appears as though the Crown is considering her case.

Let me know if you want me to develop this story.

—Sandy Pelly, Regina Office

MUCKRAKER

It is a new year. Sandy went to her hometown of Okema over Christmas, which meant obligatory attendance at midnight Mass on Christmas Eve. There, she said a prayer asking for a new and more supportive environment at work. She found that her wish came partially true her first morning back at the office. Dick Sauer is notably absent. He called in after the holiday libations to say he'd twisted his ankle and wouldn't be in all week. Someone has to cover the legislature.

"The show must go on. Someone's gotta fill in for Sauer." Frank makes the declaration, and a decision. Unbeknownst to Sandy, he'd spoken with John Kremshaw over the holidays. "Give her some tougher assignments, Frank," Kremshaw urged. "Assign her to cover the House. I'm sure she can handle it. Besides, I'm there every day—I'll keep an eye on her. Dammit, she's got the goods. Let her prove it."

That first morning back, Frank has found the opportunity to let Sandy try, and is happy to deliver the news. "Hey Sandy, Happy New Year. Listen, Sauer is extending his holiday for a week. We'd usually get Josh to fill in at the legislature, but he's on the road and Lee is assigned to another story today. That leaves you. For starters, can you handle putting together some type of political look-ahead for the coming year? A sort of political forecast, if you will?" He gives a coy smile, like he is pleased with himself.

Within seconds and a stroke of a pen, Sandy is assigned to be the political reporter. Lilly watches as Frank delivers the news. She makes a happy little squeal and claps her hands, going over to Sandy's desk as soon as Frank leaves. "So, so happy for you! And, listen, if you need me to pull any old video clips, just let me know. It'll be so great to see a woman covering politics for once. Way to go, Sandy."

Driving up to the grand marble palace that is the legislature, Sandy is both nervous and excited. Generally, covering politics is for the veteran reporters. It's a coup for her to be able to take this assign-ment, even for a week, so early in her career. She says a prayer of gratitude, grabbing her purse and notepad from the passenger seat of her Jeep before walking toward the regal-looking staircase leading up to the heavy wooden doors of the building. The morning is serene and Sandy can only hear the sounds of sparrows, no traffic noise or wind. Because she is wearing mukluks, even her footsteps are silent. The winter sunlight reflects warmly off fresh snow covering the lawn. Without realizing, Sandy holds her breath as she hoists open the door to go in, like she's diving underwater. As the heavy door bangs shut behind her, the first person she spots is John Kremshaw. He's leaning against the security desk, chatting up the security officer. "There's the little pumpkin. Nervous, Pelly?" He gives her a hug. "Here's to a happy start to a new year."

Sandy smiles, relieved to be greeted in such a friendly and familiar fashion. She sees it as a sign that the day will be a good one. Kremshaw begins to introduce Sandy to the security guard but it isn't necessary.

"Miss Pelly doesn't need an introduction, John. My wife and I watch her all the time. We love seeing you. It's so nice to meet you," the guard says, shaking her hand. "You still have to sign in though." He chuckles and pushes the guest registry toward her.

"Shouldn't be too busy today, Sandy." Kremshaw leads Sandy up the hard marble staircase, which is still covered with a dark red carpet. "This carpet should be gone by now. They only put it out when the House is in session. Don't know why it's here today. Come on up, I'll show you the gallery."

As they walk through the impressive rotunda—a big, round area that forms the middle of the building—John surveys the area. Like any good reporter or cop, he is always aware of his surroundings. He sees an MLA hurriedly walking toward them. It is then he offers Sandy some advice. "See that one?" Sandy nods in acknowledgement. "Elliott Ward. Stay away from him. Nothing but trouble and a ladies' man to boot. You wouldn't believe the rumours about how he keeps a diary of all the young pages he beds. Bad news, pumpkin. Just stay away from him."

Sandy is aware of that grapevine. Those who lead public lives often don't enjoy privacy, especially when it comes to gossip at the Press Club. But she's never met Elliott Ward in person. At first glance she finds herself being attracted to him. He is tall and handsome like the Marlborough Man. The attraction ends when Ward catches up to the two in the rotunda. Ward shakes Kremshaw's hand but ignores Sandy except to leer at her and make lustful glances at her cleavage. Ward leaves the area, making his way toward the basement stairwell.

"See, told ya. Never looks a lady in the eye, if you know what I mean." Kremshaw shakes his head in disgust as he continues to lead Sandy up to the press gallery on the second floor.

It's later that morning, when Sandy is making her way to the basement area of the legislature, that she overhears Ward talking in the hallway. On her way toward the cafeteria to grab a coffee, she sees him slouched in a corner speaking with a political staffer just inside a gallery amid old photographs of previous lieutenant-governors. Their voices are hushed whispers. But in the unusual acoustics of the legislature, Sandy is able to make out the discussion. As she listens in, it becomes clear that the staffer has overspent advertising funds promoting Elliot's governing party. That's when she hears Ward say, "I've taken care of it. I claimed the money as a bogus project in my constituency."

Sandy can't believe it. She spends the rest of the day doing research and finding sources other than Elliot and files her story. It's a gem and runs at the top of the night's newscast. Other media outlets follow Sandy's lead and run the same story the following day.

The attention makes her feel good, but increasingly the only attention she wants is Blue's. She wants to let him go, but he is still at the forefront of her thoughts, especially when she wishes to share something important, like these newfound professional accolades, with someone who is important in her life. Weeks have passed since the whirlwind evening when she both met him and learned of his unavailability. In part, it's why she's thrown herself into her work. *Blue has a girlfriend.* It bothers her that she can't stop thinking about him.

She wonders how often he picks up girls at the bar. Was she just another number or was she special to him? In that one night they spent together, she'd already come to understand what influenced his decisions in life. Sandy closes her eyes, slipping into her own little dream world, stealing just a few quiet moments. Then she is startled by a loud, booming voice and a tap on her shoulder.

"Hey, quit daydreaming there, bright eyes. Great job at the legislature, but I have another assignment for you," Frank says. He tells Sandy there are a number of new recruits for this year's police service. "Good candidates," he says. "But what makes this group special is that, for the first time, an Aboriginal has completed the program and is gonna be a cop. That's good, right?"

Frank has a gravelly voice. It gives away the fact that he smokes too much and enjoys his whiskey on a regular basis. "You take this one, Sandy. And be back by mid-afternoon. We're short of cameras today." She closes her eyes, wishing she were still daydreaming. She knows what she is about to walk in to. Maybe it will be okay. Maybe she won't have to talk to him, maybe just to his superior officers. It is more like a prayer than a thought; besides, she is wrong.

As she suspects, Blue is the Aboriginal recruit. Like her, he has boldly chosen a career that no Indian has chosen before. And you can guess that Frank wants Sandy to play up the correlation between a Native officer fighting crime and the fact that it's mostly Aboriginal people getting into trouble: where's the balance? He wants Sandy to file a story that asks the central question of if Blue will make a difference. She knows Frank will want her to depict Blue as some sort of Sir Galahad. Regardless, Sandy will see Blue again, this time on his playing field. She grabs her reporter's notebook and heads out the door.

GIRLS' NIGHT 1985

There is a lot for the girls to talk about tonight, as it was just yesterday that Sandy visited the police college. Her head is still reeling and heart still exuberant after seeing Blue again. But that big, white elephant is still hanging around and Ellen doesn't hesitate to bring it up. "So, he still got that girlfriend?"

"He didn't mention anything. And I didn't ask." Sandy went on to describe the encounter, putting in as many details as possible. "Oh my God, you should have seen the way he was dressed."

The TV crew arrived at the university just as the new recruits were finishing a workout. It took mere seconds to spot Blue, wearing only sneakers, socks and a pair of grey gym shorts. His brown skin glistened with sweat, his upper chest and arms beautifully sculpted, "Adonis-like," Sandy blushed. "I tell you, Elle, if I'd been a cartoon character, I would've started to salivate."

"You're a pig." Ellen gestures for Sandy to continue.

"I couldn't stop myself from staring everywhere. Long muscular legs. Broad, strong shoulders. Well-developed chests. And that Blue. We never slept together that night, as you know, but boy, one look at his body and I wish we had!" The girls toasted and giggled. "It was so awkward for me to pretend as though I didn't know Blue when the commanding officer pointed to him."

When Blue noticed her there, it caused him to lose his concentration. He missed a command but received no reprimand, probably because the television camera was rolling. Sandy says she scarcely paid attention to the commanding officer while interviewing him. "He said stuff like 'We are proud that our Aboriginal Recruiting Program is showing success.' He kept talking and I kept on daydreaming—it was like listening to Charlie Brown's schoolteacher. I didn't hear a word. Next up it was Blue who was beaming and standing beside me. But everyone was watching, so we had to play it cool." Blue had talked about the recruitment program, but Sandy was sure he was flirting with his eyes. The assignment ceased to exist. Sandy hardly even remembers writing it. But the story ended up taking the prominent number-three spot in that evening's newscast lineup.

As girls' night continues, the discussion flip-flops from Blue to clothing and fashion to hairstyles, family and food. Digging into the last piece of dessert at almost midnight, they agree it's time to head home. They've been through two litres of Chardonnay and are both a little tipsy. Ellen calls a cab. Sandy decides to walk as it's only two blocks. Sandy never feels afraid to walk home, even at this late hour.

It's a cold winter night. Thankfully there's no wind to make the temperature dip to uncomfortable levels. But she's wearing her gorgeous, full-length white mink fur coat handed down from her Baba. Sandy giggles, wondering if she wears the coat as a way to meet men. It always attracts their attention. Each time she wears it, people seem to want to pet it. But walking home right now, it's not her coat but thoughts of Blue that keep her warm.

She keeps thinking about all the times she wanted to call him at the police academy dorm but was too afraid. Now she regrets it. Any day now, the police academy will be graduating this year's class. Blue will be moving to another city—but not before saying goodbye, as Sandy is startled to learn when she reaches the front door of her apartment.

Blue is seated on the bench in the foyer of her building, waiting for Sandy to come home. But there's something not quite right this time. He doesn't carry the same level of confidence. When she approaches him, it's easy to figure out why. Blue smells of beer and cigarette smoke.

"I have to tell you something," he says. "It's important." She unlocks the heavy door. They walk up the creaky wooden staircase together, silently.

BLUE UNPLUGGED

'm not exactly sure how it happened," Blue's voice is apologetic. So are his eyes. "But I have a responsibility toward her somehow." Blue's drunken explanation makes no sense to Sandy. From what she is able to piece together, his girlfriend is a woman named Heidi whose bed Blue stumbled into after an accident out in the wilderness.

A few years ago Blue and his buddy Steve went cross-country skiing in Alberta's Kananaskis Country. Steve was Heidi's boyfriend. "The signs were clearly posted," Blue recounts. "*Stay on groomed trails.* That's what it said. But we didn't. We went toward the back-country. There are better opportunities for photography there. Steve loved photography. That's what got him into trouble." Blue says they found a spot that was sheltered, so he decided to stay back and build a fire, have some tea and relax. Steve wanted to keep walking to higher ground to get a shot of the setting sun. "But that never happened. Steve lost his footing on some ice-covered rocks. He fell and hit his head. He died instantly."

Blue says he didn't like the thought of the police showing up to break the news to Heidi, so he volunteered to tell her. "She sobbed. I held her for hours, talking about Steve and drowning our sorrows. And somehow that night we ended up in bed. That's how it all got started. From that day forward it was just sort of understood that I was now hers."

Blue rounds out the story further but not before fumbling with his wallet to show Sandy a photo of Heidi. It's jagged at the edges; clearly it's been in and out of his wallet often. Sandy quickly glances at the picture, feeling obligated to have a look. Blue's slurring explanation continues. "So, when I decided to join the police force and move to Saskatchewan, I asked her to come live with me but she refused. She lives in rural Alberta and I send her money each month. She hasn't worked since Steve died."

The entire story sounds weird and Sandy can't figure it out. *So now what am I supposed to do? He's hanging onto a ghost. Why?* It may be the booze that brought out the other dirty facts, but from Blue's description, Heidi has no ambition. Sandy imagines her to be trailer trash.

Blue changes the subject, picking up Sandy's hand. "You are beautiful. Truly beautiful. That's what attracted me. You have a self-confidence that allows you to be free and full of life. You deserve to be with someone who treats you like gold. I wish it were me. But now I'm leaving and probably won't get the chance."

These are the things a drunken man says just because he feels like saying it. Chances are he won't regret his slurring words in the morning, because he probably won't remember. "The eyes are the mirror to the soul. And you have the most beautiful eyes I've ever seen, Sandy." Blue closes his own eyes a couple times and says he's tired and needs to lie down for a minute. Within seconds he passes out on her leatherette couch.

She sits beside him before deciding to turn in for the night as well. She covers him up with a quilt and heads to the bathroom. Glancing in the mirror, Sandy pauses and leans her hands on the sink. *God. Why did Blue come over here tonight?* As she splashes cold water on her face, she gets an answer.

She knows why Blue showed up, intent on telling her all these things. When Heidi reached out to him, it must have been the first time Blue really felt needed. He needed to feel loved and important. She wonders if needing to feel *needed* leads to bad decisions, and whether she is making one right now by allowing him to stay.

THERE–AFTER

The next morning it is Blue who wakes up first. Somewhat disoriented, he moves the blanket Sandy placed on him to the edge of the couch. He needs to find the bathroom. En route, he sees Sandy still asleep in her bedroom. Her door is open. He hears her faintly snore and it makes him smile. He thinks she looks peaceful and he feels comfortable being there. *But what to do? Leave her a note, saying thanks for letting me stay the night and then flee the scene? Or wake her up to tell her in person?*

First things first, he goes to the bathroom, turning on the tap to let the water run as cold as possible before splashing it on his face. His hair is flattened on one side. He rubs some water over his scalp to round it out. Looking at his reflection in the mirror, Blue makes a decision. He goes to Sandy's bedroom to wake her, gently touching her shoulder. "Good morning, sleepyhead. Thanks for letting me sleep it off. Sorry about that, I shouldn't have just shown up unannounced."

Sandy reassures him that it was a better decision to stay with her than to try to find his way back to the campus. He agrees, saying he'd probably have gotten into trouble by showing up drunk after curfew. "But roll call isn't until noon on the weekend, so I still have time to sneak back." He suggests they go for breakfast. As Sandy quickly gets ready, Blue takes another look around her apartment, remembering the first time he visited. It saddens him to think that he hurt Sandy's feelings, talking about a girlfriend who isn't really part of his life anymore. Although he still sends her money, he hasn't even seen her in a couple months.

Within a half hour Blue and Sandy are at the entryway of the bus depot cafeteria. It isn't a fancy place but it's just one block from where Sandy lives. The little café can barely be called a nook since customers are elbow to elbow. The décor includes old-style Formica tables. Most of the tables have a full ashtray waiting to be emptied, plastic salt and pepper shakers and a glass bottle of ketchup. As Sandy glances around at the customers, she sees that most are eating greasy fries with their fingers. An older, properly dressed gent with impeccable manners motions them his way. "You look like you need a place to sit." He stands up. "Here—my bus is leaving in less than a half hour so I best get to the platform." He gives them both a nod and walks to the counter, leaving Sandy and Blue to take the seat he's offered.

"I really wish I didn't have to leave this afternoon." Blue's eyes are apologetic. "But at least I can get some food in you before then." He grabs the photocopied menu wedged between the salt and pepper. Blue studies the limited selection, runs his fingers through his hair, then offers another confession. "You have no idea how many times I've wished that I'd met you a couple years ago—since meeting you, I mean."

A thin-lipped waitress with a bad auburn dye-job brings over a couple glasses of water.

"Ready?" she asks without making eye contact.

"Do you have porridge?" Sandy has a hankering for comfort food this morning.

The waitress gives a hardy laugh. "Porridge? What do you think this is, the story of the three bears or something?" She can't stop snickering. "Sorry, no porridge, but the breakfast special is popular."

Sandy shrugs her shoulders and agrees that two eggs over-easy, bacon and toast will do just fine. Blue orders the same. Sandy thinks she wants the fairy tale... but while waiting for their meal to arrive, she wonders about porridge and the three bears, hoping that Blue isn't just trying her on for size. He looks handsome and well put-together this morning despite being drunk last night. She wonders if he is one of those people who can drink yet never feel the effects of a hangover. It's as though he's read her mind again.

"I feel really good today even though I had way too much beer last night." He touches just the tips of her fingers. "I think it's because I'm here with you." They eat in silence, with Blue checking his watch every couple minutes. Sandy is having trouble swallowing, trying to keep the tears back and put the food down at the same time, thinking this may very well be the last time she sees him. She almost stops breathing at what Blue says next. He fidgets and then speaks: "Come with me."

UNDERWORLD DREAMING

Sandy spends the day wandering through little shops, trying to make sense of what just happened. It's been so exhausting that once finally home, she nods off while watching a sitcom. Her sleep is fitful. She is on the couch covered by the same quilt that kept Blue warm last night. A feeling of panic jolts Sandy from a deep sleep, leaving her hyperventilating and gasping for air.

Lightning Strikes

Hard, sudden,
violent.

Walk toward
a burning bush.

One of two things
will happen.

Total destruction?
The potential for new growth?
Maybe both?

Profound
but necessary
change.

It is a lucid dream, forcing her to wake at midnight just as an owl was readying itself to fly in through her open window. In another vision Sandy saw Heidi, recognizing her from Blue's photo, signing her name in blood. *What does it mean?*

SCHVARTZE

Sandy realizes she feels sick—scratching at her forearm most of the day and wondering why. The years haven't stopped her from trying to scrape off the brown. Blue is brown: it's the reason she was initially attracted to him. But now the attraction is so strong she can't make any sense of it. From his side, the attraction must have been a fluke: "My girlfriend is white." Like a thousand other times in her life—which she would never admit to anyone—she wishes she were white. *Maybe then he'd want me more.*

It's only recently that she made the connection that her heritage has value. Employers want to hire brown-skinned people so they can claim to represent the demographic of the province. *Maybe Blue figured that out too?* It caused her to soul-search. Was she really proud of her Cree blood or was it just fashion, a means to accelerating her own ambitions? And if that was the case, was she any better than Blue?

She decides to run a bath, hoping to wash away the bad memories that refuse to die. As she lowers herself into the warm suds, she remembers a moment from her youth. A young boy from a town not far away, the scorekeeper. He noticed Sandy playing volleyball at a high school competition and made a point to introduce himself after the game had ended.

"Nice serve. And spike. My name is Gabe. Want some water?" Gabe noticed her because she was a good player. And pretty. He asked her out to a community dance.

Sandy didn't give him an answer but gave him her phone number. After that night, they had a series of phone calls, mostly Gabe calling to say hello. The conversations never amounted to anything more than superficial teenage flirting. Even so, Sandy enjoyed the attention. It had never happened before. The boys at her own school had ridiculed her and called her an ugly squaw since grade one. Gabe didn't seem to care that she was brown, so Sandy agreed to go to the dance.

Gabe picked her up in an old pickup that had a stick shift, promising her parents to have her back by midnight. Sandy got into the truck looking radiant in a crimson and sky-blue dress that she'd sewn herself. Sadly, it was not too long later that Gabe brought her back— crying. Sandy bypassed her parents and went right to her bedroom, ears still ringing with the sounds of catcalls that came her way the moment the couple walked into the dance.

"What? He brought a hooker? Those *schvartze*. It's all you can expect. And such a nice boy. What's he doing with her? Must be hard up."

Schvartze. There was finger-pointing and maniacal laughter. Too much for Gabe. Before the first dance even started, he drove home the shamed girl who never did succeed at scraping off the brown.

Later that night Sandy looked up and found the meaning of the word *schvartze*: a slang and racist term that is often used in combination with the words "lazy" and "stupid." Sandy felt as though she'd been hit with a spiked weapon—vilified, scorned, assaulted. She read further that if you are black it means "nigger." But she is Cree, so the translation is "squaw, sick bitch, stupid loser." This is how they saw her, and why he drove her home before the evening even began.

Maybe being with someone else who is brown will help make sense of all of this? Help her find acceptance and a place to belong? *He won't be ashamed of me because I am brown—like everyone else has been. He's brown too.* A prayer, if nothing else.

SOMETHING IS MISSING

Another manic Monday and Sandy wonders whether madness has indeed overtaken her good senses. But today she doesn't care. The past forty-eight hours have changed everything. Sandy can't stop smiling as she makes her way to work. For the first time in weeks she is going into the story meeting without a story idea.

It is excruciating for her to keep the news to herself: she is going to resign. Not even Ellen knows yet. Sandy has asked no one for advice. Today is the day to let everyone know that she's going to move to Saskatoon to live with Blue. Start a new life.

On the way to her Jeep a warm wind blows her long hair over her shoulders, erasing the bad images that came in her dreams. Some West African music blurts out of the radio as she starts her engine. "Guaranteed to make you happy," the announcer says. He is right. The music is energetic and cheerful. Sandy sees it as a sign that she's made the right decision. Her usual routine en route to work is to grab a coffee and enjoy at least one cigarette before getting to the office, even though she tells everyone that she quit. She realizes she doesn't want to have to hide the habit from Blue, too, which makes her decide not to smoke this morning. *If I am going to quit, may as well do it today.* She turns the music up instead.

At the newsroom, everyone is too busy to notice Sandy's arrival. She wonders if she looks different today. Sauer and McMillan are looking at the front page of the newspaper. Another reporter monitors CBC Radio. Lilly hands a Workers' Compensation Board report to the assignment editor after finding it in the morning mail. Each has the same aim—to figure out what to put on-air that night and hopefully find a good story that will lead the newscast.

The meeting begins and as usual Sauer is the first to scoff at other people's suggestions. "Just a matter of time before I leave this small place for the network," Sandy once overheard him confide to Lee McMillan. "Or maybe Montreal or Vancouver."

Sandy could never figure out that ambition. She loves the Prairies. It is the place she calls home and she is content to stay with what she knows. *To each their own, I guess.* She stirs her coffee even though she drinks it black. The swizzle stick is just for show. *Maybe I am more like these colleagues than I realize.* The thought makes her wince. Her choice of attire that day is symbolic. Sandy wore the same navy blazer and lavender-coloured skirt her very first day on the job. It is a Simon Chang design that she picked up at a second-hand store, where there is all sorts of treasure to be found if you know where to look. She wore it on the first day, and now she is wearing it on the last.

The meeting starts with the usual critique of the previous night's show. Frank leads the discussion. "That first story, Dick, was kind of weak. You should have looked for a stronger character in opposition to that bill introduced in the legislature yesterday." He continues with more personal observations, "And Lee, you've got to stop wearing patterns when you go on camera. A polka-dotted dress? Stick to conservative-looking clothes. This isn't a fashion show. Very distracting." His list of sins and omissions continues. He talks about things that work and things that need improvement, all of it with the goal of keeping people interested in watching their news and not someone else's program.

"So let's get on with today." Frank is looking for story ideas. "Simon, what's on your agenda?" He goes around the table asking each reporter, each editor and each writer for input. The discussion is typical. There are suggestions about political stories. Stories about business, the economy and education. Someone mentions something about a twenty-five-year-old cat. Most of the ideas are good. The focus turns to Sandy.

Frank has gotten used to, and expects, something hard-edged and relevant from her. She has to disappoint this morning. "I don't have a suggestion today. No ideas. But I do need to speak with you. In private."

He doesn't like the tone of her request and calls the meeting to an early end. He closes the door of his office and calls the receptionist, telling her to hold his calls for the next half hour. "The floor is yours," he says, giving Sandy a curious glance.

She adjusts her suit jacket and clears her throat before speaking. "I am handing in my resignation today," she blurts out.

He's startled. "Why, Sandy? You're doing so well. Sure, I have to admit that at first I didn't know what to think about hiring you, you didn't have that much experience. But it's a privilege to work with you. Won't you reconsider?"

"Can't." She breaks the news that she is moving, starting a new life with a new love.

"Oh boy." Frank pours her a glass of water and says, "You know, I wish you the best of luck in this, Sandy. But you need to hear a few facts. Take a close look at our newsroom. Who's there? Simon? He's divorced. Lee? Single. Rowena? Drinks too much. Lilly? Well, she's just young right now, so she doesn't count. Dick? Sleeps around with anything that walks. David? Divorced, twice. Shall I continue?"

Sandy shakes her head as Frank continues. "This business is hard on relationships. You need to be aware of that. I only hope that this Blue fellow is strong enough to support you when you really need it, as you climb up the ladder. And you *will*, I have no doubt. But really,

I do wish you the best. You're a good kid and an excellent reporter. Don't be surprised someday if the network comes calling, not just for a story, but for you. In the meantime I'll make some calls to my contacts in Saskatoon." He hugs Sandy, the way a gruff old uncle hugs his favourite niece at Christmas. The phone rings. He waves her away and takes the call.

She takes a deep breath before opening the door to leave his office. She doesn't want anyone to see that she's started to cry. Leaving is hard. Straightening her skirt, she pulls her hair to one side, wanting to regain her composure before heading back to the bull pit, which is her name for the newsroom. That is when she feels it: something is missing.

The dangly silver and hematite earrings that she put on before coming to the office this morning are no longer twins. One is missing. She doesn't feel the left one dangle as she moves her hair. It is gone. Sandy tries to quell feelings of dread. *Breathe!* she tells herself again, this time with some urgency. Sandy is superstitious and she has a theory based on nothing but intuition. During previous relationships or any major decision, when things are not going well, she asks for a sign from the spirits on what to do. Her prayers are always answered: without fail, one of her earrings goes missing. Now one of her earrings is gone again. *Why did it have to happen today?*

BETSY

ober second thoughts. Sandy hates the saying, as though she is incapable of trusting her own judgment. Just about everyone she knows thinks she's crazy for agreeing to move in with Blue. Ellen is the most adamant and she is free to be frank because she and Sandy have been close since childhood. Back then, Ellen was Sandy's only friend and Sandy was Ellen's only friend. The other kids in town didn't play with Sandy because she was an Indian and she guessed their parents didn't want their children being influenced by someone who is surely bad news. The other kids in town didn't play with Ellen either, because she was the minister's daughter. Maybe they thought that by playing with Ellen, God would know their secrets.

Whatever the reason, both little girls were outcasts and both found love and friendship in each other's laughter. For this reason Ellen has licence to say anything she wants to Sandy without worry.

"Some of the men you've been with before were wonderful and still you blew them off, figuring the best way to get over one man is to get under another one. What the hell Sandy? I love you like a sister. You have always been driven and wanting to accomplish… something."

"Yes, I know. Always needing to prove that I am acceptable. But take a look at my life, Elle. Other than you I have never been accepted by anyone, even at work—until Blue."

"You are dancing with danger, my friend."

"Well, then, it'll be the first dance I've ever been fully invited to. Ellen, if it's a mistake then it's my mistake and I have to accept the consequences. I also have to prove to myself that I am good enough at my work to make it—anywhere. I'm going to be okay. I believe. You have to as well."

"Sandy, you hardly know this guy. Have you even kissed him? I know he's handsome but what the hell? He basically led you on, gaining your interest and then telling you he has a girlfriend after the fact."

"Had," Sandy quickly corrected.

"Had, schmad, whatever. I'm just sayin' Sandy, what's the rush? I don't want you to get your heart broken again. Last time that happened, it took forever before I saw you smile again."

"I have to trust my feelings—even if you don't understand."

Sandy remembered how she had been emotionally wounded once before. It was crippling.

Sandy had fallen deeply and totally in love once, but not with a man. It was with her little sister who left Sandy's life without warning. The little girl was Saskatchewan's newest ward. She came into Sandy's home the same way Sandy came—as an orphan with the same social worker. The little girl's name was Betsy Marie Yuzicappi. She arrived one winter morning at Sandy's doorstep carrying a tattered old pyjama doll. She was four years old to Sandy's nine and another product of the Scoop. Betsy was afraid, giving the same look a stray cat would after being chased away with a broomstick. Sandy remembers eavesdropping on the discussion of how Betsy came into care.

Social worker: "We apprehended her just two days ago and she's been at the Children's Cottage since. It's not easy to find her a suitable home. Her extended family wants her to stay with Native people, but we can't find any suitable Native families and I know things went so well with Sandy that you legally adopted her. Is it still going well?"

Sandy's mother: "Of course. Our daughter is wonderful."

Social worker: "Oh. Good. Well, the fact there is a Native girl in your home may be enough to keep Betsy's relatives quiet. We're hoping you will agree to keep Betsy as a foster child until a stable permanent family can be found. You know—a white family."

Sandy's mother: "Of course we'll take her, for as long as you need. I'm just wondering, though, where is Betsy's mom?"

Social worker: "Oh. She's in the hospital recovering from frost-bite. A few toes might need to be amputated. She left Betsy alone so she could go out partying. She got so drunk that she passed out on the grid road while walking home at one o'clock in the morning. Remember that cold snap just before the melt? It was minus-twenty-three that night, with a wind. She's just lucky the RCMP were out patrolling. But don't worry. Betsy won't be going back to her. You can only give these sorts of people one chance, you know."

The social worker's tone made Sandy angry, talking about the little girl like she was some sort of lost puppy being taken to the pound. His description of Betsy's mom made Sandy think of the Grinch. In fact, this worker had that same kind of look about him: young but balding, deep frown lines, a big gut and no fashion sense.

Sandy smiled at the shy little girl, who decided immediately that Sandy could be trusted. Betsy spoke. "This is Sky," she said, holding up her pyjama doll.

"Hello Sky. Are you hungry?" Sandy asked.

"No, she's not hungry, but I am," the little girl replied.

Sandy took Betsy's small hand, leading her to the corner of the kitchen where the old Frigidaire stood. The heavy door continually made a *clunk, clunk* sound each time someone opened or closed it. Betsy's delicate brown hand reached for an orange. Sandy peeled and sectioned the fruit for the little girl, serving it to her on a plate. The little girl chewed with her mouth open.

Betsy smiled. It was a brilliant smile that changed the entire shape of her pretty face. She flashed small and perfect teeth the colour of freshly fallen snow. Sandy figured she was witnessing the same effect of when warmth touches cold: there's magic therein.

Sandy's mom was a kind and gentle woman, but blonde and blue-eyed with white skin. To Betsy, she looked like the type of person who always means trouble. White people like her always meant that someone would be leaving in Betsy's small world. So it took the little girl some time to trust Sandy's mom. But the connection with Sandy was instantaneous. Sandy's brown skin, dark eyes and black hair were recognizable and comfortable.

Betsy filled a void for Sandy too—one that Sandy didn't even know existed within her. She became attached very quickly to her little sister. They were inseparable. Sandy had never known anyone who was the same as she was—a brown girl. The little girl spoke English with an accent. She was Dakota, and loved to talk. She told Sandy stories about fishing and swimming in the lake. She talked about picking Saskatoon berries and gooseberries. And she had a vivid imagination.

"Once I ate so many Saskatoons my poop was blue!" Betsy cackled during one story, covering her mouth with both hands the way a little girl does when she makes a joke that is so funny to her alone that she might end up peeing. To Sandy, the sound was pure beauty and joy. Often they both ended up cackling, like that raven who stole the piece of cheese from the fox in the fairy tale about trust that Sandy's mom used to read when Sandy was Betsy's age. From that day forward, Sandy read the same story to her little sister each night, but not before a trip to the fridge for a piece of orange Velveeta cheese and a glass of lime Kool-Aid.

Betsy relied on Sandy for comfort and belonging. It was Sandy who was there to gently wipe the gravel out from underneath Betsy's skinned knee after she fell from her tricycle later that summer. Sandy gave her a homemade Popsicle for being brave and not crying. They watched the clouds together, laying on freshly cut grass and listening to the warm prairie wind and gentle lull of singing crickets.

There was another sound that Sandy loved: "I want a mustard sandwich, please." It was Betsy's favourite snack, and Sandy knew exactly how the little girl liked it prepared. Dry toast, mustard on one of the pieces, and squished together. Sometimes Sandy used a star-shaped cookie cutter, making the shape before handing the unique sandwich to her little sister. *Will Betsy ever get tired of that same snack every day?* Sandy wondered. But it's a question to which Sandy would never know an answer.

The years rolled by until Sandy was in grade six, and something tumultuous happened. The Grinch showed up again. He stole Sandy's little sister away. A white couple in their early thirties took Betsy out of the province after adopting her. A piece of Sandy died that day watching her little sister's crying face through the back window of the social worker's car as it drove away forever down that lonely grid road.

HALLELUJAH

est not to dwell on the past, Sandy tells herself. *How my life has suddenly changed. I've quit my job. I'm moving to a new city where I don't know anyone except Blue. Are we moving too fast?* Her head says yes, her heart says right on. Sandy keeps talking to herself during the two-hour drive to Blue's apartment in Saskatoon. *I have always done what is expected of me. I'm always worried about what other people will think—what will the neighbours think? It's been so ingrained in me. Enough! This time and for the first time I am doing something for myself. And if anyone doesn't like it, so what?*

Just because I'm a professional everyone expects me to know what I'm doing. God—you know I don't and you're okay with that, eh? You also know I don't worry about anything. I can get a job in this town. Starting over won't be so tough. If Baba were here right now, she'd say, "It builds character." (Sandy crosses her fingers.) *I have to believe that love has finally found me. God please help guide me. Baba please be by my side.* It is at this point she realizes the lyrics to Bob Marley's "Three Little Birds" is playing on the radio. She turns it up.

> *Don't worry about a thing.*
> *'Cause every little thing is gonna be alright.*

She is filled with anticipation. As she rounds the curve on the cul-de-sac that houses Blue's apartment building, she hears another special song on the radio, "Colour My World." She turns up the volume.

As time goes on, I realize
Just what you mean to me.
And now, now that you're near...

She realizes it is their song. That bad country band played it the first night they danced at the Den. She sees it as a good sign, checking her makeup in the rear-view mirror just before getting out of the vehicle and rushing in. *What will we talk about?* she frets. But talking isn't exactly what Blue has in mind when Sandy knocks on his door.

It swings open quickly, like he's been watching for her. Blue takes her hand. His touch is warm and tender. *God, he's even more handsome than I remember*, Sandy thinks. He says nothing, very gently cupping her face. He holds Sandy very close. Their bodies meld into one.

"The eyes are the mirror to the soul." It is the second time Blue has said this. He touches both her lips with his. Then he moves his mouth just to the right of hers. His tongue runs across her bottom lip, and he gently takes it in his mouth and starts to suck. It makes her shiver. "Come with me." These are the only three words that he will say for the next several hours.

Sandy sees a flicker of candlelight as they approach the entrance to his bedroom. It is mid-afternoon and occasionally the sound of traffic is heard. As they walk she takes note of the dark window shades that block out any hint of sunlight. Blue pushes Sandy's long black hair to one side. He holds it in both hands for a moment, then kisses her hair. He kisses her forehead, kisses her eyebrows, kisses the sensitive spot where her earlobe attaches to her jaw. With the flick of his tongue, he gently moves his mouth down the pulsing jugular vein of her delicate neck. She hasn't even noticed that the zipper of her turquoise silk dress is already undone. Blue brushes the thin straps from her shoulders. The dress floats to the floor, revealing her glistening skin. She can feel his fingers on her back as he pulls her closer.

His hands move down her ribcage, caressing her firm breasts, the soft flesh of her abdomen. He stops to pick her up and place her head on his pillow. He removes his T-shirt and sits down beside her. The eyes are the mirror to the soul. No lover before Blue has taken this much time, exploring her body like a grand buffet. Blue moves his mouth down each side of her torso. He takes her leg, nibbling, sucking the fleshy skin of her inner thigh.

She lets out a moan and begins to massage her own breasts, hard. "Please, please take me. Take me now." She thinks her plea has worked.

Blue stops. He removes his sweats and takes off his boxers. His sumptuousness is throbbing and hard like the rest of his body. She reaches out to touch it, exciting her even further. She wants to feel him inside, but that won't happen just yet. Instead, he grabs her hands and kisses them.

Finally, he takes off her panties. He parts Sandy's legs and puts his mouth between them, sucking and licking and kissing. When she finishes coming, he kisses and nibbles the inside of each of her thighs again. He then gives her what she has wished for. She finally feels him inside her, skin on skin. The candles have burned out now. But the afterglow is warm. Blue holds Sandy's face. Lying next to her, he wraps his arms around her body.

SECRETS

Blue wasn't next to her when Sandy woke up in the morning. He'd left a note telling her how happy he is that they are finally together. He's working a twelve-hour shift today that started at 6 A.M. She smiles, remembering the night before, moves to his side of the bed and hugs his pillow before deciding to get up and take a shower.

She has no way of knowing that Blue has reservations about them living together. He's never said anything. But before leaving earlier that morning and while Sandy was still sleeping, Blue felt the need to hide his police notebooks. They were always lying on top of his dresser, and hiding them made him feel guilty. But he had a gnawing worry that just wouldn't go away. He tried to ignore it but couldn't. Sandy is a reporter after all. He fidgeted, wondering if she would violate his privacy by going through the notes while he was gone. Best not to take the chance; if there's ever a leak to the media, everyone will suspect him. He tucked a stack of notebooks in a shoebox and put them at the back of the closet, covering up the box with an old sweatshirt. It was a secret he'd never reveal. But he needn't feel so felonious. Sandy has her own secrets.

It's after her shower that she starts unpacking her girl stuff, arranging lotions, perfumes and bath bombs on a shelf near the bathroom window. When she opens the bathroom cabinet she finds a box of tampons tucked away in the corner. She can only guess that Heidi left them there months ago. Sandy finds it bothersome but cannot bring herself to be upset. In fairness, it happened in the past, before she and Blue decided to move in together.

Then changing the sheets, she notices bloodstains on the mattress. Sandy and Blue have made love only once—last night. The stains are another reminder of his past without her and his past with Heidi. She hates the idea of sleeping in a bed where other women have had their legs wrapped around Blue's neck. His overstuffed mattress and tall box spring make the height of the bed unusually high—just the right height for him to stand up while Sandy's ankles were around his neck last night. She guesses that hers is not the only butt that's been excitedly placed at the edge of his bed. The imagery makes her uncomfortable. *We're buying a new bed. Today. I'll go buy one myself if I have to.* She's made up her mind. But it's what happens next, in the kitchen, that really hurts.

Sandy notices old telephone bills cluttering up the junk drawer. She decides to move them, but not before noticing one particular phone number with an Alberta area code. A call made November 26 of last year. A second on November 28. A third, December 2. A fourth, fifth, sixth, seventh, eighth, ninth. She guesses that the calls were made to Heidi. She doesn't want to count the number of calls Blue has made to the number but can't stop herself. Seventeen charges in one month, all made around the time that she and Blue met.

"Needy, insecure bitch," Sandy swears under her breath. Blue never called Sandy after the night they first met. He'd only shown up drunk, once. *What the hell?* She wants to rip up the old bills. Flush them down the toilet. Set them on fire. Spit on them and throw them in the trash where they, and Heidi's memory, belong. But she does none of these things. Instead, she tucks one of the old bills inside her purse. *I'll keep the number*, she thinks. She isn't sure why.

PURPOSE

Blue's day is spent patrolling and enjoying springtime along the South Saskatchewan River. It is always spectacular with crocuses in full bloom and soft buds on willow trees. But warming temperatures means more crime and new problems. Today, it's a tragic call that comes over the scanner at 1:27 P.M. Some kids were playing on a sand dune near the Victoria Bridge, one of the oldest structures in the city. They were swimming in the river even though the water was still mostly frozen. It didn't matter—these kids had been sniffing solvents since 11 A.M. and were too high to notice. Known to police, Rodney Nistawasis was the oldest kid at the scene.

He was fourteen and a typical-looking teenager. Except for today. The sniffing had caused his nose to bleed; his face was puffy and his eyes a painful shade of red. Too messed up to realize the danger, Rodney jumped in the fast-flowing river. The strong current pulled the boy under. Blue was the first to find the body about an hour later along with the rescue crew. Blue is also assigned the task of informing Rodney's mother.

A feeling of dread accompanies Blue as he goes to her home, located in a rundown apartment building in the city's west end. Upon entering the building, Blue is slapped by the smell of rotting garbage, old cigarette smoke and stale beer spilled on the rug. Being new to the force, it's only a matter of time before you have to notify someone that a family member is dead. Blue wishes that day could have been postponed just a bit longer. He knocks quietly on the flimsy, particle-board door. Rodney's mother appears wearing a pink terry bathrobe that is frayed and thin. She looks tired and, seeing Blue's uniform, her expression changes to worry.

"What's he done now?" It is then that she notices that Constable Greyeyes has such sadness in his eyes that she realizes this visit will be unlike any other police have made regarding her son. Blue's voice cracks in breaking the news. She says nothing. She goes to some forlorn place, alone but willingly, as if she's been here before. "I've tried so hard. He wasn't a bad boy, you know. Oh my God, who do I call?"

She brings out a tattered old photo album of Rodney to show to Blue, who feels obligated to stay with her a while longer. The photo album contains pictures of the boy in better times. Age six, missing a front tooth; a poem he's written in pencil crayon is displayed beside it. Age eight, Rodney looking happy standing beside a horse. It was taken at a summer camp that is sponsored by a service club. There is an old report card pasted on the page too. His grades were pretty good. The photos stop around age eleven.

"That's when he started to change," Rodney's mom weeps. In the time that he stays with her, Blue finds out that Rodney was basically a good kid, only acting up after incidents involving his stepdad. The mom explains that the stepdad tormented Rodney. "He actually used the words 'no-good lazy Indian.'" Rodney is part-Native, his father a Cree drifter who abandoned his responsibility before Rodney was even born. The story is all too familiar, striking a raw chord.

GHOST

Floating bodies resurface, to the horror of many. Sometimes memories do the same. Rodney's death and the circumstances of his life allow things that had been buried deep in Blue's memory to be re-experienced again. The drowning happened hours ago. But it is something Rodney's mom said that haunts Blue. No amount of coffee is able to drown the painful replay of something he wishes would stay tethered to the shadows.

Blue is not very tall when he is ten years old. He needs a stepstool to go rooting through his mom's bedroom closet, looking for money. That's where she hides it. He's pretty sure because that's where she disappears to each time the Avon Lady drops by with one of her orders. But his mom isn't home right now. It is after school, and Blue knows he has at least twenty minutes before she gets back from work.

There is a new GI Joe army figure at the local hardware store and Blue has to have it. He'll hide it under his mattress. No one has to know that he is going to be stealing money to buy it. He checks the pockets of her sweaters hanging in the closet. He moves a few articles of clothing around in drawers to see if there is anything underneath. Nothing. But what's this? Blue finds an old shoebox hidden near the back of a sock drawer. He grabs it and shakes it. There is no clunking sound, only the rustle of papers. Maybe five-dollar bills?

There is no money, just some old letters and a yellowed newspaper article. It reads, *Unidentified Native Man Found Frozen*. Blue reads on. The article is dated February 10, 1970. It says the autopsy revealed that the blood alcohol content in the dead man exceeded five times the normal limit. The article goes on to explain that the dead man was frozen to the ground and covered with a piece of cardboard. He was discovered by another street person checking for bottles near a dumpster on skid row. The corpse had been frozen so solidly to the ground that one of the dead man's fingers actually broke off.

The article caused Blue to have nightmares for years. In his imagination, he is always horrified when emergency officials turn the body face up. It isn't his wayward father; the face staring back at Blue is his own.

LIGHT A RED CANDLE

Sandy awakens to the sound of keys rattling at the door. She's fallen asleep even though it's only 7 P.M. Unpacking was more strenuous than Sandy had expected. "Hey, my sweet angel. You look beautiful. Napping?" Blue kisses her nose. Next he lifts a large paper bag that he's carrying, filled with croissants and muffins. "There's a small French bakery just down the street. Hope you had a chance to get out and explore while I was away today." She doesn't have the heart to say, "Yes I did and I don't like what I found."

He talks a bit about his day on the job. "Holy smokes, there was this Native man beaten up and left on the street just before I got off shift. We got the call, but by the time we got there he was pretty bad. Blood gushing out of his head. His face smashed up like hamburger meat. But he was still breathing and conscious, calling, 'Help me, help me.' We called the ambulance, but because of the street address, in a rough part of town, there was no rush. By the time they finally got there he was dead. I was so mad. I knew that if the call came in from a nice neighbourhood, and the victim was a white guy, EMS would have been there right away. But no. This was a Native man…" Blue's voice trails off.

It is then Sandy realizes why it is important to him that she is there. She is pleasant and loving toward him. It's what he needs. The exact opposite of the people he deals with during the usual work-week. Maybe that's why he was so keen to have her move in, as a little sanctuary from what is otherwise his reality as a new police officer. He tells Sandy, "When I put on the uniform, it makes me feel important. I stand out from the other Native people that I see on the street. And white people respond to me differently. They don't treat me badly, like they might when I'm off duty and wearing just my shorts and T-shirt. People trust the police. It's the best job in the world."

Sandy expresses some skepticism about his perception of people's trust.

"Joining the police is good," he says. "I think it's good that kids see me and say to themselves, 'Hey, he's an acceptable member of society,' despite all those other Indians getting into trouble. 'Maybe I'll be like him.' We're role models, you and me, Sandy. Not bums. So that's why I do what I do."

Sandy worries and wants to tell him that sometimes people won't like you—no matter how hard you try.

He seems to hear the thought, even though she doesn't say anything out loud. Blue confirms that lots of people don't like him. "Sometimes Native people spit at the patrol car. They call me a 'pig' and an 'apple'—dark on the outside but white on the inside. All in a day's work. But I have to admit it's hard to take some days. It's good to be home now."

"Amen to that. I know exactly how you feel," Sandy confides. They share a bond of mutual trauma. Is that good or bad? More importantly, can anything grow from knowing a shared hatred that has been directed at each of them? Different circumstances but the same reason: being brown. Before any other dramatic thoughts are able to creep in, the telephone rings. Blue answers.

It's a man and he wants to speak with Sandy. Blue is suspicious about a man calling but doesn't want to act out. "Honey. Telephone." Sandy rounds the corner from where she is standing in the kitchen hoping the old phone bill, still tucked away, is safely secure. Her secret. How would she ever explain if it popped out of her purse?

Sandy takes the receiver. "Hello." It is obvious that she is pleased to hear from the person at the other end of the line; their conversation is friendly and enthusiastic. She has a grin from ear to ear when she hangs up. "I start work in a couple of days!" She is exuberant. "Let's go for dinner. My treat now that I don't have to worry so much about expenses."

They end up in a Japanese restaurant even though the thought of eating raw fish turns Blue's stomach. He tries but can't get past the thought, even with her reassurances. He orders tempura instead. It is the only cooked thing on the menu. Sandy tells Blue that her old boss, Frank, had made some phone calls. By chance, a reporter at CF-Television in Saskatoon is going on maternity leave. She just handed in her leave request today and there is an opening almost immediately. Sandy is only too keen to fill it and Frank has made it happen.

It is good news for both of them. While Blue is thrilled that Sandy has moved because of him, he has also been worried that Sandy would get bored doing nothing. *Would I be enough for her if she just sat around all day waiting for me to come home? Probably not*, he admits to himself. The phone call takes away that concern. But soon enough it will cause a whole lot of other problems, for him anyway.

THE START OF SOMETHING

Sandy buys a new suit over the weekend. It is navy-coloured but this time a little sassier. The short, tailored bolo-style jacket and long skirt look very business-like yet feminine. It looks good on her. She wants to make a positive first impression. But for Sandy it is also a tradition: get a new job, buy a new suit. It signals a new start toward something better.

As expected, her new colleagues in the newsroom meet her with suspicion. But she has high hopes nonetheless. Her new boss, Lyle Hermanson, is a former network reporter from the Washington bureau. He recently moved back to the province to marry his high school sweetheart. Strong ties to home—Sandy likes that.

The slower pace of Saskatoon doesn't lessen Lyle's edge or his expectations of his staff. Viewers right across Canada know about what is happening in the Prairie region. Hermanson drives his reporters hard, insisting on network-quality stories. It pays off. Since his arrival, his small newsroom has garnered a Gemini Award for Best Reportage in Canadian Television. For a small station, it is impressive. It means advertisers are more likely to buy advertising at CF-Television, and it also gives his news team more credibility.

But today is Sandy's first day, which is supposed to mean basic orientation. Who does what? Where to go for equipment? Where is the supply cabinet? The coffee maker? The smoking room? Where to park her vehicle? She is also handed an assignment—to do a story on the lack of Aboriginal programming in the school curriculum and how it affects both Native and non-Native students in their perceptions of Canadian history. Hermanson announces, "There's an education conference downtown. See what you can piece together." A stroke of luck.

Even before being handed the story, she already knows how she wants to tell it. She's been waiting to tackle it for a while. Sandy agrees to go to the conference but the real meat of the story is something that happened to a family she met not that long ago. Sandy will tell their story even though it will require some travel out of the city, but it's not so far away that she can't manage both. She has no way of knowing that this assignment will signal the start of a new journey.

THE INFECTED BLANKET

Sandy's memory goes back to the day last winter when she met Lucy Favel and Norma MacIntosh early one Saturday morning. They were all travelling on the same city bus. Sandy had taken the bus to finish up her Christmas shopping, because her Jeep wasn't plugged in overnight and refused to start. Sandy remembers how she walked to the back of the bus, taking a seat beside an ice-covered window, relieved not to be driving. The streets were incredibly icy and the drivers incredibly frazzled. The last-minute traffic to the shopping mall was frantic.

Amidst all the haste emerged one of the best stories she's ever stumbled upon. She recalls the details now for Hermanson and makes her pitch on how she wants to handle the day's assignment. "Lucy and Norma took the seat in front of me. It was clear that they already did a fair bit of shopping, carrying large brown bags filled with plush toys, clothing and other boxes. Still, they were headed for the mall."

Sandy remembers hearing Lucy say, "I have to still buy for Davey. Then we can go to Smitty's for a piece of pie before the Old Man picks us up at noon to get us back to Yellow Quill." Lucy kept talking. "You know, I was so proud of my Jeanette at school the other day. Do you know what she did? She's only eleven, you know, and boy, did she ever get into trouble."

Sandy overheard that young Jeanette disputed something her teacher had said in social studies class regarding the story of the infected blankets. Jeanette's mom explained further: "The teacher, a white lady, told the kids that it is unfortunate that the first settlers who came to Canada unknowingly infected the early Indians with smallpox. The teacher told the students it was a mistake that the gifts they presented to the Indians carried the disease. That's when Jeanette spoke up. She yelled at the teacher, 'It was no mistake! They did that on purpose! They wanted to kill us. My mom said so.' Holy, that teacher got very mad and told Jeanette to sit down and stop causing trouble. Poor thing."

By this time, Sandy says she was leaning in to hear the conversation. It fascinated her and other passengers who'd stopped reading their newspapers or magazines, also sitting quietly and listening, as Lucy continued. "Jeanette was so confused. She came home from school that day, mad at me for telling her the story about the infected blankets. So I told her once again, that it is true. The early white people did it on purpose. They wanted to kill us. And I told Jeanette that she is right and that I am proud of her for speaking up."

Lucy continued talking about what happened the next day when the teacher came back to class again. "That teacher asked everyone to listen up and then she apologized to Jeanette. The teacher told the class that she was wrong, and Jeanette was right. The teacher said she did some research after school and found out what my girl said is true. The teacher then told the principal that they need new textbooks. And she gave Jeanette a gold star. Now that's a good teacher. There should be more like her." Lucy smiled.

Sandy loved the story. She leaned in to introduce herself as a reporter to Lucy and Norma. Lucy was only too happy to share her daughter's triumph. "We're gonna be on TV. Holy! I'm gonna have to call Jeanette," she squealed. Because the family was from the Aboriginal community of Yellow Quill, just visiting the city for Christmas shopping, Frank couldn't find a place for it in his Regina-focused newscast. But it would be perfect for CF-Television's broader Prairies mandate, and fit in perfectly with the conference assignment.

GENTILITY AMONGST RUINS

Hermanson is satisfied with the report Sandy files, telling the story of the infected blanket from a different perspective—and making the point that the curriculum needs to be updated and changed. "Good work, Pelly," he says gruffly. The station runs the story without hesitation, with Sandy saying a prayer of gratitude that her suggestion—a cultural story—hasn't been met with intolerance from her peers as was the case in the past.

But it isn't the actual story that gives her so much satisfaction; it's who she unexpectedly meets at the education conference. An Elder approaches her, greeting her like an old friend. His name is Joe Bush Sr.

Sandy finds herself being struck by the kindness in Joe's eyes. They are greenish-brown in colour shot through with amber, depending on the light. She's surprised they aren't dark brown like she is used to seeing on most Native people. Joe has many lines on his face and his crows-feet smile lines tell the story that he's spent little time frowning. He carries a heavy presence, as though wisdom is his middle name.

When she first spots him, Joe is dressed plainly in a white shirt with a beaded bolo tie. He wears jeans, moccasins and a white Stetson. From under the hat, a braid the colour of steel wool hangs down his back. He stands out from the other presenters at the conference. They seem uncomfortable, stuffed in bleached white dress shirts and tight striped ties that look more like nooses.

Joe offers his hand in introduction, and Sandy guesses arthritis might be the cause of his gnarled fingers. She wonders if he was injured in some rodeo mishap when he was younger. Joe gestures to Sandy that they ought to sit down. There is a quiet corner near the back of the conference room, where they find a couple chairs set up by a large urn filled with hot tea. Joe pours himself a cup and adds three packets of sweetener. Sandy drinks hers black.

Joe takes off his hat, rubbing his face in exasperation. Sandy knows the look. *Something is wrong*, she suspects, wanting to find out why he seems troubled. Sandy has seen the look before, in old farmers worrying about their crops when there is news of snow and only half the job done. Joe speaks. "It's been bothering me because it doesn't make any sense." As if in a church confessional, Joe whispers, passing on some forbidden message. "I heard it was no accident. The police had a hand in those girls' disappearances." Joe is a well-respected Elder who lives on a reserve not far from the city. The girls he describes are Sioux, their families from his reserve.

"They are good girls. Powwow dancers, non-drinkers and I should know—I was one of their teachers." Joe stops just long enough to observe Sandy's level of interest in what he is saying. She is keenly attentive. Weeks of tension seem to drain from him. "Finally, someone cares."

Joe tells Sandy he'd gone to the police and they said they couldn't help. "They told me people go missing all the time. Said they probably just got caught up in drinking and drugging and that they'll come home at some point when they need money." While Sandy jots down some notes in her day planner, Joe says a silent prayer—*Thank you for leading me to someone who will help you find a voice, my girls*—closing his eyes for a second, lifting both palms upwards. Sandy doesn't even notice his gesture, as she is too busy scribbling notes.

Joe continues. "The girls had just left the powwow at the Friendship Centre. They were supposed to walk over to The Nook restaurant to meet their cousin for a ride back home. They never showed up. Everyone thought the worst. We prayed they'd be found. They were found, but not the way we had been hoping."

Sandy vaguely remembers the story. It was last winter. Two youths were found on the outskirts of that city in minus-thirty-degree weather. Neither wore boots nor winter coats when discovered. Their bodies were found frozen solid in a farmer's field. One of the bodies had been partially eaten by animals, probably coyotes. Joe Bush Sr. tells Sandy she should investigate. "Somebody has to. The police don't seem to care. To them it's case closed. They didn't even do an autopsy."

She doesn't know Joe personally. She's only seen photos of him in the local newspaper because he's so busy within the Aboriginal community, usually saying opening prayers. But from the reaction of others at the education conference it's clear he's highly regarded. Sandy notices several blankets and pouches of tobacco others have given him as gifts, indicating that he is held with the utmost respect, honour and admiration (another protocol she read in a book).

Can it be true—what Joe said? And how will I piece a story like this together? she wonders to herself. Joe implies that the police were responsible for the deaths. She wants to follow the lead but can't figure out how, deciding instead to leave it on the back burner—for now. *When the time is right.* Sandy knows a story like this is dangerous to pursue but also the type of journalism that catapults careers, if the things Joe says are true.

Before leaving her company, Joe thanks Sandy for listening. He reaches into his pocket, taking out a rock. "It's from the river I've been fishing since I was a small boy," he explains, placing the rock in Sandy's palm. "Carry it with you. It comes from a good place."

But carrying around the information from Joe feels like a burden. It's now been a few days and Sandy feels frustrated about her hesitation to question Blue about it. She purposely restrains herself, mostly because she doesn't want to know if Blue might be involved— even in the slightest. If he confirms that something happened, then she'll have to investigate. If he says no, then she'll wonder if he's lying. Keeping the secret, she thinks, is like admitting to cheating and sleeping around. There's unspoken tension. It interrupts her sleep, causing fitful dreams that she doesn't understand. They seem ominous and foretell something dark. But what?

VISION, DREAM OR NIGHTMARE?

Perhaps Sandy shouldn't have had a piece of peanut butter toast before going to bed. *Maybe I ate it too late?* She has to come up with some reason for her insomnia tonight. The hours go by. Sleep eludes her. However, just before dawn she closes her eyes and drifts off. *Was it a dream, or did this actually happen?*

She has travelled elsewhere and finds herself sleeping on the floor of a school gym. *Where am I? And why? How did I get here?* All she can see is the dim illumination of the red exit sign. She isn't alone but she isn't afraid, intuitively knowing there are others in the room who are kindred spirits also seeking some type of answer.

"We're all supposed to go toward that door and that light," Sandy calls out. She can hear the sound of someone clearing his throat then asking, "Go where?"

Sandy tells him. "Out there. We are supposed to walk through that door."

She hears another voice asking, "Why?"

Sandy instructs, "I don't know, but we're all supposed to go toward the exit sign then around that corner."

"Sounds weird," a different voice from the corner says, and then the voice of a child admits, "I'm scared."

"Don't be afraid," Sandy says, standing up and motioning for the others to follow. She holds her breath, opening the door to whatever may lay in store outside.

Warmth is what greets her.

It is a beautiful summer day. Rich aromas swirl in the gentle breeze amidst a lush green meadow. There is a bluff just up the way with a single leafy deciduous tree that is the perfect size for climbing, like she did as a child. She sees a valley of vibrant wildflowers and a cold, winding brook. The other people in her dream follow Sandy, not knowing why. She knows some of them. Frank, Sean and Lilly from the Regina newsroom are here in this dream. Her friend Ellen is beside her, and Sandy thinks she recognizes others as people she's interviewed but can't remember their names, only faces. There are Aboriginal people but Sandy doesn't know most of them. Still they follow. It's like a day hike, through clumps of alders in a valley with flowering ground cover.

Suddenly someone shrieks, "Bear!"

Everyone starts running toward the brook. There is not one, but three black bears lumbering toward them. Sandy starts to run as well, eventually catching up to the others. But there is no safe place to go. On the opposite side of the brook another family of black bears appears out of nowhere, then more bears appear. Eventually everyone is surrounded by an army of bears.

Sandy is wearing a colourful shawl that she's never seen before. She takes it off wondering where it came from. "Get under it! Get under!" she instructs and sits on the outside of the shawl, holding it over the others for protection as she prays. She asks for an invisible shield to surround them all. Her mind races back to what she's been taught in the Catholic Church: all pagan religions, like Native spirituality, are evil; "the devil's work" is how one priest had once described it. This must be what is happening, she thinks, and in this dream her mind races back to a time when she is six years old and afraid. A memory within a dream.

Sandy is a little girl and she and her friends are playing a child's game called Murder in the Dark. Sandy finds the perfect hiding spot inside an old suitcase just big enough to hold her. She climbs in and closes the top. But something goes wrong and it locks. The suitcase becomes a stifling coffin as she screams and claws for what seems like hours, though it is just a matter of minutes before her friends use a small jackknife to jimmy the latch and let her out. After that day, they never play the game again.

But here in the valley of black bears, she's too terrified to scream. Her voice is gone. She is trapped in something worse than an old suitcase and there is no way out. Instinctively, she prays—for courage, for strength, for common sense, for understanding, for safety—all the while holding the rock that Joe has given her. And in that moment of silence comes a moment of peace.

Sandy isn't afraid anymore. She hears a voice. The largest of the black bears stands up and crosses the small brook toward her. The bear stands directly in front of her, speaking. "There's no need for fear. We won't hurt you." Sandy's breathing slows to normal. "We are your protection. We always have been. As long as you live in a good way, we will always come. You just have to ask." The bear relays the message telepathically. Even so, the words aren't spoken in English. They are said in Cree. Sandy somehow understands even though she is not a Cree speaker.

"Don't be afraid," the bear says. "We are your relations and we are here to bring you back to where you belong. You've been wandering for too long." Sandy feels a strong gust of wind swirling. There is a puff of smoke and the physical location of the meadow changes. Sandy is transported somewhere else, standing on a bluff by herself.

She ends up in a dark and warm place where something touches her hair. The wingtip of a bird? She can't see it. She can only feel its touch and hear its strong flight. Air keeps swirling. Next there is a soft flicker of light. Burning embers of what? Earth smells surround Sandy with a clean and rich fragrance. She can hear sharp crackles of a slow fire as the fragrance disappears in flame and smoke. A low growl vibrates through the darkness. Sandy feels something force a quick breath on her forehead, the way a child blows out a candle on a birthday cake. She faints.

She wakes up in a pool of sweat. Was it a lucid dream? A nightmare? Or was it a message from some unseen realm?

BEAR CAGE

The strangeness of her dream somehow invigorates Sandy. But try as she might, she cannot make any sense out of it even with the use of her dream dictionary. By mid-week she is back in stride, leaving her suspicions and anxiety about Blue behind and concentrating on work. The circus is in town, and an animal rights group will be protesting. Sandy is assigned to cover the story and she sets up an interview with the circus manager.

Hermanson assigns Kyle Preston to be her cameraman for the day, which encourages Sandy. Kyle is a seasoned news cameraman with ten years in the business but is not yet jaded. The job still interests him, as do the people he meets each day. Sandy can't help but notice Kyle's muscular frame as he carries the video equipment to load up into the news van. Sandy guesses that he's trying to grow his blond hair; it's pulled back in a short ponytail that touches the tip of his shirt collar.

"You know we cover this story every year," Kyle says, as the two get into the van to make their way to the assignment, "but it's different every time. Let's see what we find today." He smiles and it's somehow familiar to Sandy. She shakes her head, realizing that Kyle had been a part of her lucid dream a few days ago. And he said those exact words in the dream. The memory prompts her to run her

116

fingers over the rock that Joe has gifted her, which she now carries with her all the time, just as Joe instructed.

Sandy is delighted that the circus manager has agreed to meet with her. The rumour is that this year he'd turned down requests from all other media. "We need to set up by the bear cage," Sandy instructs Kyle once inside the main circus tent. "I need to find the circus manager, Jake Hamilton. Be right back." Sandy quickens her step toward a neon sign that shouts out OFFICE as Kyle readies the camera near the bear cage, agreeing that it's a good background for this story. Within minutes Sandy returns with Jake Hamilton. He is younger than either expects: mid-thirties, clean-shaven, blond, ruggedly handsome. *He'll look good on* TV, Sandy thinks while doing a quick survey of his collar. His tie is crooked, so she straightens it before the camera starts to roll.

"I've seen your work and it's a pleasure to meet you. I'm glad you were able to come." Jake's tone holds hints of flirting, which Sandy ignores. He gets down to business, explaining that he has a biologist, a veterinarian and other animal specialists on staff. "They travel with the show to ensure the comfort and well-being of the animals." He produces inspection reports from other cities that his circus has been to as proof that they pay attention to detail and the animals are treated well. He talks about how most of his animals are rescued from slaughter. "They were born in the wild, but left as orphans. Mostly hunters killed their mothers. The policy for most wildlife ministries is to kill the orphans unless a suitable home can be found. That's where the circus comes in."

Jake introduces Sandy to the show's star, a young black bear named Mugwah. "His mother became a problem bear in Banff National Park two years ago. She hung around the town-site once too often in search of food from the garbage containers. Even though they are supposedly bear-proof, the sow figured out a way to break into them. She started teaching young Mugwah how to do the same. Unfortunately, she charged a tourist one day. The tourist wasn't hurt, but it put quite a scare in both him and park officials. The sow was ordered destroyed. And with that, Mugwah became an orphan." Sandy identifies with Mugwah's story, having started out life as an orphan too. Her connection to the young bear is heartfelt and instantaneous.

The interview itself goes well. But Sandy knows she needs more shots of other animals as part of her story. Sandy writes down exactly what she is looking for on her reporter's notepad, tearing out the page to hand over to Kyle. Kyle, camera balanced on his shoulder, leaves Sandy behind as he and Jake head toward other animal holding pens. Sandy stays behind to compose her thoughts. She'll have to speak to the camera as a way of ending the story once Kyle gets back.

MUGWAH

Now, *how to sum it all up?* It is commonplace for Sandy to have conversations with herself. *Hmmm, I'll use the bear in the background and talk about how the show will go on, despite the protests. Yeah, that's it,* Sandy thinks, applying a new colour of lipstick. This one is called Rustic Remembrances. While reaching into her purse to look for a hairbrush, she finds a couple pieces of fruit leather. She knows she shouldn't feed the bear but she wants to. Sandy starts slowly unwrapping the dried fruit, enjoying the sweet citrus smell.

"Hello Mugwah, you handsome boy," Sandy whispers. "Look, I found a snack for you. Yum." She wonders if the bear knows the two of them have something in common. They are both orphans, both forced into situations that displaced them, taking them from their homes. She wonders if constantly searching for a place to belong hurts Mugwah too. Do animals have feelings?

The bear comes over. He snorts and gently starts eating the fruit leather directly from her hand. Even though she's never done it before, Sandy wonders if she is making a food offering to the spirit of the bear. It's something she read by an author named Lame Deer. Feeding the spirits. What he wrote touched both her heart and her intellect. He talks about "spirit" as living and tangible—something we can learn to easily communicate with. It gave her a sense of peace-fulness. If she chooses to follow her intuition, it's not so unusual to get in touch with spirit.

Lame Deer's teaching is the opposite of how she'd been raised. Her only other reference to the spirit world—as described by Aboriginal people—had come from the church. The church rein-forced that anyone is sinful and evil if they open themselves to hear spirit voices or instinctively know something. The church would tell Sandy that what she is doing right now—talking to a bear—is wrong.

But today she doesn't listen. The bear snorts again, then looks at her with his small black eyes. Sandy imagines Mugwah is thanking her. She says a silent prayer offering, prayers to the spirit of the bear: this bear—Mugwah—and the bears who recently came to her in her dream: "Please guide me toward something that will help me feel whole. Please help me find a place I truly belong, where people understand me and I don't need to constantly prove something. Please help me meet the people who can teach me. I know so little. I feel so much."

Sandy has to stop. Admitting frailty is tough, but pride is a commodity that sometimes can afford to be swallowed. She's never spoken the words that she needs help in finding her way. But she feels safe doing so here with the bear. Sandy knows it is customary to offer tobacco to someone sent to teach. *Is this the role of Mugwah? Does this baby bear know what I am thinking?* She removes a half-empty package of cigarettes from her purse, taking one out. Sandy tears the paper off the cigarette, putting the loose tobacco in her hand. Her thoughts are of strength and insight and why she needs that in her life. She sets the loose tobacco just inside Mugwah's cage, asking the bear to share his strength with her. A moment passes and Sandy smiles at Mugwah before reaching for her hairbrush in her purse. She needs to brush her hair if she is planning to go on camera. Kyle will be back soon.

At that moment, another circus employee opens an oversized door leading to the outside world. A big gust of wind flies in from out of nowhere like a bird of prey. The wind catches some loose strands that Sandy has brushed away. The hairs float in the air current and then land squarely in Mugwah's strong paws. He sniffs them and growls. Without knowing, she has just made a physical offering to the Bear Spirit.

Mugwah roars as wind continues to blow in from the open door. Sandy's spirit travels elsewhere. She faints.

RED ROAD FORWARD

Sandy. Sandy." She opens her eyes to find Jake Hamilton crouching over her, holding her hand. "You okay?"

Kyle looks worried, peering out from over Jake's shoulder. "We should call an ambulance," he murmurs as Sandy springs to her feet like nothing is out of the ordinary.

"Alrighty then," she says. "Let's head back to the station. I think we've got everything. Cute animals." Sandy straightens the sleeve of her blouse.

"Sandy, you just fainted. We heard Mugwah growl. Are you hurt?" Jake asks.

Sandy knows Mugwah will get into trouble if she admits he growled at her, so she responds, "I don't remember him growling. I've got to start eating breakfast. Honestly, I felt faint because I haven't had any food since yesterday afternoon. I just need some juice," Sandy reassures them. "Maybe I startled Mugwah when I fell."

"We have to call an ambulance," Jake insists.

"No time, and there's no need. Honestly, I just need some food." Sandy doesn't give him time to counter. She grabs her purse and the camera lighting kit that's still sitting near Mugwah's cage. She is on her way out the door, forgetting about her on-camera presentation.

"Thanks for your concern, Jake, but I really need to file this story. We're on in just a couple hours."

Kyle turns to Jake as Sandy makes her way past them both. "My guess is it's an anxiety attack," he says. "She's been under a lot of pressure lately, not that she'll admit it. New job, new city. Best to just leave it alone." Jake understands. Kyle waves to him as he follows after Sandy and feels for the keys to the news van in his jacket pocket.

They leave the circus tent and Sandy doesn't speak on the drive back. It's not surprising. She has no idea what just happened. *How can I describe feeling so overwhelmed that I fainted? And who would believe me if I tried?* Sandy feels like she's just eaten a whole box of chocolates and the sugar rush is kicking in. For a second time she reaches into her pocket, running her fingers over the rock. Ever since Joe gave it to her, it's as though the unexpected and the unexplained keep happening—like finally meeting her biological family, totally by chance, just the other day.

FINALLY HOME

Hello... Sandra Lynn?" No one ever calls her by these names.

"Yes," Sandy answers tentatively, not recognizing the voice at the other end of the line and hoping it isn't a telemarketer.

"My name is Charlene. I'm calling from up north. I think I'm your sister."

Sandy doesn't know how to respond. She gasps as a sharp sting grabs her stomach, the same way a side stitch does during a long run. She is rendered speechless, her throat expanding in an effort to hold back tears.

Thankfully Charlene keeps talking. "I hope you don't mind me calling. Seems we both know old Joe Bush Sr. He came up north last week and started talking about you, says you look just like our mother. That's how we found you, and got your number."

Charlene tells Sandy that she always suspected her mother, Maggie, had another child years ago, a baby no one ever spoke of. Apparently Maggie had an affair with the storeowner in their small community. The result was an unplanned pregnancy. "Mom moved to the city for several months back around the time you were born. No one knew why she went away, but when she returned she was never quite as cheerful." Charlene confides that's when the gossip

124

began that her mother had left to give birth to an illegitimate child. But no one ever asked Maggie directly about whether she had a baby.

As Sandy listens to Charlene's thick Cree accent and broken English, she wonders what it would have been like to grow up with her. "And why weren't you scooped up?" Sandy asks. Charlene does her best to answer. "I can't say for certain, but Mom had four kids. You were the only one taken away. I'm guessing it's because all the rest of us were born at home, up north here. Kookum is a midwife."

"What's a Kookum?" Sandy interrupts, to which Charlene chuckles.

"Oh, that's Granny. But yes, we figure you were born in a hospital down south. That's probably why you were taken." Charlene tells her their mother had passed away three years ago. "It was a car accident on a logging road." Sandy's heart drops at learning that she'll never meet her mother, but she quickly recovers upon realizing that she'll at least meet her sister. They make plans to meet up the very next morning at Smitty's Pancake House in the north end of the city, agreeing on 8 A.M.

"How will I know you?" Sandy asks Charlene before hanging up.

"You know, I am betting we'll recognize each other," Charlene reassures her.

Sandy has trouble falling asleep that night. Meanwhile, Charlene and an entourage drive all night to Saskatoon. *What if we have nothing in common? What'll we talk about? What if she asks to borrow money? What if she's been drinking?* The what-ifs are like a disease and Sandy curses old voices from her high school years and her co-workers in that first newsroom. *All Indians are greasy and lazy*, like she hasn't heard that one too many times already. But because that particular groundwork is already firmly laid, Sandy finds herself experiencing a slight hint of apprehension. She's read good and bad accounts of meeting biological siblings. She's even done stories on such encounters. It's kind of like a blind date, she supposes.

Rather than toss and turn, Sandy gets up to make some chamomile tea. It's what her Baba would have done at a moment like this. When Sandy was a child and having problems sleeping, or if she had a tummy ache or felt feverish, chamomile was the cure-all. It works every time. She falls asleep with the sweet taste of tea in her mouth and warm thoughts in her heart. She'll be meeting her family in the morning.

The alarm wakes her at 6:30 A.M. Her mind races over a to-do list: shower, baby photos, questions, questions, questions... where to start? The early morning passes quickly and Sandy pulls into the Smitty's parking lot with time to spare. Up ahead an Indian woman, shorter than Sandy and a tad overweight, is standing by a beige van smoking. She throws her cigarette to the ground and produces the same brilliant smile that Sandy wears. Sandy quickly undoes her seatbelt and leaps from the Jeep.

"Do you ever look like her!" Charlene holds outstretched arms in greeting for a sister she's never met. Once again Sandy finds herself unable to speak, overwhelmed by the attention. As Charlene comes closer, Sandy notices tears cascading from Charlene's clear, dark eyes. The women hug, and Sandy smells the sweet scent of cinnamon and fragrant floral shampoo.

Within seconds and out of nowhere, three other people appear. Another car pulls up, then there are six people. By the time they go in and start ordering breakfast, a full dozen have arrived with more on the way. It reminds her of the dream with the bears.

Each of her relatives want to catch a glimpse of Sandy, touch her face, hold her hand and speak in Cree. "Hey Larry, go get Kookum," Charlene instructs. She tells Sandy that Larry is her younger brother. Larry does as he's told, opening the side door to another minivan that's just pulled into the parking lot. He helps a very old woman make her way out. Kookum is dressed for the occasion, in a pink cardigan sweater with a floral design beaded along the neckline, a knee-length blue woollen skirt and a pair of comfortable moccasins. The Old Woman clutches a black and white photo. Once inside, Kookum glances at the picture and gives a wide smile in Sandy's direction.

"Nosisim, mithwasin ka pi-kiwiyan," she says affectionately, pointing at Sandy.

"What did she say?" Sandy wants to know.

"She called you granddaughter and says it's good that you're finally home," Charlene translates, adding her own comments. "You really do look like Maggie, our mom. You could be twins. Honestly." She shows the photo to Sandy. It is true, like looking in a mirror. Sandy and her mother have the same features: long black hair, dark skin, full lips, large dark eyes and high cheekbones. "You keep it," Charlene insists, "and these too."

She hands Sandy a small pair of baby moccasins, intricately beaded. There is white rabbit fur lining the top. "Our mother made these years ago after she returned from the city and seemed so sad. We thought maybe they were for a cousin or something. But she never gave them away, and she always kept them in a place where she could see them, on the windowsill right above the kitchen sink. Once, she caught me playing with them, putting them on my dolly and she got really mad. She took them away and told me they were special. I could never figure out why she said that until yesterday. Now I know. She made them for you."

BUCKSKINS

There have been so many changes since Blue met Sandy that first night at the bar. He sits quietly in the small living room, hearing only the sound of birds chirping to the rising morning sun. He's sipping a freshly brewed cup of coffee while Sandy is still asleep. *She was so happy coming home yesterday*, Blue thinks to himself. He feels guilty for not having joined her in meeting her biological family. *Why does it bother me so much that she's meeting new people and learning new things? And now she tells me that she's starting to have weird dreams about bears? What else is around the corner? Next is she going to cut off the head of a chicken?*

It startles Blue to admit that he no longer sees Sandy as the sweet, inquisitive girl who happens to be brown. Ever since moving here, she's sounding more like those Aboriginal women the police department hires to do Aboriginal awareness training. He thinks about one of those training sessions, held last month. What that woman had to say made Blue wince with feelings of guilt: "There are some Native men who refer to Native women as buckskins. They are ashamed of our culture, even though they are Aboriginal themselves. But they're pretty easy to spot. They date only white women, saying that Aboriginal women are here only to try on at their leisure and just as quickly be put away, at the back of a dark closet, when the men are finished with them."

It frustrates him that these nagging thoughts emerge. He forces himself to ask, deep down, whether he is ashamed of Sandy, whether he is ashamed of himself. Blue rubs his forehead as though doing so will wipe away the bad thoughts. It doesn't work. Instead, jealousy marches in. He doesn't want to share Sandy, and he certainly doesn't want to lose her to anything or anyone. His insecurity lurks in places where it doesn't belong.

It bothers him that she's reconnected with her biological family, and he guiltily hopes they won't remind him of the people he meets on the street. He also hopes her growing interest in Native culture won't cause problems down the road—if she becomes one of those militants, or pushes him to be more vocal about equality issues on the job. He is the only Native officer after all, and he fits in just fine by not purposely upsetting the status quo.

He's seen it happen before when a Native person grows up outside the culture and is suddenly reintroduced. It's like winning a million-dollar lottery. There is the potential to go overboard. Blue calls them born-again Indians, going from one extreme to the other. They wear buckskin and beadwork all the time and sometimes refer to themselves as healers.

He remembers an old alcoholic named Eli who was routinely arrested on the street. But that was months ago. Something happened. The old dude started going to a sweat lodge and has since turned his life around. Now he has some type of street ministry, helping others, inspiring people like Sandy to learn more about culture and spirituality. Sandy had met old Eli while out on assignment one afternoon. She pitched a story about him turning his life around, and later befriended him.

Just the other day she came home and started talking to Blue about the seven sacred teachings: "Universal really. To live with kindness and faith—to have a generous heart and approach all situations with humility." Sandy went on to explain to Blue that many of the people she'd met at the street ministry talking circle were like her. "So many of us don't know our own language or have ever danced at a powwow. It's good to reconnect. You should come with me next time. They meet once a week."

Blue scoffs just thinking about it, almost choking as some of the now-cold coffee goes up his nose. *Lord I hope Sandy doesn't turn out like that, buying long pieces of braided sweetgrass to hang from the rear-view mirror.* But it's something he'll never tell her. Blue gets off the couch to freshen his coffee. His thoughts race back to the article about his dad, the old drunk.

BACKPEDALLING

Blue's four-days-on-four-days-off schedule takes a bit of getting used to. Thankfully, it's day one of four days off for Blue. He wants to spend the time doing something special with the woman he loves. He awakens Sandy with the smell of fresh coffee, placing a steaming hot mug on the bedside table. "Good morning, love. Time to get up. You don't want to sleep the day away." They've been planning a trip to the mountains for a couple weeks. It's a long drive. Sandy wipes the sleep from her eyes, takes a sip of the hot brew then groggily moves from the bed. The trip to the mountains beckons. They won't arrive until late in the afternoon.

Within a half hour they are gassing up the Jeep and heading for a local coffee shop. It's cliché but not surprising that a couple of police cars are also in the parking lot. "Hey, looks like Johnson might be here." Blue has checked out the number on the patrol car parked in the coffee shop lot. "And maybe Kerzewski and Smith too. That's great. You can meet some of the guys I work with."

Blue seems excited to let his colleagues know that he too has a life outside of work. His co-workers are all married. Kerzewski's wife just had a baby boy not long ago. Blue loves the idea of showing off Sandy. She looks beautiful with her hair pulled into a long elaborate braid, the way he likes it. She wears a sundress this morning even though the air is a bit cool. It occurs to him that he's never seen Sandy wear pants; she always wears skirts and dresses. This one is a bit on the skimpy side but she looks classy.

As they enter the coffee shop, it is clear Sandy has passed the male appreciation test. All three constables wink at Blue then give smiles to both of them. Johnson speaks up. "Hey ya dog. A few days off I see? What are you up to today?"

"Hey," Blue responds. "We're headin' out to the mountains for a couple of days. Do some hiking. See the sights." He holds Sandy's hand. "This is my girlfriend, Sandy." He beams saying it. Sandy smiles. *My girlfriend*, she thinks, feeling like the queen of the world, or at least the queen of his world. But that feeling lasts for only a second.

"Oh, you're the one from Alberta. So you'll be heading back toward home?" Johnson is not trying to be hurtful. Sandy realizes he has never met Heidi, only heard of her, so has no way of knowing which girlfriend is which.

But her heart still hits the floor. "Oh no, that's not me." It is the only thing she can think to say, going from elation to despair within moments. It may be an unconscious survival skill that kicks in next. Sandy isn't sure why, but at that precise moment she thinks about a petticoat, of all things—a piece of clothing specifically designed to cover up detail. She wishes for an emotional petticoat to do the same thing right now as she recalls another time of feeling this shocked, during her first job interview.

She was applying for a position of chase producer at one of the city's most listened-to radio stations. Whoever got the job was expected to come up with ideas for stories to talk about on the air, do research, make phone calls, book guests for the show and prepare a question line for the host. From there, the host of the show would take all the credit. And the host of that particular program had a bad reputation. Sandy had heard that he went through producers faster than she uses a bottle of shampoo. Despite the warning, she applied.

The name of the host was Walt Bramble. The day of the job interview, Walt looked gruff, reminding Sandy of a troll, with black nose hairs nearly touching a big brown mole fixed just above his top lip. His eyes were mean-looking and he refused to shake Sandy's hand when she entered the room. Instead, he grunted as though her very presence had offended. Sandy felt like shrinking when he barked out a command: "Well, sit down already." Walt proceeded to chastise Sandy for even putting in an application. "You're not even qualified," she remembers him sneering.

She instinctively responded accordingly, "Well, why did you ask me to come in for an interview?" Her confident query took him off guard, making him uncomfortable.

"You have next to no experience and yet you think you can handle this type of journalism?" He was trying to intimidate and Sandy couldn't figure out the purpose in that. She found it disturbing to find such a treacherous undercurrent in someone who couldn't be much more than thirty.

Sandy explained to him that she had been watching the news every night since she was a child. She told Walt that she knew how to identify a story.

"But that's television news. Pablum. Do you ever read? What's the last book you read?" Walt grumbled.

"Dylan Thomas's collected short stories and a textbook on script writing," she answered.

Walt's lips cracked into a sinister smile. "Don't get your hopes up, kid. There are others way more qualified than you. I'll call you either way tomorrow." He dismissed her with a flick of his hand. Sandy thanked him for his time then got up from her chair to leave. That's when the slip happened.

Up to that point, Sandy was still very much a farm kid, running around all the time dressed in an old denim skirt and a T-shirt. But thankfully, during a sewing class in high school a couple of years earlier, Sandy was forced to design and sew a skirt and blouse ensemble. The lines were not perfect, but the outfit was nice and presentable enough, even for a job interview. The only problem was the material for the skirt was somewhat see-through. Sandy needed to wear a petticoat or slip underneath. She didn't own one, so the day before the interview she went to a second-hand store downtown. She found one that fit, though it was quite old and the elastic on its waistline was worn.

Sandy was mortified when right there in Walt's office, the slip fell down around her ankles the moment she got up to leave. Walt laughed. Sandy apologized but she didn't blush. The pigment of her dark skin doesn't visibly allow that type of emotion to show. Still, she felt humiliated and small standing there like that. In retrospect it was a funny and bizarre moment, a twist of fate that Sandy got the job of chase producer. Walt said the reason he chose her is because she didn't blush, she didn't seem flustered. Little did he know.

Now, standing here in front of a bunch of cops, the same type of shock sets in. Except this time there is no petticoat anywhere in sight. Does anyone teach the art of backpedalling? And is there such a thing as graceful retraction of a major blunder? It is obvious that Johnson's question made Sandy uncomfortable, and that her reaction made Johnson feel terrible for asking. Blue too. Sandy guesses this is how a Catholic priest would feel if he miscalculated putting the host into someone's palm, dropping the communion wafer on the floor instead. What would he do? Pick it up? Ignore what just happened? Or just say a prayer that no one noticed?

She breaks the silence. "It's okay. I'm gonna go order." She directs the comment toward Blue, but doesn't look him in the eyes. "It was very nice meeting you guys." There. She acknowledges them individually, especially Johnson.

Sandy hears mumbled discussion coming from their table as she places the order. "Two coffees please," she manages to choke out. It isn't easy to speak; there is a knot in her throat and in her gut. She can't stop herself from eavesdropping.

"Oh geez, man. I'm so sorry." It is said in hushed tones, just above a whisper. Sandy knows what Blue and his buddies are talking about. She orders some orange juice to go too. "I'll meet you in the car," she croaks out, leaving the shop.

When Blue finally makes his way out to the parking lot, there isn't much that either of them can really say. He takes the wheel and the two drive in uncomfortable silence for a long time. Sandy nods off into a fitful sleep and toward a dreamland she'd rather not have visited. In this dream, Blue does not pass the "turkey test," a test from a story Sandy remembers from her childhood.

THE POTENTIAL FOR POISON

Sandy was ten years old and sitting around the old kitchen table. Her Baba was cutting up onions for turkey stuffing. The old Catholic priest from Sandy's hometown was there. His name was Father Hebalto, a cantankerous old bastard. He had a penchant for drinking the offering wine, and ordered cases of the blessed alcohol every week. But funnily enough, there were never any empty bottles in his garbage can. Sandy didn't like him because he didn't let the kids play hopscotch. "Playing with numbers like that summons the devil!" he'd say.

But Sandy didn't listen and she and a couple of the other girls snuck around. It made Sandy think she was a little witch—gone into hiding to practise her craft—giggling with each stroke of chalk. *1–2–3–4–5–6–7–8–9–10*, arranged in a pattern that Hebalto claimed would summon hell on Earth. The girls danced in secret, pinky-swearing to tell no one and delighting in the forbidden; counting, leaping and laughing out loud, praying not to be caught by Father Hebalto.

Meanwhile Baba watched from a distance—continuing to dress the turkey. Hebalto was very particular about his food preparation, instructing her to leave the bird out on the counter overnight, at room temperature. "That way, it closes up the pores on the thing, locking in juices for when it goes into the oven to roast."

"But that will cause food poisoning." Baba voiced her concern about salmonella. Regardless, she reluctantly but obediently did as the priest instructed, placing the raw bird on the counter beside the sink for its overnight transformation. It sat there on an oversized platter staring at Baba as she closed the door to the priest's home, crossing herself that the turkey wouldn't spoil and telling the priest that she would return tomorrow.

The next day at dinner, the turkey was a grand-looking main dish, presented in its roasted perfection in the middle of an elaborately set table. It was the kind of presentation you'd see in a *Better Homes & Gardens* magazine photo, the bird trimmed with parsley and radishes adding a splash of colour. Still, Baba was hesitant to serve it to Hebalto and the other priests who drove in from neighbouring prairie towns. The turkey looked irresistibly tempting: brown, plump, juicy. Its mouth-watering aroma provoked pleasing anticipation as Hebalto made the first cut into its crisp skin. But Baba was fretting and pacing. If salmonella had set in, there was only one way to find out. As Father Hebalto put fork to mouth, Baba held her breath.

Anticipatory angst.

Sandy's fitful dream switches from past to present day. She says a silent prayer. As she prays, Hebalto's face changes and is replaced by the face of Blue.

Baba says now she knows for sure that the risk of poison is real: it has sat too long in an unhealthy and unsafe environment.

Sandy jerks herself awake, bumping her head on the glass of the window just as Blue reaches over to turn up the volume on the Jeep radio.

BARE CLAUSE

Minnewanka Loop. It's one of the first road signs anyone sees driving into Banff. "Sounds like some short cartoon character!" Sandy laughs out loud. Blue smiles. *The Rockies are spectacular in any season,* Sandy muses to herself. *Even more so during this season of love.* She blushes at the thought, realizing it sounds too corny to say aloud. The day is warm. Sandy welcomes the cool mountain breeze on her face as they pull into the town-site. Her window is down and so is her guard. As expected, they arrive in late afternoon.

The bustle of Banff never slows. In wintertime it's the skiers who flock to the mountain resort. In summertime it's the hikers. And during the in-between season of late spring, it's the lovers. There is no snow as ground cover anymore. It has all melted except for the ever-present snow-covered mountain peaks. The alpine meadows below are showing hints of green.

Blue seems pleased as they drive down Main Street. Sandy is agitated. "Shit. There are no rooms available anywhere." She furrows her brow. NO VACANCY—the same neon message bellows from each hotel. "We may have to drive back to Canmore. It looks like everything is booked." Sandy prays this rocky start is not a precursor of the rest of their trip.

"Oh, come on now," Blue smiles. "We don't have to worry. I say we start our visit with a trip to the candy store."

"Shouldn't we find a room before we do anything else?"

"Oh, plenty of time for that, my love." Blue points up the street, driving toward the only parking spot available, near the candy store. He wraps his arm around Sandy as they stand outside the huge glass window. Inside, they watch chocolatiers preparing sweet treats. Fine Belgian chocolate cascades like a small waterfall from machines that remind Sandy of the cream separators she's seen on the farm. They go into the store.

"Two bear claws, please," Blue puts in his order. "Milk chocolate." There is a confidence surrounding him that Sandy doesn't understand. "It's worth the drive just to get one of these." He smiles after taking a bite. A string of warm caramel drips from his chin as the two make their way back to the Jeep. "I can drive. Give you a bit of a break," he says, holding the passenger side door and offering his hand as Sandy steps back inside. He drives straight to the front doors of the Banff Park Lodge. "Let's check at this place, maybe there's a room for us."

"But there's a 'no vacancy' sign here, Blue."

He gets out of the Jeep anyway, circling the vehicle to open Sandy's door. "My lady." He slowly runs his hands down her waist as she opens the hatch to the Jeep. He kisses her hair then takes her suitcase out of the vehicle. "Let's go in."

A pleasant young woman with long red hair greets them as they approach the reception desk. "May I help you?" Sandy expects Blue to say they haven't made a reservation, but instead he announces with pride, "Blue Greyeyes and Sandy Pelly." The front-desk clerk checks her file, smiles and takes out two room keys. She hands them to Blue.

As they walk up to the second-floor guest suite, Sandy has to ask, "How'd you do that?" Blue explains that back at the coffee shop, Constable Johnson suggested that he make the call and the reservation. "It's the least I can do," he said.

When they reach the doorway, Blue bends over to kiss Sandy, licking a small bit of chocolate off the side of her bottom lip. Blue's tongue stirs feelings of desire and they go in. Blue draws her closer, taking off his shirt then undoing the back of her dress. Sandy can feel herself starting to swell with excitement and passion.

He pulls her body closer. She feels the shape of his chin then brushes her hands across his strong shoulders. She loves looking into his eyes. "Lay down Blue," she instructs. Sandy unzips his jeans and puts her mouth near his navel. Seconds later her full lips electrify him, unleashing sounds of tortured pleasure.

Blue quivers as she runs her full lips up and down. He tells her to stop—"I'm ready." She knows but continues. He makes the primal sound she longs to hear. She feels his surge at the back of her mouth and swallows, laying down beside him and running her fingers lightly across his chest. It makes her want to take him there again.

Sandy wraps her legs around him. His hands tightly hold her legs in place. She starts to sweat, listening to Blue's breathing. Heavy. Fast. She pays attention, wanting them both to combine their love at the same time. He is ready. So is she. They mix in a single, glorious expression of passion. Sandy has never been more satisfied. She whispers it as a prayer of thanks. They shower together before heading out on a hike.

At 5:15 P.M. they are at the base of Sulphur Mountain. "The last gondola returns from the summit around 9 P.M., so we have to leave right now if we want to catch it. Otherwise, we'll be forced to walk down the mountain trail in the dark. On second thought, that might be kind of fun," Sandy says. The hike up takes about two hours. The ride back down is free. "We probably won't see anything bigger than a chipmunk. Besides, no self-respecting bear would come here—too many tourists."

Sandy feels silly admitting to Blue that she suffers a phobia. She considers forests to be an enclosed space. She is used to the wide-open plains and feels trapped when she can't see beyond a few feet. It occurs to her that it may be a metaphor of how she, deep down, feels about him too. Still, they start their climb. The crunching sound of loose gravel on pavement causes Sandy to hear voices in her head. It is her instinct offering advice—which she doesn't appreciate right now: *Be aware of your footing. It's so easy to get hurt. You must choose your lovers carefully, lest you risk falling in love with them.*

Shit. Where did that come from? She forces her mind to stop wandering by slapping at a mosquito that has landed on her forearm. It is likely the first bug of the season. Early evening in the Canadian Rockies, with snow-capped peaks casting long shadows, it's easy to assume that temperatures dip significantly with the lowering of the sun. But that doesn't happen tonight. This is Chinook country and the mercury still reads seventeen degrees, very warm for this time of year. Blue is in his shorts and T-shirt. Sandy wears a short mustard-coloured dress, light enough to stay cool but heavy enough to absorb any sweat brought on by something other than their passion. Blue wears his runners and Sandy is wearing her favourite beat-up hiking boots along with thick grey work socks. She loves these socks: they remind her of times when she and Baba used to make sock puppets when Sandy was a kid. They also help guard against blisters.

But what will guard her from phantoms? The random negative thoughts she's been having about Blue keep surfacing. She hopes he has no more dark secrets. But Constable Johnson, back at the coffee shop, sure gave the impression Blue and Heidi are still together. She thinks he keeps things hidden—the way these trees hide oncoming dangers, like bears.

Sandy heaves a sigh, hoping that the exhalation of air might blow away her thoughts. She can't figure out why after so many moments of togetherness and intimacy, the doubt keeps creeping in. Instinctively, she finds herself reaching into the fanny pack she's wearing so that she can feel the smooth edges of her special rock.

Blue smiles and reaches for Sandy's hand to pull her up a slight incline. From there, he insists that she walk out front, "so I can protect you." But that isn't the reason. He wants her to lead the way because he likes to watch the way she moves. Her strong, slender calves stretch out with every step up the steep mountain pathway. He comments on her long hair flowing in the wind.

The air smells wonderful, full of pine, damp moss and alpine flowers, mostly edelweiss. Small flowers are just beginning to awaken from their long winter slumber. She sees the small shoots of Indian paintbrushes, which will turn a bright red soon enough. There are delicate purple and yellow flowers that have just recently opened their buds dotting the trail as well. The bloom of colour is small but lovely. Over the next days and weeks, they will be in full bloom. Sandy wonders if she and Blue might be too.

Blue talks about an Elder that the police service has just hired as a consultant. "I drop in on him once in a while. He seems nice." It lightens Sandy's dark mood. She hopes it signals that Blue is taking more of an interest in learning about Aboriginal culture. It makes Sandy happy to know that he knows someone like Joe. She smiles, remembering their arrival at the National Park earlier in the day.

Some dream catchers were hanging in a store next to the chocolatier. They looked interesting, so Sandy asked, "What are these?"

Blue knew the answer. "Oh those. They are called dream catchers, from the Ojibway people. If you hang one in your bedroom window then bad dreams won't be able to pass. Bad thoughts get caught in the webbing. In the morning, when the sun rises, the bad dreams melt away." Sandy didn't know this, though upon closer examination the word-for-word explanation that Blue gave was written right next to the *Made in China* sticker.

We can learn together, she keeps telling herself, as they continue to climb toward the summit of Sulphur Mountain. The view is breathtaking. Sandy hands her camera to a Japanese tourist who agrees to take their photo—of two young lovers smiling, with a perfect mountain vista at sunset as the background.

A couple days later it is time to leave Banff. They drive away, windows down, letting in crisp mountain air.

SUDDEN STORM

It has been a long but lovely drive back home, the sun setting over the ever-changing and living sky. Sandy is tired and looking forward to sleeping in her own bed tonight. As they pull up to the apartment building, an angry storm looms—a storm standing on the sidewalk, smoking a cigarette.

Heidi throws down her cigarette and attacks as soon as the vehicle comes to a halt. "Blue, who's the frickin' Indian princess?" Blue seems frozen in fear. He doesn't answer. Heidi looks at Sandy, and hisses venom at both of them. "Who the hell are you, bitch?" She escalates the insults, calling Sandy a "fuckin' bitch" right in front of Blue.

He does nothing. He says nothing.

"I'm Sandy. Who are you?"

"I'm Heidi, you piece of shit. Get your hands off my man!" She shoves Sandy like she wants to start a fight. Heidi smells disgusting: a mix of cigarette smoke, bad breath and stinky armpits.

Again Blue does nothing. He just stands there, aghast.

Heidi continues to swear. "Who the fuck is she, Blue?"

From Sandy's perspective, Heidi had been a monstrous presence even before they met. She might seem attractive to some, with bobbed blonde hair and a tall, thin body. But Sandy sees her as something that ought to be chased out of town with crosses and holy water. Heidi looks like a biker chick, with dried-out bleach-blonde hair and black roots. There is a tattoo of the Tasmanian devil just above her left breast. Her fingernails are chipped with red nail polish. Her front tooth is chipped too. And now Heidi is chipping away at Sandy's happiness and dreams of love and belonging.

"You bastard!" Heidi screams at Blue. "I come here to surprise you, and this is what I get? Male slut! You fucker!"

Heidi slaps Blue hard across the face. She moves to slap Sandy as well.

Finally, Blue does something. He grabs Heidi's arm. "Don't."

Heidi starts to cry hysterically and collapses on the sidewalk. Sandy holds her breath, asking herself what the hell is going on.

That's when Blue makes a choice. The wrong one. He holds Heidi, not Sandy, his eyes showing complete sadness and utter confusion. Sandy is appalled by how easily he acquiesces, remembering his words "I have a responsibility toward her somehow." It didn't make sense the first time she heard it. It doesn't make sense now.

He disappears into their apartment and Heidi follows, into Sandy's home. Sandy just stands there on the sidewalk, empty and alone. The only thing embracing her now is the cold blanket of twilight.

The Jeep engine is still running and Sandy gets in, wondering if she'll be able to drive. Tears obscure her vision. She's been hit in the gut with an emotional sledgehammer and feels like throwing up. Sandy turns up the radio. Leonard Cohen is singing.

I'm aching for you baby. I can't pretend I'm not.
I'd love to see you naked, in your body and your thought.

She turns it off and drives to a nearby convenience store. Even though it is foul, the old habit of smoking during crisis kicks in. She needs some nicotine but even more than that she needs a friend. She goes to find a payphone down the street.

FALLING APART

Ellen, I don't know what to do. If anyone ever needed a girl-friend, now is the time." Sandy wishes she could see her friend, but for now the phone call must suffice.

"Move back home, Sandy. We all miss you here, and I doubt you'll have a problem getting your old job back."

Through her sobbing, Sandy considers but decides against a move backward. However, she does decide to move out of Blue's apartment and get her own place—and she's certainly not going back to Blue's tonight. Sandy admits to Ellen that she is scared, wiping a tear and reaching for one of her newly purchased cigarettes.

"You need to get your own place, Sandy. I can drive up and help you look if you want," Ellen offers, "but you need to get out now. Go stay with a friend tonight. You shouldn't be alone." Sandy agrees and after hanging up she immediately dials Kyle's number. Since their first assignment together they'd become fast friends. She is grateful for his generous response of allowing her to stay at his place for the night, maybe even a few days.

Upon Sandy's arrival at his home, Kyle's first reaction is to take a frozen pizza from the freezer and place it in the oven. "I am guessing you haven't been eating much lately," he states, "so I'll make you something to eat."

She gives him a half smile and nods. While the pizza is baking, Kyle starts making a salad. He pours two glasses of milk and sets one in front of Sandy. "You can stay as long as you need to. I'm glad you're here. Your friend Ellen is right. You shouldn't be alone at a time like this."

Sandy doesn't have much of an appetite but she manages to swallow most of her salad and half a slice of pizza. As they eat, they talk about relationships. Every now and then Sandy chokes back tears. She discovers that Kyle is divorced but is casually seeing a new girlfriend at the moment. He tells Sandy it isn't serious, and she wonders if the girlfriend knows that. She begins to cry about Kyle's admission that he's seeing someone just to avoid loneliness. *Is this how Blue feels about her? Is this how men feel in general?* For a moment she wonders if it is questions like this that drive people to suicide. The thought stays with Sandy into the night. It's troublesome enough to cause more bad dreams.

RUSTY SCISSORS

Anytime there is stress in Sandy's life, it replays as a familiar black and white dream sequence. Sandy is brushing her lovely mane of thick, long, black hair. As a child, she braided it or put it in rollers or pigtails or ponytails and used clips to hold it off her face. She loved the feel of it blowing in the wind and how she was able to hide behind it by pulling it over her face during games. Her hair was a source of joy, strength and identity, all of which are taken away one rainy afternoon.

In her dream, as in her real life, Sandy is a reporter. She is still at her old job in the dream, maybe a way of saying that moving back would really be moving backward. Frank is away at a conference and leaves Sauer in charge. In this dream, Sauer has fangs. Sandy is on assignment in a farmer's field. The grasshoppers are particularly bad, especially for those trying their hand at organic farming, the topic of the story she is supposed to be filing. Sandy can smell the earth. It is so dry and parched that it looks sore. Everyone is praying for rain. Rich black topsoil, with its essential nutrients, has blown away with the hopes of the farmers.

As Sandy readies herself to go on camera, a small miracle occurs. First it comes as drizzle, quickly developing into a heavy sprinkle. Sandy makes the decision to speak to the camera as the rain falls.

Strands of her long hair keep blowing onto her face and neck with the breeze accompanying the rain. Eventually it turns into a downpour.

When Sandy returns from assignment, Sauer takes a look at the videotape, chastising her appearance. "My lord girl, you look godawful. Too ethnic and unkempt with that hair. No one has long hair on TV. Or haven't you noticed?" Sandy figures he is just goading her until he makes an unreasonable demand. "It's unprofessional. It gets cut today. Otherwise you are fired. I'm serious." In the dream, Sauer holds a pair of rusty scissors. He turns into a faceless ghoul who sounds a sickening chortle as he begins hacking away at Sandy's beautiful mane.

She awakens on Kyle's couch in a panic, but not for the worry that her hair is short. She finds herself sobbing, knowing that in her dream her long black hair began to change colour—from black to blonde.

NEW BROWNSTONE

Sandy reaches in her purse for a cigarette but this time the package is empty. She's been smoking a lot lately. It is near the end of the month now and time to get off Kyle's couch. She arranges to take her belongings out of storage and find a place of her own, though some of her items are still at Blue's. Every morning a freshly folded newspaper is delivered to Kyle's doorstep. Sandy goes to retrieve it even before grabbing her morning coffee. Kyle has left her a fresh pot. Sandy likes that he puts just a pinch of cinnamon in the grounds before brewing.

As she opens the door Sandy is greeted by the sound of birds cheerfully singing their morning songs. The wind is calm, the temperature is pleasantly warm for an early Saturday morning and there are no traffic sounds. A wonderful start to the weekend. Sandy hopes her good fortune continues as she begins to search for a place to rent. She opens the newspaper to the classifieds.

Within the hour, Sandy is viewing the apartment that will soon be her new home. It is within walking distance of the TV station— and again, she chooses to live in an old brownstone. It is a large one bedroom with hardwood floors, vaulted ceilings and radiators for heat. It reminds Sandy of her old apartment in Regina. She is starting over and decides this familiarity of surroundings will be good, helping her get back on track at work and hopefully in other areas of her life.

Still there has been no word from Blue. They'll have to meet up at some point. The city is only so big and besides, some of her things are still in his apartment—if he hasn't thrown them out by now. She notices she still has his key and sighs, fastening the key to her new apartment on the same ring.

BROWN ENVELOPE

There is no one currently living in her new apartment, so Sandy talks the landlord into letting her move in before the start of the month. On Friday night she picks up a bouquet of fresh flowers, some food and wine before walking home. The plan is for a quiet evening, maybe some TV. Grateful for Kyle's help in getting her moved in, she was hoping the two of them could celebrate with a home-cooked dinner together in her new place. But Kyle is out of town on a late assignment, so she dines alone.

Sandy struggles with her bags of groceries before turning the deadbolt to go in. She's arranged her new apartment with style. Each piece of pottery has been properly placed, paintings are hung in areas that will best reflect natural light and her area rug is unfurled in front of the brown leatherette couch. She smiles as she glances at the colourful potted plant on her coffee table. Ellen sent it as a house-warming gift. But the hardwood floor sounds hollow and cold as her heels click across the floor into the kitchen area. She finds a cork-screw and opens the bottle of wine she purchased on the way home. Sandy pours, offering herself a toast.

"Welcome to your new home," she says to no one, raising her glass in the air then taking a sip of the Cabernet Sauvignon. With

Kyle's help and encouragement, she's managed to pull herself together enough to get back on track at work, and figures a little celebration like this will do no harm.

Her feistiness at work comes in spurts now, but thankfully at the right times. Her story before coming home tonight was an investigative piece about a Boy Scout leader recently accused of sexual assault. Kyle's nephew is a Scout, which is where the tip came from. Her research uncovered that this Scout leader had engaged in inappropriate sexual touching before, in another province. It could have been prevented from happening here except for a fundamental flaw—an oversight made by an unqualified nineteen-year-old. Sandy managed to find out that a young lady was filling in at the Scout office and neglected a crucial part of her duties: background checks, criminal records checks and previous employer reference checks. But because she was new to the job, she didn't know the procedures. She was also the troop leader's niece, which is how she got the job in the first place.

The background checks sat in a file because the young lady was too embarrassed to ask for help and too proud to admit she didn't know the steps. A brown manila envelope containing photocopies of records and a description of how the oversight occurred was anonymously delivered to Kyle, helping Sandy construct the story. It led the newscast.

She makes a toast to this accomplishment, too, while eating her salad. The main course is pilaf rice, perfectly seasoned lamb chops and baby carrots. It should taste better but without Blue to share it with, it is only food. And it is her only meal today. There is also no one to call. Kyle won't be back until the morning and Ellen is working this weekend. Sandy is with her solitude, which isn't a good thing. *Here's to a beautifully cooked meal. And a perfectly fucked-up life.* It is Sandy's next toast. Alone. By this time the bottle is empty.

She grabs her keys from the foyer table and heads out the door. For a moment she considers joining her new colleagues who have invited her to join them this evening. She has proven that she is now one of them, a solid journalist. And tonight they are congregating at the Artful Dodger, an English pub that is only a few blocks from where Sandy lives.

Like the Press Club in her former city, the Dodger is the place where the media elite meet up every Friday night. The mahogany wood atmosphere is comfortable and encourages open conversation. And the members of the press who flock in at week's end are certainly good for business. They down enough pints to fill a septic tank. The cab companies do well too. But the liquor store is closer and Sandy finds herself walking there instead, picking up a pack of smokes at the convenience store along the way. She doesn't feel like she would be good company tonight, knowing the booze she's already consumed would make her candid, divulging details of her personal angst to her unsuspecting new colleagues.

There are only a couple customers at the liquor store, who also look tired and worn. Sandy walks to the Canadian wine section and finds two bottles of Merlot and a bottle of Zinfandel. On the way through the checkout, she spots a small bottle of Smirnoff and decides to pick it up as well. On her way back home, a street person stops her to ask for bus money. She gives him five dollars. "Go crazy," she says, handing him the bill. He takes the money then says a word she doesn't recognize: "Meegwetch." She looks him quizzically in the eye, as if to ask what that means. That's when he recognizes her.

"Hey, you're the one from the TV," he says in a shy way. "I'm glad there's finally an Indian on TV. Right on." He puts out his hand to shake. She doesn't take his hand, but instead gives him a patronizing smile and hands him an additional two-dollar bill from her pocket. He isn't offended and accepts the extra cash with the wave of his hand, "You know, you have a responsibility to be a leader for our people. I'm honoured to meet you." He seems genuinely proud to be in her presence and chatting with her.

"A leader for what?" she mutters under her breath, having no idea what he is suggesting. Still, she nods in uncomfortable agreement before turning away. She doesn't want to talk to anyone. Solitude is her friend this evening along with the cold sting of night air. Sandy quickens her pace, asking herself a second time, "A leader, eh? Why not? I suppose I could lead myself right out of this place, away from Blue and straight to the network." She mumbles, but it is more like a grumble. The thought about moving startles her. She's never wanted to leave the Prairies before, let alone make such a suggestion aloud, even if there was no one else around to hear it. A jumble of logic reminds her of times in the past when she'd leave a place early to get ahead of the weather. Her mind wanders back to a memory as she briskly continues to walk, hands in pockets.

"There's a storm coming in, sweetie," her Baba said on a visit home once. "If you're going to make it back safely, you better leave now or think about staying another night." So Sandy cuts her stay short in an effort to get ahead of the storm. But it never works. She always seems to get caught right in the thick of it, having to pull over at the side of the road while torrents of rain remind her who's in charge. It's a piece of bad luck that seems to follow her.

Sandy quickens her pace again, pulling her sweater close to her neck. The wind is picking up, causing her eyes to water as she walks. Her thoughts keep wandering. Usually when she walks by windows where the drapes are left open, she finds it interesting to catch a small glimpse of someone else's life. Tonight, though, it is excruciating for her to see the smiles of happy children reminding her she doesn't even have a cat to go home to. She crosses the street, coming to another home with shades drawn. Inside is an older couple playing a board game, reassuringly comfortable in each other's company. The scene she sees through another window makes Sandy uncomfortable and sad: two young lovers slow dance in their living room amid candlelit ambience. *These are bits of my dream*, she thinks, as tears once again begin to well. She wipes them away with the back of her hand, a doleful look on her face as she repeats to herself, *I don't even have a cat to go home to.*

Minutes later Sandy is fumbling with her keys. They feel like sharp bits of ice; the wind has wrapped cold fingers around the steel. Sandy selects the right one, inserting it into the keyhole. The wooden door heaves a sad, hollow sound again as she walks back in. Taking the key out, Sandy wonders if she is unlocking anything else. Her Baba always told her to look for the silver lining even when things go wrong. She reaches for a silver corkscrew instead. Her pain is still profound. Numb that. Numb that. She opens the second bottle of wine.

Another fleeting thought comes. The street person she just saw is about her age, maybe just a bit older. "A shame," she says out loud before taking another sip. "Wonder what put him over the edge? Probably love." She stares at the warm glow of the Merlot then takes a gulp. If Blue's silence doesn't kill her, the alcohol just might. She toasts the air, taking a second gulp. She goes to the telephone and picks up the receiver, dialling Blue's number, wondering if that little piece of magic they shared is gone. There is no answer. *What the hell am I supposed to say to him anyway?*

She decides to take a bath. The fragrant suds in the oversized claw-foot tub provide a couple moments of relief. "You know, before I met Blue, everything was fine." Sandy is talking to her shadow, cast dimly on the bathroom wall by way of candlelight. "I didn't need anyone. What's happened?" She feels a warm rush of air that comes out of nowhere, the same feeling she had in a dream the night she met that Elder, the feeling of a wingtip of an invisible bird. *What was the Elder's name again?*

"Oh, yes, Joe." A tear rolls down her cheek. Sandy takes another sip of wine. She holds her breath and stays under for as long as her lungs will hold out. She wants to confess to Blue that he is the one that she's been waiting for all her life, that she's never felt so connected to a man, that she's never wanted a man to touch her the way he does… It's like everything she did before was a rehearsal for Blue, she thinks, remembering the moment of their first kiss. She can still feel it, warm on her lips.

She longs to dial the telephone again. She wants to tell Blue that she's never been so open to a person's touch. She wants to go there again, with him. "A beautiful gift. That's what I read in a book." She wonders if talking to herself out loud like this might be a sign of madness. Or is it good therapy to purge in this way, even if no one is around to hear? It worries her. "The most precious part of me doesn't belong to me at all. It is my love for you," Sandy whispers before sinking below the water one more time.

It is 11 P.M. when Sandy crawls out of the tub. She decides to turn in for the night, the wild and glamorous life of a television personality. The thought makes her chuckle. Or maybe it is the wine. After towelling herself dry, she decides to put on some perfume that Blue had commented on as one of his favourites. She closes her eyes and imagines feeling his lips touching her neck as she dabs on the fragrance. But she needs more comfort. That's when she remembers her long, red, fleece nightgown. It was a gift from Baba the Christmas before she passed. The nightie, soft and warm. She had one just like it when she was a kid.

Sandy goes to find it, digging through dresser drawers, looking through a couple of as-yet-unpacked boxes. She checks her closet. No nightie. Then she remembers—it is at Blue's. Next comes a thought that is not rational. Sandy could easily wear something else to bed tonight. But no. The wine has influenced her too much. She has to have her special nightgown. So she decides to go over to his place and collect it and some of her other things. She still has his key. Thinking she may need someone to talk her out of this plan, she calls Ellen for advice.

LOGIC IN ABSENTIA

Sandy is disappointed to hear Ellen's answering machine with its monotone voice message, "Hi, I'm not here right now…" Sandy doesn't leave a message. She wanted Ellen to talk some sense into her. Instead there is only silence. She accepts the lack of anyone to convince her otherwise as a message that she should go to Blue's.

Sandy gets dressed, grabs her keys and calls a cab. The cold night air slaps her hard as she stands there on the sidewalk waiting for the cab to arrive. It reminds her of the scene with Heidi. She remembers feeling hurt, watching Blue walk away from her, taking Heidi into their home. As she wipes away the tears she hears a kind voice call out, "Miss? You call a cab?" Sandy nods and gets in, checking her purse to make sure there is enough money to cover the cost of the ride.

The drive over to Blue's is a blur of headlights and neon signs. Some sort of self-help talk show drones on over the FM radio. Sandy isn't sure how to feel right now. *What if he's home? What if he's with someone else?* The thought terrifies her but she is determined to go through with it anyway. She pulls a cigarette out of her purse and asks the cabbie if it is all right to smoke. He says yes. She lights up then leaves him a good tip when she gets out.

He is intuitive. "Do you want me to wait a while?" He is a nice young man, probably in his early thirties. He is wearing a wedding ring.

"No, I'll be okay. But thanks."

There is no light on through Blue's window shade. Sandy wants him to be home. She trembles, turning the key to his apartment door then switching on the foyer light. It is one of those old fixtures that starts out dim and lights up to its sixty-watt capacity over the course of a few minutes. Everything looks pretty much as she last remembers it, like no time has passed at all. An old TV guide sits on Blue's small, white plastic living room table. It is dog-eared at the corners and smattered with stains from having been used as a coaster for coffee cups. She can see a half-filled pot of cold coffee at the edge of the counter in Blue's small kitchen.

He isn't home. Sandy takes a deep breath, wipes her feet on the multi-coloured rag rug that greets people at the doorway and heads to the storage room to find an empty box. Her first destination after that is the bathroom. It saddens her to collect her fragrant bath oils and shampoo, conjuring images of the time she and Blue bathed together on the second day of their mountain visit. She closes her eyes and for a moment can almost feel his hands caressing her back and shoulders. She gathers a few pieces of jewellery and hair ties. They are exactly where she left them. The box of tampons is gone.

As she enters Blue's bedroom, she is convinced that she feels a rush of warm air again. It feels inviting, as though he is physically there. She picks up one of his shirts and smells it. His scent is strong, like he left it there just that afternoon following a workout. She holds it close to her heart. She briefly thinks about taking it with her so she can smell his scent whenever she needs to feel close to him, but she puts it back in its place. Instead, she collects only a few of her own articles, including the red nightgown. She glances around the room. It brings her a smile to see his favourite yellow T-shirt draped over the back of an old wooden chair that is sitting underneath the window. The shirt is prominently displayed like a piece of artwork. Sandy knows why. She feels special at being reminded of the most sensuous and romantic thing that no man before Blue has ever done to her.

It was the night before the couple left to visit the mountains. Sandy was hotly excited and glistening with sweat when they made love. He whispered, "You smell beautiful. I love your scent." He used his T-shirt to wipe away her sweat. The T-shirt retains that scent. The soft feminine smell that Blue towelled from between her breasts, off her ribcage and under her arms and the husky, sweet aroma he lovingly gathered from between her legs. The memories are now preserved by the scented cloth that sits so near to his bed. He never washes that shirt, keeping it close.

Oh my lord. Thank you. He still loves me, Sandy wants to believe, until something else catches her attention. Blue's chequebook, of all things. It is sitting there on the night table, just underneath the light switch. She glances at it and starts to cry. What she sees is a duplicate cheque that he's written, dated just a few days ago, of two hundred dollars made out to Heidi. "Maybe they never broke up after all," she whispers as tears cascade from her eyes, smudging mascara. She turns off the light but not before placing Blue's apartment key on the night table, right beside the chequebook. Then she leaves.

Sandy finds that the cab driver is still outside waiting. Intuition. Some men, even strangers, are so good. She gives thanks for this small blessing. She doesn't remember the ride home, but when she gets back the first thing she does is put on the red nightie. Time for another glass of wine. She pokes herself with the corkscrew while opening a fresh bottle. A small bit of blood forms a ball on her fingertip. Her thought process is as dense and red as the liquid. She picks up the phone again and starts dialling Blue's number.

Ring. Ring. Ring. No answer. Sandy frets, waits and drinks some more. After a few more glasses, she does something really stupid.

Sandy searches for the forsaken phone bill that she tucked away ages ago. Heidi's number. She dials it.

"Hello?"

"Hello yourself, you stupid cunt."

Silence. "Who is this?" Heidi asks.

What transpires next is a diatribe of shame ending with "He's fucking me again. Not you. Don't you get it?"

Click. Static.

CHANGING OLD PATTERNS

Sandy wakes up to the sound of the telephone ringing. She checks the clock—it's 10 A.M. For a moment she panics, thinking she is late for work, until she realizes it is Saturday. "Who the hell is calling me before noon?" she groans. Another ring. She answers. Her head is pounding. Whoever is on the other line must think they dialled the wrong number, her voice is so hoarse and raspy.

"Mornin' Sunshine. You still up for brunch?" It is Kyle Preston. He mentioned to her during an assignment earlier in the week that he has a Saturday morning routine. "I always go to Kelly's Diner. It's one of the oldest restaurants in the city. They make the best waffles and sausage." Kyle has a great smile that he shows just almost every time he speaks. Kelly's Diner is a small establishment, and if you don't know where it's located, tucked away on a side street just off Broadway, it is easy to miss. Because of that, tourists never clutter the place. Instead, it is a regular and appreciative crowd that frequents it.

Kyle had also told Sandy that Kelly's Diner was the place he went the morning after he first lost his virginity, and that the décor hasn't changed much in that time. "Neither has the clientele. There's something comforting about that black and white tile floor, the chrome fountain-seats and those old elaborate light fixtures." A lot has

happened for Kyle in that diner. It has been the backdrop for celebrating career successes, and for lamenting breakups and nursing
hangovers. All of it happens over a big cup of hot coffee.

Kyle is hoping Sandy will also recognize the diner's charm and
make it part of her routine too. He regards her as a little sister and
knows she needs a friend. Sandy has shared bits and pieces with
him about her situation with Blue. Kyle never asks unless she volunteers the information first. Kyle is a reformed alcoholic, so he never
suggests that he and Sandy meet at a place like the Artful Dodger.
It isn't his style to review the week just passed. He likes to look
forward. And he sees a bright future for Sandy, so long as she doesn't
get caught in the same trap that he's seen so many other young journalists get destroyed by. He has seen too many spirits falter and then
wither because of the purveyors of fine spirits: young reporters who
are unable to handle the pressure, success or expectations. He will
do what he can to prevent Sandy from becoming another casualty.
They agree to meet at Kelly's Diner within the hour.

What the fuck am I doing? While hanging up the receiver Sandy
wonders why she's agreed to meet him. She should have made up
an excuse. She feels like shit, and the thought of eating right now
is the furthest thing from her mind. But she is happy to hear from
him. Besides, she doesn't want to nurse her broken heart with a
hangover and spend the day feeling sorry for herself. She did that last
night. Sandy gets up, goes to the bathroom, sticks her fingers down
her throat and forces herself to throw up. Twice. She jumps into the
shower, obviously a new addition to the old building. She is grateful
for this small renovation. Some Visine in her eyes, some mouthwash,
and off she goes. Kyle will be waiting at Kelly's Diner.

"So, did you meet up with those bums last night?" It is Kyle's best
guess. He easily recognizes her day-after shuffle. Plus she is wearing
sunglasses, something she rarely does. Sandy's eyes are her best
feature and can make the people she interviews tell her just about

anything. She doesn't give him an answer about the sunglasses, instead ordering a big glass of water and a coffee. The waitress brings both within seconds.

"I think I did something terrible last night." She grasps the hot mug with both hands and slurps her coffee. She is trembling a bit.

Of course Kyle's first thought is that she woke up with someone she didn't know. He has a gift for using humour to get through difficult conversations like this one. "Aw c'mon Sunshine, coyote ugly happens to the best of us!"

That makes her chuckle, causing her head to pound even harder. "Oh no, not that."

Kyle likes knowing that he can make her smile even when she feels this bad. She manages to get through her story without crying. She tells Kyle that she called Blue's former girlfriend and said the most horrid things. "Why would I do such a thing?" Then she becomes silent and looks out the window. Two young lovers walk into Kelly's Diner at that moment, their afterglow from the night before still surrounding them. It makes Sandy wonder if her aura right now is equally as telling.

"I'll order you some breakfast," Kyle says. And with that she gives him a half smile, in part for helping her not to make some insignificant decision about white or brown toast. But more so she wants to let him know she appreciates that he never suggests to her that everything is going be all right. He simply listens to what she needs to say without casting judgment or interrupting. When it is clear that she has finished talking, he changes the subject. Not dwelling on the negative is his way of moving forward. Kyle talks about a boat he purchased earlier in the week. Today is pickup day.

"As soon as we finish up here you should come with me, Sunshine. We'll take it for a spin out at the lake," he says, suggesting they go to a provincial park not far away.

She agrees to join him. "I have no other plans, thanks. It'll do me some good to get out of the city." Besides, she secretly worries that if she doesn't go with him she might end up at the Artful Dodger. A couple of the other cameramen invited her to join them Saturday afternoon, to get rid of the hair of the dog that bit you. She doesn't even want to be tempted.

A couple hours later they arrive at the lake. Sandy braids her hair, asking Kyle if she can borrow the CF-Television ball cap that she spots in the back seat of his two-cab pickup. She doesn't want to deal with a tangled mess later because of wind from the boat. "Hell, sweetie, you can keep it. I've got about a dozen of them. I give them away sometimes when I'm on a shoot." He is like a kid at Christmas with his new toy. His energy is infectious and that makes her feel better. She is glad that she's joined him. The effects of her hangover are easing off a bit thanks in part to some weird concoction at Kelly's Diner. In addition to breakfast, the waitress brought over some vegetable-like beverage. It had a kick to it, which made Sandy guess that it contained cayenne or pure lemon juice, or both. Kyle ordered it, assuring it would help. "But make sure you drink it all in one gulp." She did, popping a couple more Tylenols afterwards.

Now with the sun and a slight breeze, the soothing rustle of leaves in the wind and the smell of the lake, Sandy sees things more clearly. Blue hasn't contacted her. She doesn't know why. But she doesn't regret giving him back his key, even though she essentially broke into his place to do so. She left no note for him explaining, she just left the key. Still, she feels a lingering sadness. Is something fundamental missing from both our lives? Or just from mine?

It is at this moment that Sandy thinks about little Betsy. She has never confided to anyone at work that a piece of her died the day the little girl was taken away. But this past week while thinking of a story pitch, Sandy has realized she has the tools necessary to find out what happened with Betsy. Her role as a reporter gives her the authority to phone up the right people within government and ask tough questions, as part of a story. Where did Betsy end up? Is she okay? Does Betsy remember their time together?

Sandy could find out what she longs to know while cushioning it as a story. But instead of making a pitch she just called up the Department of Social Services to inquire about whether their old social worker still worked there. Bingo! The Grinch hadn't retired yet. Sandy called him.

"Of course I remember you. You were one of the few cases I had where a child was officially and legally adopted."

There was a bit of small talk and then Sandy asked about Betsy's adoption and whether he kept track of how she ended up as well.

"I wish I could give you some good news about that. But I can't. I kept in touch with the family that adopted Betsy. It wasn't like your story."

He explained that as Betsy grew in to her adolescent years, there was family breakdown. She started skipping school and ran away from home a couple times, only to be returned by the RCMP. Having grown up in a small town near Prince Albert, police were usually able to locate her in the city—except the last time her adopted parents called to report her missing.

Betsy left home one day and never returned, couldn't be found. No one has seen her since her sixteenth birthday.

Sandy could barely say goodbye to the social worker after he told her this news.

Her thoughts are interrupted as Kyle exclaims, "Hey! Buddy! Come check out my new baby!" For a second Sandy isn't sure if Kyle is talking about her or the new boat. His next statement makes it clear. "I finally broke down and bought one. Hell, you're only young once," he says to his friend.

"Buddy," as Kyle greets him, is a respected member of the nearby Dakota Sioux First Nation. It's the same community where that Elder lives, the Old Man who approached her with his concerns about missing girls some time ago. Now what was his name again? Her short-term memory is not good right now, even though she asked and answered herself that very same question just last night. Hangovers have that fuzzy memory effect.

Kyle's friend is Amos Bear. Amos possesses a kind and gentle manner. He looks to be in his late twenties, of average height and build, with a masculine square jaw and a shiny, long, black braid. His smile is genuine and friendly. Amos immediately recognizes Sandy from the TV and puts out his hand to greet her. She shakes his hand and smiles as well, finding herself being drawn to Amos, but not in a sexual way. Amos holds a different, powerful allure. She can't pinpoint it and it leaves her stymied. His very presence reminds her of ancestral spirits, like the day she met Mugwah and travelled out of her body. Within those next moments she goes elsewhere again, leaving the conversation and the lake in both mind and spirit. Something about Amos opens some type of portal.

Sandy hears the hard rumble of thunder followed by a downpour of cold, hard rain. It causes her to close her eyes. In that darkness she hears a voice speaking in a language other than English. She hears the low growl of Mugwah and feels a blast of his warm breath on her neck as he snorts, like a bear in the wild might do just before charging. Then the rain lightens. Sandy opens her eyes and sees Amos. He is standing beside the bear as though the two are brothers. Amos is wearing face paint like Indian warriors she's seen in movies. A gust of wind brings her back to the present. She feels lightheaded.

Sandy listens in on the conversation between Amos and Kyle and figures out that Amos owns the gas bar on the reserve. He's come to the lake this afternoon to meet up with some Old Woman. "Yeah, she came from up north. My auntie's friend. She's camping for the weekend, and my auntie said I should meet her. She's got some smoke-tanned bags, moccasins and beadwork for sale. Tourists always like that at the gas bar." Amos is there to buy her work. He shows some of the items to Sandy and Kyle as the fragrant smell of the smoke tan fills her nostrils. The smell is pleasant and familiar, the same scent that has come into her dreams a few times now. Sandy picks up a small change purse with baby blue and royal blue–coloured beads, asking Amos, "How much?"

"Take it," he smiles. "I get the feeling it's your first piece of smoke tan? And I feel good knowing it comes from me." He resumes his conversation with Kyle. "So yeah, I tell the Old Man I want to meet up with this Old Woman, but mostly I'm at the lake because I want to take a break for a bit, before my day gets too busy." Sandy notices that the familiarity between Amos and Kyle holds some type of brotherhood. They talk about intimate subjects.

"How is the Old Man's diabetes?"

"Oh, really good. No problem. He's been watching what he eats and he's doing a lot of walking. He'll be dancing later today," Amos answers. It catches Sandy's ear, *dancing*? She doesn't quite follow. Amos fills in the blanks.

"There's a big powwow happening out at the rez today. First one this summer. You two should come," he smiles. "A whole bunch of people will be coming over to my house for some food sometime before tonight's Grand Entry. My cousin Henry got a deer last week, so lots of stew and dried meat. You're welcome to join us." Amos gets a sly look as he continues the sentence, directing his comment toward Kyle. "Even if you are a monias! Ay!" Amos winks and sticks his tongue out slightly between his teeth as he makes, what Sandy guesses, is a joke. As both men laugh, she just gives a polite smile. Amos gets back into his blue pickup truck and drives away.

"What's a monias?" she asks Kyle.

"You're joking, right?" As they get into the boat, he answers her question with a question. It is a defining moment. "Have you ever been to a powwow?"

"No. No one has ever invited me."

"Holy shit, Sandy. No one needs to be invited to a powwow. You just go. Anyone can go. Anyone can dance. It's a celebration. A very public display of the pride of being Dakota, in the case of Amos." He pauses. "And in answer to your first question, a monias is a white person in the Cree language. Amos knows you're a Cree, so he made the joke in your dialect." Sandy can sense that Kyle is bursting to know something else. "Other than doing stories, have you ever spent any time with Native people at all?"

"No. I've never met any. Well except for Blue of course."

It saddens Kyle to realize that he probably knows more about Sandy's Aboriginal culture than she does. He knows that she reads a lot and listens a lot, but she's never had any actual experiences. He feels a sense of loss for Sandy, along with his suspicion that she can still be made to feel ashamed of being Indian, which is why she searches for threads of truth to help her find a place of belonging. But in a newsroom? Well, she found him anyway. And he can introduce her to other people like Amos. He first noticed her shame in being brown in a wisecrack she recently made while they were driving to an assignment.

Sandy was poking fun at how some Native people pronounce certain words. "Why do they all sound like that? They say things like 'fissin' instead of 'fishing'?" Her tone made it clear to Kyle that she saw her oratory skills as superior.

Kyle wasn't about to let it slip by. "Sunshine, anyone whose first language is not English always has an accent. Like Francois, our editor at the station. He speaks English with a French accent and I have never heard you make fun of him. A lot of the Aboriginal people who are here in the city come from communities where they speak Cree or Saulteaux or Dene. That's their first language, not English. That's why they have the accent. You should know that."

Sandy felt ashamed to admit that factor hadn't even occurred to her. Kyle has made a concerted effort to embrace Native culture, spirituality and traditions, and his knowledge doesn't come from books. The fact he is non-Native doesn't matter to teachers like Amos, whom Kyle met by chance.

"Mother Earth is here for all of us," Amos said when he and Kyle met a couple years ago. They are the eight words that changed Kyle's life, and thoughts about life. He knows the deep importance of the knowledge to which he has been privy. He is now determined that Sandy will know too. The water reflects warmth from the afternoon sun. It feels good on her face and neck as Kyle continues talking. "Sunshine, we're going to that powwow." He smiles and turns the boat toward shore.

REAWAKENING AT THE REZ

It is the perfect moment to begin anew. Sandy is excited and frightened at the same time. She gives Kyle a worried look as they step out of his pickup truck and onto a dusty parking lot. Drums call in the distance. Kyle examines her face. "This is your place, Sandy. People talk about reclaiming their culture all the time. You gotta start somewhere. This is a good place."

Sandy finds herself wishing that she met Kyle years earlier. He ruffles his blond hair, putting her at ease. *If he fits in here then I will too.* She wonders if she'll know anyone else. "Will Amos be here for sure?"

"He wouldn't miss it," Kyle responds. He tells her the story of how the two became friends. "I met Amos one day, just taking a drive out here. Wanted to see the landscape. His gas bar has a sign on the grid road that says they sell Native arts and crafts, so naturally I stopped."

That's when Kyle learned that in addition to being an entrepreneur, Amos is a Grass Dancer. Kyle liked the story, so he pitched it one day at the morning story meeting. Despite the fact he isn't a reporter, Kyle had been experimenting with putting together vignettes. He calls the series "The Lives of Our People," a montage of images, music and the voices of people explaining why they love to do the things they do. He's highlighted gardeners, artists, bakers and others. Upon meeting Amos, Kyle instinctively knew that Amos' story would fit in perfectly with the vignette series, which runs at the end of the newscast each Friday evening.

By this time Sandy and Kyle are seated on the hard wooden bleachers surrounding the dance arbour. "What happens now?" Sandy asks as she pulls her little automatic camera from her bag.

Kyle explains, "Amos tells me that the Grass Dancers enter the powwow arbour first. Today it is largely symbolic. But Amos says the Grass Dance is one of the oldest on the Plains. In the time before European contact, the Grass Dancers served a useful and necessary purpose. They were the first on-site when a new camp was set up; they prayed to the Spirit World for guiding them to where game could be found, food gathered and love shared. Then they'd dance. In doing so, they were also flattening out the area so the teepees could be set up. The same principle remains today, even though you don't live in teepees anymore."

Sandy is fascinated as Kyle continues with detailed reverence. "After the Grass Dancers, everyone enters. There are hundreds, some-times thousands, of dancers. It's the coolest thing to experience." Sandy understands as she feels the place fill with energy and pride. She snaps her camera as a parade goes by of the most elaborate colours and beadwork and headpieces of porcupine quills and eagle feathers.

"What do you call that type of costume?" she whispers to Kyle as a group of women wearing metal cone-shaped bells on their dresses dance by.

"Those are Jingle Dress Dancers," he answers. "And by the way, don't ever call their outfit a costume." Amos had told him that one too. "A costume is what a clown wears," he says. "So always refer to their dress as an outfit or regalia. If you say the word 'costume' to an Indian at a powwow you're likely to get slapped."

It is a good piece of advice for Sandy, and something she wishes someone had mentioned before. In a report only last month, she referred to their outfits as costumes, not knowing she'd insulted her own people. It makes her wonder why no one wrote a letter to the station. "How am I supposed to know these things unless I'm told?"

Kyle watches her transformation with wonderment. He can't guess how Sandy might react to cultural immersion. He's witnessed other Native people slink away as though being touched by fire, too afraid to allow themselves to open up. They are the lost and lonely who cringe from the sidelines and listen as others rail on that Aboriginal peoples are pagans, heathens and devil-worshippers because Native spirituality is an earth-based following and not Christian. The lost and lonely have ingested the name-calling, essentially sentencing themselves to Stereotype Hell. It is a place where they believe the lies told to them by the church and others that Natives are sinners and won't amount to anything. It is a self-hatred that lies just below the surface.

Kyle has met Aboriginal people like this in his work as a photojournalist. He can never figure out why anyone is afraid to explore his or her own reality and culture. His thoughts turn to genetic memory, the same innate instinct that leads salmon back to their birthplace. Will Sandy's genetic memory carry her today? He hopes it will.

Perhaps it is that instinct, combined with the warm Prairie sunlight that wakes something up, and Kyle is delighted to witness the metamorphosis. Sandy blossoms from a closed green pod into the vibrant orange prairie lily that she is. Wildflowers.

Kyle has pondered much about Sandy over the past week. He will never tell her his honest opinion that losing Blue might be the best thing that ever happens to her. Kyle has never liked Sandy's relationship with Blue because it seemed out of balance. She is going out of her way to learn about the culture while he seems to be running away from it, choosing a career that punishes Aboriginal people instead of nurturing them. Kyle's plan all along was to take Sandy to the powwow this weekend to keep her out of the bars and away from those other hooligans at the station. If she makes a habit of hanging out with them, her life will be a constant discussion about work and work only over pints at the Dodger before waking up with a hangover. He speaks from experience.

But Kyle managed to move forward and now wants to share with Sandy something positive to occupy her thoughts and time while she gets used to the fact that Blue is gone. The powwow is just that medicine. It was learning about Aboriginal culture that helped Kyle to get grounded and find balance, when he first decided to quit drinking. Although in doing so, Kyle has to admit, he was taken aback by racism that he didn't expect.

"You're a wannabe." Someone once mocked him when he went to his first spiritual ceremony with Amos out at the rez. Naturally it made Kyle uncomfortable because it was true. He'd sometimes wish he'd been born Native instead of white. What he'd learned from Amos and his family felt right. Kyle endured the name-calling until one day Amos spoke up after overhearing a slur.

"Wannabe what? Whole? Spiritually enlightened? Shit man, don't be such a jerk. Everyone has the right to honour Creator," Amos scolded. That happened at a round dance. The group of teens who mocked Kyle apologized. Amos reassured Kyle, "As long as your heart is good, I'll help anyone find their way back to the Circle. Who knows, maybe you were an Indian in a previous life." Amos explained that Aboriginal people who discriminate are no better than racist whites. "I can never figure out why some do that. Exclusion keeps us apart. The only way we can truly move forward is to understand each other. That's what my dad says."

Ever since that day, Amos has been introducing Kyle as his brother. It's led to community acceptance. Others at the rez understand the relationship, and the name-calling has stopped. Kyle wishes that similar kind of magic for Sandy.

Sandy is dumbfounded as she continues to watch the dancers filing in. Then she silently cringes, realizing something huge. She's never been around any large group of Indians celebrating culture like this—ever before. It makes her feel ashamed that usually her exposure to Aboriginal people is only as part of a story. She sees them on the streets, drunk or homeless—too often living with violence and poverty. Young single mothers who struggle. Her only other image of *Autochtone*, as her Francophone editor calls them, are the contemporary suited chiefs. They never look totally comfortable, smothering their spirits with a pinstriped jacket. And the only reason Sandy has ever met any of these people at all is because of her work.

Such irony, she thinks, making the connection that the environment where she works, which has often been hostile to her Aboriginal culture, is also the place that has provided her with a vehicle for learning. It has been her only real link to her own culture—not books. And how ironic, she thinks, that it is a white guy who is introducing me to my own Native heritage. She studies Kyle's face and his prominent smile lines. He has a small pointed nose and a square jaw. Sandy watches his clear blue eyes gaze reverently upon the passing dancers. It is at that point she decides she'll regard him as her brother too, just as Amos has done—even though she doesn't fully understand the significance yet. It just feels like the right thing to do.

FEELS LIKE HOME

By this time, all the dancers are assembled and the opening prayer is spoken. Sandy points to the Elder officiating the ceremony. She recognizes him. "Hey, there's that Old Man. What's his name again?"

"Joe," Kyle responds. "He's Amos's dad." Joe raises his eagle feather fan in the air as the beat of the big, bison-hide drum sounds. After that everything goes blank for her. She is transported out of body again.

She can feel the heat of a warm Saskatchewan breeze as strands of her hair touch her face. "Touched by the fingers of God," she remembers a catechism teaching once saying. She experiences brief moments where she is enveloped in a kaleidoscope of sheer colour followed by a blanket of darkness. Sandy hears a familiar grunt. It doesn't scare her. She knows it is Mugwah. He is very near to her, so much so that she can feel the soft ends of his fur brushing up against her arm. She listens to his soft voice. She smells campfire smoke. Through all of it there is the constant beating of the drum. Beating. Beating.

Her heart rate increases. Called by the drum.

Sandy opens her eyes, sensing the darkness has disappeared. The colours that greeted her in thought are now physically swirling right before her eyes. The multi-coloured ribbons at the end of a Fancy Dancer's shawl brush over her face and hair. Sandy is no longer in the stands. As she glances down at her feet it is startling for her to find that her blue and red flip-flops are replaced with elaborately beaded moccasins. Sandy realizes that she's joined the dancers. The moccasins on her feet bring a tear of joy. They look exactly like the baby moccasins that her sister Charlene gave her on their first meeting, except these are larger.

In her hand she carries a feather fan just like the one Joe held in the air seconds ago. There is a turquoise ring on her hand as well. She no longer wears the pretty sundress she put on that morning; it has been replaced by a white deerskin dress that hangs three-quarters length. It is heavy like a blanket.

She glances next to her and sees Joe. Beside him stands a man Sandy thinks she recognizes but cannot place. A black bearskin robe is draped over his head in place of the feather bonnet that she sees most of the other male dancers wear. Drums beat. She feels the wings of a bird brush past her shoulder. There is the tremendous energy of women and the sound of silver cones sewn on dresses; the healing energy of the Jingle Dress Dance.

She looks into the face of the woman dancing next to her. It is the face of Sandy's biological mother, Maggie, whom she's never met in person; a face she's only ever seen in a photo. The woman smiles momentarily just before the unexplainable occurs: the woman's face changes into that of a fierce, roaring black bear. It is the threatening roar of a mother bear protecting her baby.

Once transformed, the black bear speaks. "My name is Black Bear Woman. Kaskiti Maskwa Iskwiw. Here—take this." The mama bear places a black bearskin robe over Sandy's shoulder. "It is yours. Always has been. Wear it for protection. Wear it to remember where you come from. Wear it to honour your roots. Wear it so we can always be together. You've finally come home, Sandy. Osam kinwisk kiki spiwitan. We've been waiting for you. Kisakihitin. I love you, Nicanis, my daughter."

Sandy faints right there in the bleachers.

"Sunshine. You okay?" A look of concern is on Kyle's face and his query breaks Sandy's trance.

"What?"

"Where'd you go there, girl? You fainted for a few seconds. Heat getting to you?" It is early in the summer, yet the arid heat clings like the hot days of July. Temperatures exceed plus-thirty the day of the powwow, but Sandy knows that it is not the heat that has affected her. As she re-enters real time, Sandy realizes she's travelled again. Not knowing why it keeps happening or what it means, Sandy becomes frightened this time.

"What's going on, Kyle?"

He thinks she is talking about the powwow, "Oh, don't worry. It's just the Grass Dancers." Kyle points with his chin. "Hey, it's Amos." He motions toward a striking figure moving in perfect rhythm with the drum. Sandy can't take her eyes off him. Amos's outfit is blue, yellow, white and red. He is entranced by the drum, stepping in time.

"What's that thing on his head?" Sandy manages to croak out, electing not to describe to Kyle what just happened.

"It's called a roach," Kyle offers. "It's made from porcupine guard hairs." The long hairs sway back and forth with masculine grace and beauty, looking like wild grasses swaying in the wind. As Sandy watches Amos, she is struck by his transformation. Earlier he looked like a regular guy wearing a ball cap. But here, she would never have recognized Amos if Kyle hadn't pointed him out. He seems so different, larger than life.

A lump forms in her throat. Sandy tries fighting back tears, but a few cleansing drops come out. Kyle notices and puts his arm around her. He says something eerie, something too coincidental: "Welcome home, Sunshine. You've been away too long." All she can do now is sit and watch. Kyle understands her stunned silence and decides not to question. They sit and watch this visual feast for the rest of the afternoon and into the evening.

Kyle gets up once to get them drinks and Indian tacos. The taco looks like a giant, regular taco on a large piece of fry bread instead of being on a tortilla. It is the best thing Sandy has tasted in weeks. She is thankful that her appetite seems to have returned. Taking another bite of the greasy taco, Sandy says a prayer of thanks for sharing in the pride, as Old Men and Old Women move slowly, keeping to the beat of the drum. They hold their heads high, wearing fantastic beadwork, white buckskin outfits and long headdresses made with hundreds of feathers.

Sandy feels a great urge to get up from the stands and join the dancers. She longs to be among the handsome brown-skinned men with long black braids. The thousands upon thousands of ribbons, which flow from their outfits, continue to sway in the wind. She wants to be beside the children who dance in perfect form beside their mothers as though they learned to dance before learning to walk. The longing makes Sandy realize that her anxiety at attending the powwow was foolish. She worried about not belonging. As she takes a slow sip of water, Sandy is overwhelmed at knowing this is exactly where she belongs. She is home. It provides a warm feeling of satisfaction—until something troublesome happens.

An ominous figure pushes his way into the centre of the dancers. He's wearing a potato sack that covers his face, carrying a stick and wearing beat-up clothing that is ragged and torn. He starts to yell and howl and frantically runs from big drum to big drum to big drum. He visits each drum group and after he leaves, they each begin to play, but all different songs and all at the same time. Once all those drums get going it doesn't sound like a powwow song. It sounds like noise. Sandy raises her voice, asking Kyle, "Who is that? What's going on?"

Kyle calls the clown-figure a witago. "Amos told me this type of contrary dancer shows up sometimes at ceremonies or powwows. I've only heard about a witago—never seen one until today. He's here to wake people up, to remind people that money and status are never as important as community and family. He's a reminder to force you to choose—go on with your life as if nothing has happened, or accept the challenge and change your life to benefit others." With that information, Sandy feels certain that the witago showed up specifically for her benefit. *How will she choose?*

ABANDONMENT ABOLISHED

Things start settling down at the powwow around 11 P.M. Sitting there in a sundress and sandals, Sandy should be chilly. The warm summer day is quickly replaced by a cool night breeze. But tonight, cold air does not slap her. The darkness does not envelop Sandy in any unkind way as it has in the past. It isn't allowed.

She's been surrounded all day by something stronger. She feels groggy again, like she's just woken up. That's when she realizes she is sitting alone. A familiar voice calls out. It's Kyle. He is carrying two cups of hot mint tea with sugar and walking toward her. Amos is with him, still wearing his Grass Dance outfit.

"Sunshine, where have you been? You disappeared for hours. I was thinking it was about time to call the cops." It is an inside joke. Kyle used to kid Sandy by saying that when she and Blue were still together. He realizes the comment this time may open a wound, which isn't his intention. He quickly changes the subject and hands her the tea. "It's a good thing I spotted you from over there," he gestures. "I was thinking it's probably time to leave soon." Sandy takes the tea and smiles quizzically.

She has no idea what Kyle is talking about when he says she's been gone for hours. But Amos knows. He says six words to Sandy, six words that change her life: "You need to see my dad." Amos gestures to Sandy that she ought to go with him. He turns to Kyle. "She'll be okay. I'll make sure she gets home all right." Kyle nods in agreement.

Kyle turns to Sandy. "You'll be okay, Sunshine. Go with Amos and then call me in the morning if you need to." Kyle understands that there are certain spiritual practices that are not shared outside of the culture. He accepts this protocol, even if he doesn't always agree. Kyle leaves the arbour carrying his cup, and disappears under the dark blanket of night.

Sandy isn't quite sure what to make of it all. Her first thought is that Kyle has just ditched her and that maybe Amos is trying to pick her up—"snag her" as she heard some teenagers joking about earlier. She thinks she should be angry but that's not how she feels. Instead she just feels weak, like she has run a marathon. Maybe it was all that dancing I did? The bewilderment of pragmatic thought frightens her. This is her first powwow. She wasn't a participant, not a dancer, only a spectator. She had danced only in her imagination. Yet she feels weak as though she's taken part physically. It is all very confusing. She follows Amos.

It is only once they leave the perimeter of the arbour that she feels her skin rise. Amos notices that she is cold and puts the blanket he is carrying over her shoulders. The blanket is elaborate in design. Blue, pink and yellow in the shape of a big star. It resembles the shawl that Sandy saw herself wearing the first time she travelled out of body when she met Mugwah.

"It's called a star blanket. Special. My dad told me to give it to you. Somehow, he knew you'd be visiting today. Your first blanket, I'm guessing? I can tell. You're home now, Sandy. Consider this blanket a gift." The way he says it brings her as much comfort as the blanket itself. Déjà vu—she's been here before too. It confuses her almost to the point of panic: the star blanket, Amos, the mint tea. Logical instinct warns her to bolt but her feet keep following Amos.

"It's okay," he reassures. "You'll understand once you meet my dad." They walk to his truck, get in and drive in silence. She feels safe and at peace with Amos. As she looks out the bug-spattered windshield, Sandy can't remember ever before having seen so many stars. She wonders which one is there to guide her, and marvels at the most brilliant display of northern lights.

Amos notices. "The Old People say the lights are our ancestors looking down on us. I think they showed up tonight because they wanted to dance like the rest of us." His humour reassures her that nothing is out of the ordinary, including her memories and inexplicable experiences of the day. They continue the drive down a dusty grid road.

Minutes later they arrive at a modest-looking home. It is typical reserve housing: a white bungalow with no garage. Sandy notices a small garden planted to the left of the house and daisies planted alongside the walkway that leads to the front door. Inside the home, she can hear the murmur of pleasant conversation and heartfelt laughter. She looks forward to meeting the people in there. But that's not where she and Amos are headed.

Instead, he directs her elsewhere. Pointing with his lips, he gestures toward a small shack-like structure about a hundred metres away. Sandy understands and starts walking toward it. As they walk, he hands her a cloth pouch. Inside is some tobacco. "Give it to my dad once you enter," Amos instructs.

SERENITY AND STRENGTH

Sandy, the Grandmothers have been walking with you this day." That's how Joe Bush Sr. greets Sandy as she and Amos enter the small building. He is seated on an exquisitely hand-carved cedar chair.

She hands him the pouch and smiles. "Joe, it's good to see you again." She thanks him for giving her the tip about the missing girls, admitting that she hasn't yet found the time to follow up.

Joe nods. "When it is time and when you are ready it will happen." His voice trails off and he motions for Sandy to be seated. Even though she has no idea why she is here, seeing the Old Man's familiar face eases her tension. She's done too many stories about young women falling victim to sexual assault. The thought had crossed her mind, but as she shakes the Old Man's hand that worry disappears.

Joe speaks. He starts by telling Sandy that she needn't be afraid. "I watched you leave the arbour earlier tonight," he says, "and I followed you. You were being led by the spirits and walked for about a quarter mile toward a grove of birch trees. It's the same spot where a sacred bundle was opened fifty years ago. I was there then. So were you, even though you probably don't remember. I mean, your soul was there. It's always been connected to the Grandmothers."

The hair stands up again on her neck and arms. The pupils in her eyes dilate at hearing his words, the same way a cat's eyes would in the darkness.

"Come sit, Sandy. We need to smudge." Again, the Old Man gestures that she should take a spot on a blanket that's neatly placed on the dirt floor. It is another star blanket, but bolder in colour: red, orange, yellow and bright green.

"Will it hurt?" Sandy asks him, not knowing what smudge means.

This question causes Joe to smile, but not in a way that makes her feel silly. "No. If you've ever been to church, it's kind of like when the Catholics burn their incense at Easter time," he reassures. He puts some type of herb into a large shell and lights it on fire. It sparks for just a second and then a sweet-smelling smoke drifts toward her.

She knows the scent, having experienced it numerous times since she began travelling out of body. She remembers the smell from lucid dreams. It is the same earth scent that greeted her at the powwow and the same smell from her trance. Joe fans the smoke with a large feather. It has orange, green and white ribbons attached, as well as some beadwork near the feather's base.

Joe starts to quietly sing. Like Gregorian chanting, Sandy thinks. It is her only point of reference for this type of sound. He instructs her further. "You need to cup your hands and direct the smoke over your head, your heart and the rest of your body, Sandy. That's smudging. And say a prayer to those who surround you. Thank them for this day and for showing you the way home." She does as instructed. Amos quietly moves the shell toward himself, repeating the same motions. Next the Old Man smudges. He speaks again.

"You had a vision, my girl. You have medicine, and you don't even know it. It's very unusual that someone coming back to the Circle would be welcomed like this. Most people aren't invited to cross over until they fully understand. Sometimes it scares them." Joe lights a pipe and continues speaking. "If you're not ready when the vision comes, some people remember the words of priests and nuns saying that the old ways are bad. Then they get frightened and leave again, never to return. But you? You came back. That makes them happy. That is why they have shown you so much."

Sandy wants to ask who *they* are, but before she can mouth the words Joe answers, "*They* are those in the spirit world, Sandy. They say they like you. They say you are a kind woman. That's why they left you a gift." Joe points to Sandy's ears. She didn't put a pair of earrings on this morning before meeting up with Kyle. But as she slowly moves back her hair, she feels earrings dangling near her neck. It startles her. The path to the spirit world is closer than she could have ever imagined and it is veil-thin.

Sandy's face goes ashen and she begins to sob. But not out of fear. Joe fans some more smoke toward her. His presence calms her in a way that ensures total trust. Nothing bad will happen here. She knows that. She gathers the courage to look him in the eye as he explains further. "They tell me that your mother brought those earrings for you. She made them for you when you turned sixteen, but only now did she have the chance to give them away. They tell me that you never met her. But since she passed over, she's been watching out for you. They tell me she's very proud of you."

The idea that Sandy and her biological mother have today somehow connected brings her much warmth. A pleasant breeze blows just at that moment even though they are indoors. It is the same gust of air she's grown to trust. She takes one of the earrings off to examine it. It is elaborate in design. Beadwork and porcupine quills. As she studies it, Sandy realizes that she's seen the earrings before, in a dream. There were bears in that dream, too, hundreds gathered around her. They repeat, "We will always be here for you, as long as you continue to do the right thing." She never knows what it means, so she asks Joe.

"I can't interpret that for you, my girl. Sometimes dreams are as individual as each person. You will know in time what it means. But

I can tell you one thing. When an animal speaks to you like that, it's a good sign." He goes on to tell her that it is no coincidence that they met earlier that year. "I knew the moment I saw you that we were supposed to meet. It's because you are supposed to tell the story about those missing girls and stop it from ever happening again." ·

Sandy nods, acknowledging his words and feeling curious to find out where he'll go with this, as he continues. "They told me to find you, to tell about the girls and our suspicions about the police. Bring peace to their families by telling the story. That's always been your role." As Joe talks in general about the role of storytellers within Aboriginal culture, Amos serves Sandy some berries, water and rice.

Joe motions that she should eat as he continues talking. "The gift storytellers leave behind is courage and strength. In turn, it allows our people to embrace our cultural roots and identity." Joe talks about the role of storytelling and how in ancestral times it was the main form of communication. He talks about how early settlers and lawmakers tried to kill traditional ways and spiritual practices, making them illegal, and that Duncan Campbell Scott was a "no-good man." He goes on to explain that it was Scott, a senior federal bureaucrat in the 1920s, who outlawed dancing and traditions.

"People were arrested and thrown in jail for smudging, like you just did. That's why it's important to be proud, and to follow the ways of the drum. People had to go underground to keep these traditions alive. Now it's our job to keep them strong, to resurrect them and to pass them along. A lot of people have forgotten." Joe is sad when explaining how too many people have forgotten the old ways.

His words prompt Sandy to wonder why all Aboriginal people don't return, like she has. Joe reads her mind and answers, "Too many have been taught to be ashamed. But with you it did not stick. The shame. Not anymore. They tell me you have been having dreams since you were a child. Dreams you never understood. Now that you are a woman, it's time for you to understand." Joe pauses to look into Sandy's eyes, to gauge her reaction.

Not only does she understand, she feels it. He continues. "Only those who are truly strong enough are given this gift of storytelling. It is a responsibility not to be taken lightly." It unnerves her because if she interprets correctly, choosing journalism is actually more pre-destiny than free will. After the discussion, Amos drives her home.

Back in her own bed, it takes her just seconds to fall asleep and it is the most deeply restful slumber she's had in weeks.

SUMMER SOLSTICE

A significant time of year. The longest day and a time to celebrate the light of consciousness within. Sandy looks forward to renewal.

"Pelly, you're on night shift this week. Do your best to try and make boring policy meetings, well, not sound so boring," Hermanson says, smiling. He is just on his way home for the day, throwing a ball cap over unkempt hair.

Sandy missed the morning meeting, having been shifted to come in late. It is a new workweek and she has no intention of following what is assigned and expected. The time has come to follow Joe's lead, see what she'll find about the missing girls. "Kyle my camera tonight?" she asks.

"The dynamic duo? Yes, Preston is your man for the rest of this week. He asked that his schedule be changed. You two up to something?" Hermanson jokes just before waving his hand goodbye.

Sandy checks through the mess on her desk to see if she has any messages. "One of these days I'll have to clean this up," she murmurs to herself while grabbing an old Styrofoam cup. Lipstick stains line the top. Old coffee still in the cup, it leaves a round brown mark atop an old city council agenda that has been sitting on her desk for days. She throws both in the trash, takes off her brown suede jacket and hangs it on the back of her grey office chair. The chair is ancient and always makes the same sound each time she gets seated: *screech*, like an old screen door on a turn-of-the-century farmhouse, announcing that someone has arrived.

Fitting. Sandy feels new and invigorated from her honest soul-searching. She's finally admitted that she's been living too long in a place of profound sadness, having been conditioned to turn away and despise what is most precious. What's she been seeking? An identity. She found it at that powwow, and the feeling was strengthened even further in getting to know Joe.

She checks a small pile of messages on her desk. Amongst them is a note that Blue has called. She crumples it slowly and, with the sadness of letting go, throws it into the trash. This is a new day. Blue has already proven to be distraction enough. *No more*, she promises.

Kyle breaks her train of thought, sneaking up on her and slamming a brown paper shopping bag down on her desk. Sandy squeals. A few loose papers hit the floor. "Hey, Sunshine. Ready to go?" His eyes beam, as though the two of them have successfully pulled off someone's surprise party. "Check for yourself." He motions toward the brown bag.

Sandy grins, opening the bag slowly and quietly, so as not to call attention. "Oh my God. It's so red." She closes the bag quickly, grabbing it and hurriedly strolling toward the bathroom. Kyle can't stop grinning. His sister is a beautician who also deals in wigs. She lent him a bright red wig with cascading curls after Kyle spun a yarn about wanting to take his girlfriend to a surprise masquerade birthday party.

What brought this on—this urge to go undercover and put herself at risk? It's because Kyle confided something troubling over the phone earlier that day, before coming on shift. "Amos told me the problem is more widespread than you think." He went on to describe an actual account, sharing what happened to a young girl from the reserve where Amos and Joe live.

"Amos said she was at the Exhibition with a group of friends. Somehow they got separated, so this girl decided to walk to her auntie's over on the west side. It's a long way to walk, but she'd already spent all her babysitting money at the fair and didn't have enough for a cab. Not even enough to make a phone call. She should have called collect but didn't think of it at the time. So she walked— over the bridge, through the business district and got just past the core when Amos says the police stopped her. He said they thought she was a hooker because she was wearing short shorts and a tank top and she is Aboriginal. What the heck, it was a hot day and she's a young girl. The poor girl was scared and told the cops that she lost her friends. She said the cops then offered her a ride. They were cops, so of course she felt safe to get in."

Sandy was sickened by the story as Kyle continued to recount what Amos confided. "Seems once she was trapped in the patrol car, the cops started telling her that she was a sick little bitch who doesn't deserve favours like a ride home. They told her she needed to be taught a lesson. The girl said they expected her to have sex with them. The young cop actually said, 'If you spread your legs for us, like you do for johns, then maybe you won't end up like the rest.'"

Sandy trembled with anger as Kyle kept talking. "For God's sake, she's just a kid and probably a virgin at that. Amos said they drove her out of town but when they opened the car door she bolted. In addition to being young, she's also a cross-country runner and quite an athlete. She escaped just west of the city dump and hid until dark. What's ironic about all of this is that where the cops dumped her is closer to her auntie's than it would have been if she'd continued walking from where they picked her up downtown."

"Is she okay now?" Sandy was genuinely worried. "Did she report this? It's a crime."

"No, she's scared," Kyle answered.

It was at that point that Sandy wondered if he was pulling her leg. "You're full of shit, aren't you? Why would Amos tell you a story like that?"

Kyle's stern tone made it clear he wasn't yanking her chain. "I suppose he may never have told me the story—except, he saw that you were with me."

"I don't understand," she said.

"Think about it," Kyle expressed. "The girl told him all of these things in confidence, during a ceremony. It's a moral violation for Amos to repeat it—being told a confidence during ceremony is kind of like being a priest in a confessional but you're right, it is a crime and he felt he had to say something. When he saw you with me, he figured you might be able to help. He said you are someone who can provide a voice for those who are not able to speak for themselves."

"And?"

"Man! I totally understand why some are exasperated with you white Indians." Kyle immediately regretted the comparison, knowing it hurts her. He softened his tone. "Sorry about that. Let me put it another way, because I know you have just started learning. I mean no disrespect but—I repeat—it's like if you went to a priest in a confessional, the information is supposed to remain private. Most times it stays confidential, but here a crime was committed. Amos didn't feel right about staying silent. He wants to know if you will investigate." Kyle paused. "I know he didn't like repeating the story, but I agree with him, it's a story that needs to be made public. The cops can't treat our young girls like this."

So Sandy is now pulling the long red wig over her own lovely mane of hair, fitting it near her ears and tucking in any remnants of black. She and Kyle have agreed to embark on a sting operation, hoping to catch the dirty cops on tape, with Sandy, posing as a prostitute, as the bait."

Sandy opens her purse, pulling out some heavy rhinestone costume jewellery that she picked up at a second-hand store. She applies Fire Engine Red lipstick then exaggerates her eyeliner, painting the lines in heavy swoops like an Egyptian princess. She uses a grease pencil to paint on a fake birthmark on her cheek, just up a bit and to the right of her lips. By this time, all other staff is gone for the day. Regardless, Sandy peeks around the corner as she leaves the bathroom. The only one there is Kyle, leaning against her desk and reading the newspaper.

"Convincing?" Sandy inquires, showing him how she has painted on tonight's makeup. She feels cheap.

"Not quite," he replies, holding up another bag that his sister gave him. He reaches inside, pulling out a short red skirt. It is made of rubber. He puts his hand in the bag a second time, producing a white satin tube top that has the insignia of a silver crucifix embroidered down the front. It is easily the sluttiest-looking garb that Sandy has ever been expected to wear.

"Shit, man. Where does your sister get stuff like this? And why?" she exclaims.

"You know," Kyle admits, "I've never asked because it occurs to me that I don't really want to know why she has this stuff. Just put it on. Oh and Sunshine, you're going to have to wear these too."

Sandy holds back a cackle, taking a look at thigh-high boots that are supposed to resemble black patent leather but are really made from some type of cheap synthetic. The boots have an open toe and go almost all the way up Sandy's legs to just below the short skirt. It rounds out the effect, just in case anyone isn't sure that she is trying to look like a hooker. "You are a sick bastard. You're enjoying this, aren't you?" Sandy chides as Kyle motions that it is time to leave.

"Honey, if you want to catch a fly..." he jokes, knowing full well that both of them are embarking on something that is exactly the opposite of a joke.

THE STROLL

Red rubber is hot in more ways than one, Sandy thinks, feeling uncomfortable, out of place and scared standing under a Twentieth Street lamp. Her features look harsh under the dim streetlight as her red skirt shouts out that she is open for business. Sandy knows she should feel safe enough but feels little comfort in knowing that Kyle is close at hand. His camera is aimed from the window of a nearby photography studio that is closed for the day. The owner agreed to allow Kyle to use the site for the stakeout, feeling it was his way to take part in action—however small—toward addressing growing concerns about crime in the area at night. Kyle also arranged with a separate business owner to allow for a time-lapse camera to be set up atop his roof to record the goings-on from another angle. Sandy knows she is well monitored, but it doesn't bring her a feeling of safety.

A moustached man slows down in his dark blue Mustang, delivering the answer—unearthing her own memories of being a teenager and being mistaken as a prostitute. As he decelerates with interest, other passing motorists take no notice, making Sandy feel invisible. If they happen to glance out their car window they look right past her, toward some cheap window display of lawn furniture and silk plants, rather than making eye contact with her. She is just a hooker after all.

Sandy's stomach turns. It may be the heavy smell of exhaust or the fact that she begins to grow paralyzed with fear, forcing herself to swallow bile. She waves toward the studio where Kyle is hidden. She hopes his reaction is quick, and that he'll charge out to save her if need be. The man in the dark blue car has rounded the corner, passing her a second time. This time he stops just ahead, indicating his interest by tapping his brake lights three times. Sandy approaches, keeping a safe distance on the sidewalk.

"Hey beautiful. Lovely night," he smiles and his teeth are yellow—so is the wedding ring on his left hand. "How much?"

Sandy surprises herself at the ability to give an answer. "Two hundred dollars, darlin'. Half an hour."

The moustache scowls and swears. "You brown cunt, I can get ten of you for that price!"

Sandy slams her hand on the hood of his car. "Well, fuck you too!" She holds up her middle finger for the moustache to see as he speeds off. He doesn't go far. Sandy notices his dim brake lights tapping thrice a couple blocks up. The faint sound of a car door slamming signals that he's found someone willing to settle for his offer of twenty dollars. Dignity is not at a premium here.

She never really pondered it before, but tonight—standing here terrified by the enclosing darkness, frightened by any movement, disgusted at what lurks in the back alleyways of people's minds— Sandy understands why most street walkers are either stoned or drunk. They need to be to numb the pain.

Her gut tells her to run. This plan to get an exclusive, undercover story is not worth the risk. Sandy begins to sweat out of nervousness and because the tight-fitting rubber skirt is uncomfortably hot. Yet she trembles, feeling chilled, the way she felt as a young girl taking shortcuts down dark alleyways at night, worrying about whether vampires are real. It causes her knees to lock, forcing her to lean up against a lamppost so as not to fall down. The air is heavy, a culmination of the day's heat and dirt settling on the roadway. The seemingly ever-present breeze is quiet tonight, allowing the filth to settle, stinging Sandy's nostrils.

Rather than fidget she decides to take control, reaching for one of three emergency cigarettes she has tucked away in the pocket of the small, white bolo jacket she decided to wear over the revealing tube top. The only item of value in her purse is a small audio tape recorder—no keys, no ID, no money. She doesn't want to be carrying anything else of value in case she gets mugged.

She gives herself permission to light up. A pack of wooden matches is the only other item in her purse. She wonders how stereotypical she seems right now—Aboriginal girl leaning against a lamppost, wearing a short rubber skirt and smoking a cigarette. She hardly takes a couple of puffs from her smoke when another vehicle stops. It is a police car that pulls up into the loading zone near the front doors of the business Sandy has claimed as her territory for the evening.

"Bit early, isn't it?" the young policeman remarks. Sandy throws her cigarette on the sidewalk, crushing it out with the heel of her boot before looking at him inside the squad car.

"Oh, I'm just waiting for the bus," she lies, then takes a closer look at the young constable. She wants to bolt. She knows him.

It is James, the badly behaved boor who was Blue's dorm-mate during basic training. Sandy tries covering her face with some of the long, loose ringlets from the red wig, hoping James will not recognize her.

He speaks. "Well, if you're lost and you need a ride, sugar, we can help." By this time James has exited the vehicle without closing the car door behind him. "You shouldn't be out here anyway." James runs his hand against Sandy's ass. "Nice. But let's be real, you ain't waiting for no bus." He grabs his baton, grimacing, then propping the weapon under her chin, forcing her gaze. "Got any ID?" James snatches her purse. One of the fake red fingernails she attached with glue comes loose but makes no sound as it hits the hard sidewalk below.

James is just about to open the zipper to the purse when the other officer, who is driving, bellows, "Fresh meat, Leroy?"

James forces the small purse back into her hand. "It appears so. Never seen this one before," he answers to his partner before turning to Sandy. "Whaddya say we acquaint you with the rules? No time like the present."

With that, James hangs his baton back on his belt and grabs Sandy by the elbow, jerking her toward the police car. "We'll take you for a ride, all right." He opens the back door, pushing her with such force that Sandy worries her wig might loosen. If it falls off he'll surely recognize her, so she doesn't struggle.

While this drama unfolds, the rhythm of the street continues without her. No one seems to notice or care that she is in danger. Motorists continue to drive past without slowing down, without wanting to witness. She thinks about Kyle, hoping he can abandon his post quickly enough to be able to follow closely in his truck. But it all happens too fast. James slams the car door to a close before Kyle has time to get down to street level.

A panicking Sandy thinks about being enclosed in a tomb or a coffin or a locked suitcase. It is surreal as she sits in the back seat, the dispatcher's voice over the police radio droning as a blur of city lights flashes by. Sandy feels like she ought to fight, try to somehow escape. Her breathing accelerates to the point where she worries about hyperventilating or even fainting. The seat cushion is hard, like it may be only a thick piece of plywood covered in thin cloth. There are no door handles and no way to open the windows. She is trapped. A heavy steel mesh separates Sandy from the dirty officers up front.

The sick smell of old vomit, urine and feces that wafts from the worn carpeting on the back seat floor is parallel to the evil deeds committed in that car. Are they planning on raping her? What is she trying to prove tonight? That she's a super reporter? Sandy privately scolds herself. She realizes she might die. It causes her to regret that she hasn't told people—like members of her biological family, her friends, Ellen and Kyle—how much she truly loves them. Panic deepens, as does the feeling of helplessness, which manifests as a single teardrop falling from her right eye. She doesn't wipe it away, allowing the cool, damp sensation to momentarily distract her from the reality that she is in for torture—physical and emotional.

But in her moment of panic, she remembers her small tape recorder and quietly opens her purse to turn it on. An odd thought enters. She concludes that as long as the car is moving, she is safe, albeit confined. So long as city lights shine from outside this window, it signals a reprieve from what looms. Her thought is confirmed with James' next statement. "Hey you bitch, hope you've got some condoms in that little purse of yours. I feel like playing sink the sub tonight. Get ready to take it up the ass!" His laugh is diabolical, like he might suffer a mental illness. His partner chuckles in agreement as the cruiser inches to a stop at a red light. It is the last stoplight before the city limits, heightening Sandy's level of dread.

She notices a change then as James shifts, stiffening his back. His posture moves uncomfortably—the way a cat would in self-defence—as he glances at the rear-view mirror. "Son of a bitch!"

"What?" His partner expresses concern.

"There's a fucking patrol car pulling up beside us." James wipes a thin bead of sweat from his upper lip as he speaks. "It's okay. Just play it cool," his partner reassures as James turns to Sandy with menacing regard. "One peep, you cunt, and you're dead." James barely finishes the sentence before opening the passenger-side window. Sandy doesn't know whether to feel relieved or further victimized to see that it is Blue behind the wheel of the approaching patrol car.

TURNING A BLIND EYE

Every bad thought Sandy harbours about Blue disappears as he pulls up beside the dirty patrollers. She's relieved to see his face and wants to reach out to him, wants to pound on the windows, rip off her wig and yell for help. She wants to, but can't. James' threat of death leaves her frozen with fear. She barely has the strength to swallow tears that have somehow fallen inside her body rather than stream out. His words, hurriedly spoken before the window came down, keep resonating. *One peep and you're dead.* Sandy believed it to be more of a promise than a threat. She remains silent, even as Blue's window opens and he starts to speak, "Need any help?"

Sandy feels like throwing up, her thoughts racing and mired in jumbled logic. *If Blue recognizes me, will he help? Will they beat him up if he tries to help? James says he'll kill me—will he kill Blue too? Will they make it look as though I killed him?* Her thoughts race as James smiles toward Blue, acting as though nothing is out of the ordinary.

"Hey, Greyeyes, shouldn't you be answering a call or something?"

Blue enjoys the banter. "Naw. Dispatch has been quiet all night." Blue pauses. "Here's hoping it stays that way." He crosses his fingers

200

then makes the sign of the cross over his heart. "I see you guys are busy?" Blue motions to the woman in the back seat that he can't see very well, but assumes is a street whore.

James responds with a rotten lie. "Yeah. It's actually a story with a nice ending. She's pretty shaken up, by her pimp I suppose. She wants us to take her to that halfway house, for ex-street walkers, so that's where we're headed." James pauses to see if Blue might buy it. The halfway house is located in the inner city, not on the outskirts.

Blue frowns. "Isn't that in the core area?"

James' partner already has stage two of a lie ready to unleash, "It is," he pipes up from the drivers' side. "Only thing is we need to make a quick detour. Asshole-face here scratched his contact, so he's gotta rush home to get a new pair before we get back on track." It sounds reasonable, but Blue knows it's a lie because of a conversation he had with James the first day of basic training.

Blue remembers James bragging that he was accepted to the police force while his cousin was not, and all because James has twenty-twenty eyesight. James' cousin suffered from astigmatism and needed corrective surgery before the force might consider him. So James does not wear contacts. Blue wonders why he's lying. Still, he doesn't question.

Blue's posture tightens, but he forces a smile and gives a quick salute, indicating the conversation is over. He rationalizes that this is none of his business. Besides, the light is just about to turn green. Both squad cars leave the intersection, headed in different directions.

"You think he bought it?" James asks. "I worried we were had there for a second."

"Of course he bought it, why wouldn't he?" His partner smirks. "He doesn't know a thing about our..." he nudges James with his elbow and winks, "...arrangement." Any hope Sandy held quickly fades, watching the headlights of Blue's cruiser slowly disappear.

EMPTY

Her heart hurts, coming to terms with the ugly realization that the practice of violating hookers may be as old as the police force itself. *How many of them are involved, or know?* She can't help but ask herself, *Why didn't Blue stop to help me? He must have known something isn't right here.*

James starts up again with his abusive diatribe, "Yes, you sick piece of shit, your chances of being saved are now gone, ha!" He slaps his knee. His partner chuckles. Sandy hasn't paid much attention to James' partner since being picked up, still coming to terms with the fact that James himself is so intricately involved in something so evil. She knew he gave off bad vibes when they first met all those months ago, but she would never have guessed he is this beastly.

She glances at James' partner. He looks to be in his forties, with a small potbelly, greying hair at his temples and skin the same colour. He wears a neatly trimmed moustache and smells faintly of aftershave, like he showered just before coming on shift. Sandy never caught his name. He speaks. "It's our brotherhood, partner, and what keeps these Indian whores in line. Fuck them once—or as often as you wish, really—and let them know who's boss. Besides," he nudges James, "wife's so frigid and old. A man needs a piece of fresh meat every now and then. In fact, we *deserve* fresh meat."

The two laugh, and Sandy can only imagine spit hanging from both their lips like rabid dogs. James turns toward her. "You are in for the fuck of your life, sweetheart." He makes a vicious croaking sound.

Meanwhile, Blue is not so stupid or naïve. He knows James doesn't wear contacts. Blue also knows James does not live in the west end. He's dropped him off in City Park, the neighbourhood just adjacent to the core, at least twice since joining the force. Blue feels sickened but doesn't know how to react. He's heard the rumours. He's heard that cops fuck prostitutes, an unspoken way of letting their pimps know that they will be allowed to stay in business and the dirty cops will turn a blind eye so long as the pussy is free. He's often rationalized that it can't be true. But these past few moments verify to him that it probably is, especially considering the rumour that it's always young Native girls who are picked up.

Blue feels compelled to investigate. He turns off his headlights and doubles back, following the patrol car carrying the girl. The car heads toward the outskirts of the city. His question is answered. Blue watches in disbelief as the city patrol car leaves city limits— out of their jurisdiction, its red taillights growing ever dimmer as it continues toward an unknown destination, definitely not James' place.

Blue noticed a young Native girl in the back seat yet did nothing to stop her from being escorted out. It sickens him and forces him to pull over to the side of a lonely grid road, coming to a stop. He puts his hand over his mouth and strikes the steering wheel hard in disgust. He knows he's chosen to remain silent and now some young woman is going to suffer as a result. The brotherhood extends in insidious ways. In his silence, he knows he has just condoned the violation. He feels nauseated but swallows, taking a deep breath, and decides to carry on with his patrol by rationalizing, *There is nothing I can really do about it, is there?*

IN PERIL

Sandy admits to herself that she's too afraid to speak, that she can hardly even breathe. She is mortified to realize that some girls, Aboriginal girls, choose this terrifying life voluntarily. What could possibly be worse in their home life that they would come out here and allow themselves to be treated like this? Sandy wonders if their disconnection—similar to hers—might play a part.

Sandy shivers at the thought of being a cold case file. It sparks another plan: *In case the worst does happen, I will scratch out their eyes if I have to. I will fight. It'll leave some evidence under my finger-nails. Skin. Blood.* Tough words.

Still, she has no control over her gag reflex as the car slows to a stop. It's a dark and lonely grid road and Sandy tastes the putrid bitterness of puke in her mouth. It sickens her even more to force herself to swallow. She can see a gully and a small creek running under a bridge. There is an old cemetery just beyond. Sandy can see crumpled and falling-down headstones and old wooden crosses. A full moon disallows darkness from fully engulfing those details.

"Here we are," James heckles. Only the crickets, hiding in tall grass, will be witness. The night is still but for their lowly chirping or the occasional sound of a frog. James forces Sandy from the back seat with a jerk of her arm. It hurts, leaving her to wonder if he may have dislocated it. Panic arises again, and she wonders if pleading for reason might be a way out. But noticing that James has already removed his belt, which carries his gun, flashlight and baton, Sandy knows there is no room for talk. She swings at him, jerking away as hard as she can.

"Bitch!" he scowls as her fist jabs his throat, hard. He temporary loosens his grip, enough for her to pull away and bolt. She had enough foresight in the car to remove the high-heeled boots that she wore earlier in the evening.

She heads toward the creek, under the bridge. Her red wig is now dishevelled and partially obscures her vision. She bounds like a deer pursued by wolves. A few steps down the gully she lets out a piercing scream of terror as she falls into the arms of someone else who's there, obviously awaiting her arrival.

But it's no boogeyman. It's Joe Bush Sr. Sandy almost knocks the Old Man over. "Hey little one," he reassures her. "It's okay. You are safe now." She recognizes his voice and her heavy breathing slows, though her heart continues to race.

"Joe!" The dim illumination of a flashlight reveals that he is not alone under that old wooden bridge, which still smells of fresh creosote even though the structure was built decades ago. Amos is with Joe, as are two other large men Sandy recognizes as security guards from the powwow. Her quartet of safety has set up lawn chairs near the creek. Along with Joe's old border collie, Rose, they appear to be fishing under the bridge to the flickering light of a small citronella candle.

As quickly as Sandy ducks to safety, James is in close pursuit. He stops short, almost toppling over, when he encounters the Indian posse. He can't have anticipated their company. There are no vehicles parked on the road alongside the creek bed.

"The fish like to bite at night," the Old Man smiles. "Best to put out bait just after sundown if you want to catch trout."

James doesn't know how to react, and spits out a command. "Unhand the witness!" Sandy moves in behind Joe now. James continues, "What are you people doing here?"

"Fishing." Joe picks up a net that is on the rocks. "And you?" A tense silence threatens—the situation could go either way. It is James' turn to sweat.

In the time it takes for a frog to croak twice, James thinks up a plausible lie, finally responding, "This girl is a witness. She told us that a john had driven her out here a few days ago, beat her and took her money. We are investigating and she's our witness."

"Well, my name is not John," Joe responds, "but I recognize this girl." The Old Man hates to lie but figures he'll be forgiven for this one. "She's Theresa-Ann Lafayette—from our reserve. We've been worried about her for days, since she disappeared at the Exhibition." He pauses. "Thank you for bringing her back to us." Joe clears his throat.

It is a way out for James, and he knows it. "Well, I'll leave her with you then." James says, then looks toward Sandy. "Miss, we've got your statement, you led us to the crime scene. That should be good for now. If we need anything further, we'll be in touch." And with that, he leaves. The older officer hasn't moved from the side of the patrol car, likely stricken with the fear of being caught. This time there are witnesses. Four of them, under the bridge.

After James retreats to the car, and the sound of the engine starting up means that harm is no longer present, Sandy turns to Joe and cries. "How did you know?"

Before answering, Joe scolds her. "You are a stupid girl, putting yourself at risk like that." He reaches out to hug her, wanting to make the point but not be too harsh. She's already been through enough. Before he can answer her question, the group is startled by a set of headlights that flashes atop the bridge. Sandy panics, worried that it might be James and his partner again, this time returning with guns drawn. They hear a car door slam and heavy footsteps sound. Whoever it is, he is running.

Sandy feels like melting when Kyle rounds the corner. "Holy shit! Sandy, it got out of hand so quickly. I'm so sorry. I'm so sorry. I finally caught up to that police car but they were driving out of here without you in it. You okay?"

"She's okay now," Amos pipes up. "And what the hell are you doing out here alone? I thought you said there'd be others watching out for her too."

"Enough," Joe responds. "It's over and now we know." He gently removes Sandy's red wig, wiping a tear from her cheek. She is still trembling but has gathered her wits enough to ask if anyone has a cigarette. The ones in her jacket pocket have been crushed. Thankfully for her, one of the tall security guards grabs a cigarette from a pack in his jean jacket, hands it over and lights it for Sandy. The small flame reveals smudged mascara. She's been crying. She takes the cigarette, inhales deeply and exhales ever so slowly before asking again, "How did you know?"

He tells her that under this bridge is the same spot the police took the young girl. "They had no way of knowing she knows the area. People from the reserve really do come here to fish. It's where I've been fishing since I was a kid. When Amos told me that you and Kyle were planning a sting operation, I knew this is the place where they would take you." He pauses. "The place has a sadness to it now. Too bad."

He directs his next comment to Amos, "Maybe we should smudge it? Ask the spirits to cleanse the area and bring back good energy. Those cops won't be coming back here again, that's for sure." Joe leaves Sandy's side, going over to the lawn chair that he set up beside the slow-moving creek, and picks up a flask. He pours some liquid, handing a metal cup to Sandy. "Have some tea, my girl, and promise me that you will never do something so dangerous ever again." Joe picks up another river rock and hands it to Sandy, the same as he did the first time they met.

GATHERING STRENGTH

It is Joe's suggestion that Sandy take a few days off work, an idea to which she wholeheartedly agrees. She doesn't have the strength right now to relive what happened by telling anyone. She doesn't have the strength to explain to her boss that she pursued a lead on a great story and that it nearly killed her. Kyle agrees the idea is a good one, and volunteers to tell Lyle Hermanson that a family emergency has come up and Sandy will be away for a while.

She hasn't stopped trembling and tells Joe that she doesn't want to go back to her apartment, even though James has no way of knowing it was her hiding under the red wig and heavy black eyeliner. Joe makes a suggestion—that she stay with him, a place where she's safe and accepted. They are already sitting at his kitchen table when this decision is made, Sandy wrapped in a soft throw that Amos retrieved from the other room. But she can't stop shivering. Amos isn't sure if it is from a chill, the trauma or bad memories.

"You should try to eat something too," he says, pointing with his lips to a wooden bowl in the middle of the table filled with oranges, apples and bananas. She shakes her head to indicate no. Joe peels her an orange anyway. "You need to eat something."

She sincerely and silently offers a thousand prayers of thanks that Joe had the foresight to anticipate she'd need help. She feels safe and protected in this warm kitchen but feels foolish in her red rubber skirt. She thanks Creator for the blanket to cover up her shame. "If it's okay with all you guys, I really need to lie down now."

"You go rest," Joe agrees. "The guest room is all made up." He helps her from the heavy wooden chair and walks with her as far as the stairwell. Just before heading up, Kyle makes a promise. "By the time you wake up, Sandy, you'll have some fresh new clothes to wear. I'll pop by your apartment." He feels his jacket pocket, searching for her keys. "I'll leave right now, in fact. You get some rest."

A small green banker's lamp is the only light in Joe's guest room. The bed frame is wrought iron painted white. Sturdy. She expects the bedspread motif to be some type of Aboriginal design, the same way the rest of Joe's house is decorated, but it isn't. In contrast, the décor here is more an old English style—heavy floral-design bed coverings and elaborate antique wallpaper, the floor tiled in black and white, each tile with a fleur-de-lis symbol in the centre, and an ornate copper kettle placed in the centre of the dark wooden dresser. The kettle is used as a vase holding a bouquet of silk gardenia. *Lovely room*, Sandy thinks, peeling the tight skirt from her thighs before sitting down on the bed. She puts on a long fleece nightie that is on a chair, slips under the covers and closes her eyes. Her head feels the comfort of the soft feather pillow. Another tear slips out; Sandy realizes she doesn't want to admit the truth. It hurts too much, like being poked with a red-hot branding iron.

No matter how the night's events replay in her imagination, she is repeatedly horrified that Blue did nothing to help her. He must have known something wasn't right. Yet he just let them take her away to be tortured, raped and maybe even left for dead. Rightly or wrongly, she partly blames Blue for the ordeal, even though the decision to take part in the stakeout was hers and hers alone. Even Kyle attempted to talk her out of it early on, saying it was too dangerous.

But she didn't want to listen, thinking only about the accolades and recognition she'd receive in breaking the story.

Her heart hurts, but she can't bring herself to call for help, even though Joe and Amos are within earshot. Physically, she experiences chest pains. She applies pressure with the palm of her hand and the pain subsides only to be replaced by erratic breathing that feels almost like hyperventilating. *Probably one of those anxiety attacks I read about*, she tells herself. A faint knocking at the door whisks away the worry. "Come in."

It is Joe. "Here, drink this," he says, handing her a bitter-smelling brew, explaining that it is sage tea. "It will calm your nerves and help you to sleep, Sandy. You really do need to rest. What's done is done. When you are strong enough you can tell us what happened. But for now, just know that you are safe." He places the fine bone china on top of a coaster that is on the bedside table. Before leaving he tells Sandy that he will say prayers for her tonight.

She falls asleep, though it's debatable that it brings her very much rest. Sandy flops around like a fish on a rock, talking in her sleep. "No. No. I promise!" She kicks her legs as if trying to run, causing the heavy quilt to fall to the floor. But it won't stay off long enough for her to get cold.

Kyle has come back, agreeing to stay and watch over her in the night. He grabs the quilt from the floor and places it back over her. He loves her like a sister and they share a deep friendship. Ever since Sandy was forced into the squad car, he's been kicking himself for not moving faster from where he was posted. Because it wasn't possible to reach the street in time, he couldn't follow as closely as they had planned.

GATHERING MEMORIES

Kyle nods off sometime during the night, only to be nudged at daybreak. Joe, carrying two hot mugs of coffee, wakes him, offering to take over the vigil. "You go home, take a shower and have something to eat," he says, offering a heavy mug to Kyle.

He smiles and nods, taking a slow sip and agreeing to head back into the city. But he has no intention of going straight home, already having decided today is not a day for the office. He makes his way to Sandy's apartment, wanting to collect more items for her. Besides, caring for Sandy in this small way makes him feel better, considering the constant lamentation in his head that refuses to quit replaying. *Stupid, stupid plan.*

Once outside and in his truck, Kyle reaches for a water bottle, usually stored in a cardboard box between the driver and passenger seats. The bottle isn't there and he makes a mental note to pick up another one at the corner store before heading back out of town. He is parched, and a bit stiff from sleeping in a chair all night. Kyle makes it back to the city in record time and finds his way to Sandy's apartment, putting the key in the door and going inside.

In general she keeps a lovely home, Kyle observes, but today it seems empty without her. He glances at her chrome and glass coffee table while taking off his boots. He remembers helping her move it in. The coffee table is new, replacing the old Coke crate she used before. Kyle prefers the wooden box. A silver metal vase holding wilted flowers is almost lost in the jumble of unopened mail and magazines surrounding it atop the table.

He isn't sure where to start in collecting items that will bring comfort to Sandy. He knows she loves fragrance, because she always smells nice—either of sweetness or spice, so he makes his first desti-nation the bathroom. Because he grew up with a sister, Kyle knows the items Sandy cherishes the most are likely to be on display there, maybe in a basket. He'll take those for sure. His hunch is correct. Upon turning on the wall switch, he spies a large basket with a handle, balanced on a small wicker vanity. In it are items like hand-made soap, a perfume container in the shape of a large nose, some bath crystals and an array of all sorts of styles and colours of hair bands. He opens the vanity where he finds an empty plastic bag and throws a few hair bands and bath crystals in.

The next destination is Sandy's bedroom, where her red fleece nightie is prominent just near the foot of the bed. Why didn't I grab this last night? Kyle guesses it has nice memories attached to it, which is what she needs right now. He places it in the bag on his way to her closet. After parting the sliding doors, he decides that a warm sweater, a plain denim dress and an oversized pair of grey sweat-pants should suffice, throwing in a large pink T-shirt as well. It's been calling to him from the closet floor.

Turning to leave, Kyle notices a black and white photo framed in dark mahogany. It is on her bedside table, which is the old Coke crate. The photo is yellowed a tad but shows a handsome couple dressed in their Sunday best. Kyle guesses it is probably Sandy's grandparents. He places it in the bag as well, wondering if maybe he should call her family and suggest they come and stay with her for a while. The hardwood floor sounds as he turns back toward the door. Walking past the living room table again, Kyle sees a little pink address book, which he takes just in case he decides to call her kin, deciding to give it more thought before letting anyone else know what happened.

Moments before shutting off the hallway lamp and closing the door, he sees another framed photo, this one on the mantle. It is a happy moment captured of Sandy and Ellen sitting in a restaurant. It too becomes a part of the collection of memories in the shopping bag. Kyle gently closes the door.

Back in his pickup, he decides it is time to get something to drink. He neglected to pour himself a glass of water at Sandy's. He didn't even go into the kitchen. Not a problem. There is a 7-Eleven convenience store nearby.

As always, Kyle checks to make sure he is still six feet tall when he walks into the store. It is a habit for him to glance at the measuring tape pasted to the side of the door. Just in case the store is robbed and the assailants flee, the clerk can take note of the height-indicator in order to give police a description. Today, the clerk greets him with a friendly smile. She is a young Aboriginal girl, maybe seventeen or eighteen. Kyle returns the pleasantry, happy to know she is working here at the store and not out on the stroll. He also hopes she is here part-time while going to school, but isn't about to ask.

Kyle heads toward the cooler. On his way to pay at the cash register, he notices a bucket filled with red and pink roses. A sign indicates they are being sold for charity. He knows Sandy likes flowers. He smiles to himself at the thought and chooses one of each flower for his friend.

"Will that be all?" the young clerk inquires.

"Oh, one more thing." Kyle is embarrassed to do so, but selects a *Cosmopolitan* magazine from the rack. He often sees his sister reading it and figures Sandy might like it too. An afterthought influences him to buy a pack of cigarettes. Last thing Sandy needs right now is a craving for a smoke and not have it satisfied. She will keep quitting until she finally quits, and that's good enough for Kyle.

He scampers into his vehicle, placing the magazine and the flowers on the passenger side before getting in. Prior to putting the truck in gear to exit, he glances in his rear-view mirror. He almost pisses his pants, seeing the image of a police car driving by. Kyle gasps. Are they out legitimately patrolling or are they just out strolling? He wonders if Blue is the driver then briefly wonders if maybe he should call Blue, letting him know what has happened. This thought only makes him angry. Kyle decides a phone call isn't necessary. Blue will find out what has happened soon enough.

CALL IN THE TROOPS

Kyle interprets finding the photo of Sandy and Ellen as a sign. He dials Ellen's number from the pink address book once he gets back to Joe's. He tells Ellen what happened, asking her to come and stay for a few days. "Sandy needs you right now."

It is now less than twenty-four hours since that call and here he is at high noon, standing at the bus depot platform and waiting for a girl he's never met. He feels a bit silly but it doesn't matter. Sandy's mental health and welfare are more important. Besides, she's talked about Ellen so many times he feels like he already knows her.

Ellen exits the bus, glances around and wonders who is behind the voice on the telephone. Because Kyle's seen photos of her, it takes seconds for him to recognize her. "Ellen!" he bellows from afar. She approaches, her hand outstretched in greeting. Kyle ignores it, going in for a hug instead.

"Such a pleasure to meet you too," Ellen gushes. "Sandy didn't tell me you are so handsome." Kyle blushes ever so slightly, longing to make some type of similar comment but feeling restrained. He is taken aback by Ellen's charm, not expecting her to be so forthright. Like Sandy so often does, Ellen wears a fashionable sundress, lime green with yellow, even though the day's temperature is cooling.

Hanging from her forearm is a denim jacket. Kyle guesses that the two women likely shop at the same stores. Ellen, banishing any residual discomfort, looks him straight in the eye, saying with great compassion, "How is she?"

Her questioning breaks Kyle's momentary trance. "She's doing much better. And I know that seeing you will do her a world of good."

At this point, Ellen holds up a small paper bag. "These will help too. I brought some baklava from Meeka's. It is our favourite haunt back home."

"I know, Sandy's told me all about your girls' nights. She'll love it," he smiles.

By this time, the attendant has started pulling luggage from the undercarriage of the bus. Kyle isn't surprised when he sees a bright pink leather suitcase. "I take it that one is yours?" he points as Ellen nods in agreement.

In turn, she points to Kyle's large blue pickup truck parked across the street. "And that, I am guessing, is yours?" He laughs while his cheeks turn a nice shade of red. He carries her suitcase across the street and puts it into the back of the pickup, all the while wondering why Ellen makes him so nervous. It is he who suggested Ellen come visit, telling her why it is important. Now here she stands, in an act of love and friendship for Sandy.

"So, what should we do first?" he asks after entering on his side and just before turning on the ignition. Ellen suggests they stop for a coffee.

SISTERHOOD

H
ey beauty," Ellen whispers, quietly entering the room where Sandy is staying, "look what I brought." She holds up two paper cups. "Dark roast—and baklava—but the dessert is in my purse right now. We can have it later." Ellen sets the cups on the bedside table, beside a full mug of now-cold coffee, and kisses Sandy's forehead. "You've been through a lot. Too much for one girlfriend."

"Elly?" Sandy hopes she isn't dreaming again.

"Of course it's me, sweetie." Ellen straightens Sandy's bangs, the way she saw Sandy's Baba do it years ago when they were kids. "When Kyle called and said you needed a friend, I jumped on the first bus here."

"Kyle called you?"

"Yes, he did."

"I'm glad," Sandy whispers. The two hug and on cue Ellen feels compelled to tease. "Beautiful one, you need a bath." They laugh. "I can either run a bath for you or give you a sponge bath. Your choice."

"You can run one in a bit," Sandy suggests. Glancing around the Victorian-style guest room, Ellen spies a pack of smokes in the bag Kyle gave her, along with some bath bombs and Sandy's other clothes. She suggests they head outside—not so much to smoke, but she figures Sandy probably hasn't been outdoors since the incident.

As the two sit on Joe's front deck, Sandy marvels at the caress of warm sunshine on her face. The breeze smells of fresh rainfall, along with the sweet tang of freshly planted crops and the newly shaved grass of summer.

"I don't need to know details. I'm just glad you are here and safe." Ellen pats Sandy's hand. Simultaneously, each takes a drag from their cigarette. Ellen rarely smokes but today she makes an exception. For the first time since the horrific experience, Sandy smiles and attempts to run her fingers through her hair. Ellen notices the tangles. "You need a brush, honey. I'll do it for you when we get back in the house. You're okay now. You're strong and whether you know it or not, you have all of our strengths, combined."

Ellen points toward the inside of the home. "We all love you Sandy, and want to see you get well. But I think the first thing you need to do is get out of bed. I took a week off, you know. I'm staying with you, at your apartment, won't take no for an answer. If you need me to stay longer, I will. It's time for you to regroup. There's been way too much going on for just one person to handle. I'm just sorry I didn't come sooner."

Sandy knows what Ellen is speaking of. Ellen had suggested that she visit right after the breakup with Blue. Sandy was adamant it wasn't necessary. In retrospect, maybe it was necessary. But that doesn't really matter at the moment. What is important is that Ellen is here now

Sandy starts to sob, confiding that she is still afraid to go back to her place because James might find her. Ellen replies, "You know what? I am guessing that guy's been walking around more afraid than you these past few hours. I mean, think about it—he got caught— there are witnesses. Not only that, you got it on tape, didn't you?"

Sandy nods, wiping a tear. She ceases to cry and her breathing returns to normal as Ellen continues. "He's the one on the run, now,

Sandy. Not you. You didn't do anything wrong." Again, Ellen pledges her support, with both women knowing that once Sandy leaves the sanctuary of Joe's, another ordeal for her lays just around the corner. Sandy will have to go to the police with the information. There will likely be a trial, where she'll have to testify, reliving the terror.

The least of her concerns is how her boss will react, knowing she assigned herself to something so dangerous. It is a great story. Hermanson will be a little disappointed at her lack of common sense, but proud that she was so eager to excel.

"So, where are the tapes now?" Ellen asks. It takes Sandy a moment to respond. "You mean the video tapes? I'm sure Kyle has made many copies by now. I am also guessing he's hidden them in many different safe locations." She pauses to take a long drag from her smoke. "But there is an audio tape he hasn't copied yet. I still have it."

"Where?"

Sandy tells Ellen about the small tape recorder. It has not yet been removed from the small purse. "I haven't found the strength to take it out and listen yet."

"Did you want to listen now?" Ellen asks.

"May as well. We've come this far." Ellen volunteers to retrieve the purse from the guest room. It allows Sandy time for quiet reflection. She marvels at how good it feels to stretch out her arms, reminiscent of a bird in flight. She closes her eyes, takes a deep breath and counts her blessings once more. There are so many.

When Ellen returns Joe is with her, carrying a tray that has two bowls of tomato soup with a side of bannock. "Glad to see you outside, Sandy." He smiles, setting a bowl on the old wooden patio table in front of her. "Eat first. We can all listen to that terrible thing together once you've regained a bit of strength."

"I know you're okay," he continues, "but is your friend on her time?" Ellen hears the remark but doesn't know that "on your time" is an Aboriginal way to inquire if a woman is menstruating.

So Sandy pipes up, "Hey Elle, Auntie Flo visiting you right now?"
Ellen laughs, with a shake of her head indicating no.

Joe doesn't quite follow but nods. "Good. We can all take part in a smudging ceremony then before we listen. Ask the spirits for strength too." He turns to Sandy. "You have an auntie coming to visit too, as well as Ellen?"

The women belly-laugh, throwing their heads back and clapping their hands. Ellen explains by repeating a story to Joe. "I mean no disrespect laughing like that. It's just so funny because it reminds me of an old roommate. I can still see him, heading out to play tennis and wanting to know if I'll join him. I tell him I can't because I am expecting my Auntie Flo to show up anytime now. Next thing I know he's at the door with a packed suitcase, so I ask him where he's going. He tells me he'll stay with a friend for a few days while my auntie visits, to give us some privacy. I didn't have the heart to laugh out loud, nor did I have the heart to admit that 'Auntie Flo' means *having my period*. I let my roommate leave and had the place to myself for three days!"

It is Joe's turn to laugh. He isn't embarrassed, commenting, "I've never heard it said like that before. Learn something new every day."

Once Sandy finishes holding her ribs, she has to thank her friends. "I haven't laughed like that in such a long time. It's perfect, given what we have to do. Thank you." The comic relief lessens the dread, which festers like an infected wound. Ellen slowly removes the small tape recorder from Sandy's purse. Sandy stutters, "I don't know if I can do this."

"You have to, Sandy," Joe reasons, a look of concern on his face. "They are just words on a tape recorder now. The danger has passed." Sandy wipes a speck of nervous sweat from her upper lip before hitting the play button. Joe lights a braid of sweetgrass, fanning the smoke toward the women and praying in his language.

They listen but do not offer commentary. What's on the tape is too dramatic and sad to respond to immediately. It is like watching something die. The sombre mood is worsened as Joe begins to tremble and shake as if experiencing a seizure, his face turning the colour of cold granite. It is his turn to travel out of body, the spirits physically taking him to the place in time where the crime occurred. He is transported to under that bridge. He cries out and slumps to the floor. Sandy and Ellen stand there, not knowing what to do. Their logical response is to call an ambulance.

That's when Amos shows up. "Don't worry"—he has a look of concern but it's clear he's not panicked—"he's with the spirits right now. They are showing him something. He'll be safe."

WITNESS

I hope she's okay." Kyle keeps repeating the words to himself as he drives, praying the prairie wind will carry thoughts of positive energy to Sandy. After dropping Ellen at Joe's, he somehow knows that the time has come for Sandy to listen to the tape recorder. He knows it will sicken her, just as watching and making copies of the videos nauseated him. Now he is going back to the scene of the crime. Sandy's time away from the office is coming to an end too. Hermanson expects her back just after the long weekend. Kyle knows he will need a story to be produced soon. He has already shared with Hermanson bits and pieces of what happened.

In order to recreate the events as a narrative, Kyle decides to get some shots from under the bridge. He drives toward the lonely spot along that grid road. Once back at the scene, he fastens the top button on his jacket and turns up the collar before opening the back door to retrieve his camera. Kyle makes the sign of the cross, walking toward a place that seems barren and sad, like the land itself is still weeping, having been witness to what happened there. The creek is grey. Kyle imagines he sees thin shards of ice forming at the water's edge, giving the appearance of tears. He listens to the cracking sound of cold grass under his boots as he makes his way down the embankment and rounds the heavy creosote-stained beams that lead under the bridge.

"Don't come any closer!" The menacing command startles Kyle. "I said, stay where you are!" The command repeats. It is James and his weapon is drawn.

"Whoa. Settle down," Kyle speaks quietly, amazing himself that there is no flutter in his voice. He is terrified at having stumbled upon this desperate soul. He wasn't expecting to see anyone, let alone James. *He's going to kill me*—the words keep rolling over in his mind. Kyle slowly sets his camera on the ground, keeping an eye on James' shaking hand holding the gun. James lowers the barrel of the pistol.

"You here looking for me?" His words are flat and absent of emotion.

"No," Kyle manages, trying to maintain his composure and not show fear.

"Because I don't mind if you are here looking for me." He makes eye contact and Kyle notices James' wild expression has disappeared, replaced by a darkness that gives his eyes the look of something dead. James makes a request. "You pick that thing up," motioning with the gun toward the camera. "You'll want to record this."

It takes only moments for Kyle to place the camera back on his shoulder, but in that time he can only think to pray. He prays for safety. He offers prayers of gratitude for having lived a life filled with love and rich in experience. He says prayers for James that his fury will diminish. He says, *Please help*, more times than he can count. Finally, he has completed doing as he is told, picking up the camera and placing it on his shoulder.

"Now, turn that thing on." Kyle hits the play button and focuses just in time to record James putting the barrel of the gun to his temple and pulling the trigger.

Kyle has no recollection of what passed from the time of James' suicide to being held by Sandy at the side of the grid road. Kyle had somehow made his way up to the road and called for help. He is still in shock, zombie-like and without memory. Sandy is there because of Joe. After listening to the tape, Joe was hit by a premonition. After going limp and experiencing a shortness of breath, he murmured, "It's Kyle, he needs our help," explaining that they all need to get into his truck right now and drive to the bridge. "Kyle is in trouble," Joe repeated.

By the time they arrived, a squad of police cars was already at the scene along with two ambulances. Sandy finds Kyle wandering near his truck, muttering gibberish. She grabs a blanket from the back seat of Joe's vehicle and wraps it around him, whispering reassurances to Kyle that everything will be all right—the same as he did for her just days ago.

DEFINING MOMENT

The media doesn't cover suicides—not even of police officers—so the ordeal goes unnoticed by most, as do the circumstances leading up to James taking his own life. It won't be that way for long. Sandy knows why James shot himself, and so does Lyle Hermanson once she explains. Hermanson doesn't react the way Kyle and Sandy first guessed he might, which would be to expect a news report immediately. He gives her several days to check the legalities of the tape recordings and follow up on hearsay, which is what led her out onto that street corner and into danger.

"We can air the story when it's ready. No rush, no one else will have it," Hermanson says. He is kind, compassionate and well aware that Sandy is still fragile. They chat and then set the air-date for Wednesday, July 10. It allows a few days for news promos to run, highlighting to viewers that this exclusive is worth tuning in for.

Joe tells Sandy that her bravery has elevated her to the status of warrior in the eyes of their people. He's planned a special stew and bannock dinner tonight in her honour. He also plans to explain in detail what to expect of a certain sacred ceremony.

Joe is planning a naming ceremony for Sandy that will be organized in the days to come. Sandy's never been to any ceremony like this and she's keen on learning what she needs to do to prepare. But mostly, she looks forward to the chance to wash her spirit clean. Too many negative things have been happening. If that bad energy somehow attaches itself to her, she knows the ceremony Joe is planning will be the place to get rid of it.

Sandy wants to suggest to Joe that Kyle attend as well. What he's seen is soul-damaging as well, watching someone kill himself. She wants Kyle to feel the protection of this ceremony too, as well as to benefit from and the prayers of those around him. Kyle's been seeing a counsellor with the employee assistance plan offered at work. She figures it will help with any logical explanation he may be seeking, but Sandy knows turning to Aboriginal culture is where he'll find what he needs to help him through this period.

Wednesday the tenth arrives quickly. When the story airs, it has an instant impact. Viewers call to say they had their suspicions about dirty cops as well, but no facts to back up their claims. Prostitutes call to confirm. "It happened to me too," they say, but are too afraid to repeat it on camera. Sandy is proud to have broken some code of silence but she is still shaken that people have lost their lives because of it.

The days that follow are mayhem for the police department as it is inundated with inquiries and interview requests. Chief Gavin Draves agrees to none of the requests, instead arranging a news conference where all media are invited to attend. The news conference is being held in one of the large gyms within the police service building. Sitting under hot spotlights that have been set up by no less than twenty television crews from all over the country, Draves sweats profusely. Radio and newspaper reporters have set up their microphones too. Reporters were asked to submit their questions before the news conference starts. But in true form, the journalists abandon protocol and start shouting queries the moment Draves gets seated.

"How many people knew about these sex rides outside of the city before the story aired on TV last week, Chief?"

Draves doesn't have time to answer before another reporter yells, "How long has this type of thing been going on?"

"How widespread has it been? Did you know about it personally, Chief Draves?"

Draves ignores all questions. He reads a short prepared statement then is escorted out of the room by uniformed officers. Sandy is dumbfounded as she rereads the statement over and over—seeing nothing in it that gives her hope.

In response to the investigation by a local media outlet, our department has found there has been no wrongdoing by our general force. The footage released by the media outlet in question, and a subsequent investigation into another young woman's claims, reveals that the allegations are limited to two members of the police. Those specific members are the late Constable James Leroy and his partner Constable Edward Dufresne. The police service has not received complaints or had suspicions about this type of violation by police officers until the report was aired on a local TV station. Constable Leroy is now deceased. Constable Dufresne has since resigned his duties as a police officer. This file has been handed over to the Royal Canadian Mounted Police, and it is now up to that policing agent to determine how to proceed in this matter. If you have any information regarding this matter, please contact the department.

PICKING UP THE PIECES

Sandy receives an invitation extended by the crew immediately after the news program is over. "Let's celebrate. Last one to The Dodger is a rotten egg." Jason, the production assistant for the news, makes a point of specifically asking Sandy. "Hey, listen. I know you might be busy tonight, but please join us. Just for one. You're the lady of the hour after all."

Sandy is grateful but chooses to decline. "Thanks, but I can't. I've got to visit my dad tonight." She is referring to Joe, who has told her he will traditionally adopt her as his daughter at the naming ceremony—a type of adoption that comes without legalities but with a binding of hearts that is even stronger.

Her first stop before visiting Joe is to pick up Ellen, who has stayed in the city to offer support to Sandy since the incident. Ellen and Kyle have been getting very close; it warms Sandy's heart that her two best friends are getting along so well. Traumatic situations can either destroy relationships or pull people closer together, and she's grateful it is the latter that has manifested. Now Ellen is walking toward tradition too, even though like Kyle she is not Aboriginal. Sandy asked Joe if it is okay to include Ellen in tonight's visit.

"Certainly," he agrees, saying Sandy and Ellen are more like sisters than friends. "Family is family and is always included." With that, Joe gives an answer to Sandy's question about including Kyle, even though she hasn't yet spoken it aloud. "And make sure to tell Kyle to come. He is welcome tonight."

The drive over to Ellen's new apartment takes only minutes. "I'm excited and nervous," she explains, stepping into Sandy's Jeep. "What exactly is going to happen?" The drive out to the reserve doesn't take long, but there is enough time for Sandy to explain that Joe plans to hold a naming ceremony for her soon. "But first he needs to meet and describe the process of what's expected beforehand. That's the reason for tonight's dinner. Plus, Joe probably just wants the company," Sandy smiles.

She does her best to define a naming ceremony. "He tells me that a spirit name is one place to go when I need strength and guidance. I sure could have used it a while back." Sandy pauses. "Joe says I've been carrying my name since the beginning of time. He told me an example of the deer person. The teachings say the fawn is gentle and compassionate when faced with anger and hate. The fawn has a deep belief that love can overcome anything and that's how she reacts even when others try to harden her. It is that gentleness that allows deer people to touch hearts."

"Wow, Sandy. Sounds like quite a responsibility." Ellen is fascinated.

It's at this point, Sandy admits, that she's not sure that she carries the spirit of the deer. She figures Joe is more likely using himself as an example in describing a deer. He's the one who is always gentle and compassionate. "He says because I'm visited so many times by the black bear maybe that's my animal spirit guide. We'll find out during the ceremony." Sandy asks Ellen for a smoke. The two light up and continue driving in contented silence. They've quit smoking in theory only, as their thoughts wander in different directions.

Sandy feels gratified to be a part of Joe's family. There is so much she wants and needs to learn. Her questioning of Joe is relentless, always prefaced with the words, "Joe, I hope you don't mind me asking, but…" He always answers fully, in descriptive detail and with great patience and kindness toward her. Joe's attention to her has bothered some on the rez—the worst exhibition of that happened just before the summer solstice. Sandy gets a little sad at the memory, recalling the upsetting row.

EVER SICK

andy had dropped off a photography book for Amos at the gas bar because Amos had told Sandy he'd been trying his hand at taking pictures. Amos was thrilled, trading a pack of smokes for it. "On the house," he smiled. Sandy felt good to be accepted by him.

It was after that delivery that the verbal assault happened. As Sandy headed back to her Jeep, stinging words were coughed up like blood by a hard-edged-looking woman. Sandy had seen her before, smirking and sneering, privately nicknaming her the Lardass. It was a nasty thought but she was so vulgar and brash that Sandy found it appropriate to give her a nickname that reflected the offensiveness of her behaviour. The Lardass always pulled her hair back into a greasy ponytail. She rarely smiled. Sandy couldn't understand the woman's intolerance.

The Lardass was foul, yelling from across the gas bar parking lot, "Who do you think you are? White girl! You think you're better than me because you work on the TV? You think you're smarter than me because you wear fancy clothes and drive a fancy truck? You think you're one of us now?" Spit had dried in the corner of the Lardass's mouth. "Well, you're not one of us and you never will be. You're just a wannabe like those German tourists. They dress up in powwow regalia too! But they don't know the first thing about bein' an Indian because they're not, and neither are you!"

The attack provoked tears. That woman clearly wanted to take away Sandy's power and make Sandy doubt her own journey toward self, her culture and her people. The Lardass had Sandy right where she wanted and kept ranting. "That's right. You're a disgrace. A joke. You were put into that white world because you're not worthy of being an Indian! And now I hear you are making an outfit. Gonna dance at the fall powwow? Well, let me tell you, it ain't right. You're not ever supposed to dance."

Sandy said a prayer, saddened that the wrath of racism she'd so often encountered from white people was now coming from her own. Her own Aboriginal people saying she doesn't belong?

"You're no dancer. You think that just braiding your hair makes you an Indian. You're an apple. Hell! You don't even know how to show proper respect for an Elder. You're always askin' question after question of Joe Bush Sr. Don't even know that you have to offer tobacco to an Elder before you ask a question! Don't even know! Don't even care!"

Suddenly the woman's Gatling-like assault stopped as quickly as it began. The next thing Sandy knew, Joe's hand was on her shoulder. He told the woman that family doesn't need to make an offering. "Sandy is my daughter." With that the Lardass slithered away as Joe motioned that they go back inside. "Have a coffee," he said. Once there, he gave Sandy a red lollipop and said, "You have to quit smoking, my girl, not good for you."

Sandy could feel her anxiety lessen once inside the gas bar. Amos poured them a coffee while Joe attempted to make sense of what just happened. He talked about jealousy, and how it is the most destructive of all the emotions. He called it a mental illness that is more destructive than hate. He shared a secret, saying that this woman had only recently returned to the community and to the culture herself.

She too had been removed from the rez as a child. Joe explained it was because her parents drank.

"She was probably treated badly in the foster care system. She may have been called bad names and was brainwashed into believing she's no good. I know you have heard it too. You see Sandy, if we believe those lies, it will kill us." He explained that was what was happening to the woman. "Maybe she is still ashamed of her parents. Maybe she is still ashamed of the colour of her skin. Maybe she still believes what some of those hateful people said to her. She hasn't had anyone to teach her the old ways. Hasn't asked or tried to meet anyone since moving back here. She just keeps to herself. That can cause damage. And now she drinks and it makes her feel guilty. Then you came into the community Sandy, and you are not so ashamed of yourself, not like her anyway. You have accomplished a lot by yourself and that makes her mad."

Sandy's thoughtful excursion ends just as Ellen finishes crushing out her smoke, breaking their comfortable and familiar silence. "Penny for your thoughts."

Sandy offers a short pause followed by an explanation. "I'm just grateful, Elly, that's all. Sitting here and giving thanks to Creator, for new wisdom, new insights and new experiences. But mostly I'm saying thanks for helping me find my new family. That includes you too. I'm going to start introducing you as my sister. After all, you have been like my sister ever since we were kids. I love you."

DUCK'S FLY MOON

It's been more than a month since the stew and bannock feast. Joe suggested they wait a few weeks before holding her naming ceremony. "Best to wait until the next full moon is nigh to arrange for your ceremony. The full moon is one time when a woman's power is at her strongest." Sandy likes the explanation and the timing. It marks a new direction in a new season. Autumn has always been her favourite. She loves the symphonic sound of geese flying overhead and the sound of crisp leaves being raked and piled high. She loves the earthy smell of damp moss and rotting leaves. She even loves the feel of the cold north wind. Autumn always signifies great change for Sandy.

Today, a lone bald eagle flies directly over her vehicle as she drives. It's going to be a good day. She smiles to herself, recalling an Aboriginal teaching that Joe mentioned. "The bald eagle watches over the spirit of Aboriginal peoples because it flies higher than any other bird. It is able to communicate between the Earth and the Spirit World." Sandy cherishes those words, which Joe spoke just before giving her an eagle feather. It's hanging from her windshield for now. Sandy remembers other gifts of autumn from years gone by.

At age five, it was autumn when Sandy found Andy, the stray dog, who stayed with her for the next twelve years.

At age twelve, it was autumn when her time began, signifying her passing from childhood into womanhood.

At age twenty-four, it was autumn when she got her first full-time job in television, signalling a major advancement in career—her journey into being a storyteller.

Now it is nearing autumn again, and Sandy is excited about the possibilities. Her summer has been fantastic. She found her way home and she learned to dance. These are her thoughts, and they make her smile as she heads into a mall in the city's west end.

She feels revitalized, here to pick up some items for tonight's feast and ceremony. Her positive energy prompts her to walk through the large mall to the grocery store near the back of the building, instead of parking close by like she'd normally do.

The feast tonight honours the Duck's Fly Moon, she is told. She plans to make potato salad, knowing it mixes old traditions with the new. She longs to invite her parents, the ones who adopted her, but decides against. They won't understand and this is her world, not theirs. She gives thanks that they raised her with love. It is that love, the nourishing memory of warmth that includes her Baba, that allows her to move forward.

As a child, Sandy remembers giggling, glowing and absolutely loving to watch Baba whip up a batch of potato salad, all the while talking to Sandy about life. "Boy," Baba would say, "the garden this summer is good. Look at all of these potatoes! So, tell me sweetie, how was school today?"

Baba then roasted up an entire head of garlic, not missing a beat and taking in every word Sandy spoke about school. Baba washed and peeled and cooked the spuds, cooling them and sprinkling them with vinegar "for extra flavour." Frying up the kolbassa was also part of the recipe. "The secret family recipe," she'd chide. "My Baba taught me how to do this. Now I am teaching you. It comes from a long line." Sandy loved Baba's potato salad. It tasted heavenly, which was little wonder considering how much fun the two always had as one prepared while the other watched. Both laughed. They weren't just making food.

Sandy hopes those who come to tonight's feast will also enjoy the special salad as much as she always had. She figures Baba will probably be with her in spirit. It makes Sandy smile. She's taken a few more days off work, wanting to fully enjoy this significant point in her life.

As she nears the food court, she catches a glimpse of love and kindness that causes teary emotion. An old couple is sitting for an early dinner. The old woman is in a wheelchair, wearing a purple dress with a red brooch on her lapel. The old man who is with her is dressed in overalls and a denim jacket. Sandy doesn't know what is wrong with the old woman, but she can't feed herself. Sandy is over-whelmed watching the two. It all starts with a single french fry.

The old man smiles at his wife and gently puts a fry up to her mouth. The old woman gazes back with a look of trust and love. The wrinkles surrounding her mouth widen as she opens it to receive the fry. This dance is a regular part of everyday life they both accept. Sandy doesn't have a tissue in her purse and has to use her sleeve to wipe away a tear, thinking, *That's the kind of love I want. The kind that's real.* She gives a silent prayer of thanks for having just witnessed such beauty and continues toward the grocery store. Thoughts of the old couple stay with her. But the daydreaming catches her off guard for the harsh reality staring at her across the produce aisle.

As Sandy stands there minding her own business and selecting the perfect, firm head of garlic for her salad, she feels a presence—a sad one that gives her the chills. She feels compelled to look up. After four months of no contact, she spots Blue. He is standing near some mangoes and staring directly at Sandy. She freezes.

"Sandy. How have you been?" He doesn't wait for a response. "There's so much I've been wanting to say to you, but are you okay?"

"Blue." It is the only word she is able to speak, as though a dagger of loneliness lunged in from somewhere, slitting her vocal chords and preventing her from speaking further. Tears well up in her brown eyes and she grabs a napkin from one of the fruit sampler trays. The alternative is to use her sleeve again. She turns away from him and quickly heads for the exit door.

Blue follows as Sandy almost sprints through the mall and out to the parking lot. Just as she is sliding into her Jeep, he grabs her arm, the same way he did the first night they met. Back then it was to prevent her from falling on ice. This time it is to prevent her from falling away from him. Sandy says nothing.

"I need to explain what happened," he says. His eyes hold a look of genuine concern. Blue says he's tried calling her many times since finding the key she left behind. "I tried you at home and at work. I kept hoping you would answer. You didn't. And this is too important to just leave a message. I even dropped by your place one night. I guess I should've tried harder, but I was scared." As he'd done before, Blue leaves the most important piece of information for last. "Heidi is pregnant." The words come out with embarrassment and shame.

He goes on to tell Sandy that he recently got a phone call from Heidi. He describes her as being hysterical, calling him an irresponsible asshole. She had just found out that she was pregnant. "And this little bastard is yours!" she hissed. Blue admits he still isn't convinced the child is his, but that she's already five months pregnant. Heidi demanded money, yelling, "I'm having an abortion, you fucker!"

"So, I wrote her a cheque and sent it off." "And James," Blue says. "I don't know what to say about that."

It is irrelevant now. It's at that precise moment that Sandy is distracted by a presence other than Blue. He keeps talking. Sandy can only hear the roar of Mugwah. It makes her feel faint, like she is short of breath and drowning. Although she can't see her bear, she knows Mugwah is nearby. She can feel his spirit, as real as feeling sunlight on her face. Is it a warning? What is he trying to say? If it is a warning, will Sandy finally listen?

IN SINISTER COMPANY

She hurries into her truck, starts the engine and drives. From the rear-view mirror, she watches Blue get smaller and smaller until he disappears. It is excruciating, driving off and leaving him. Blue stands there, gawking, but takes no action, the same as he has done before. He doesn't follow, his inaction reminiscent of another time, with Blue content to witness misery and doing nothing to stop it.

Good thing the traffic is not heavy today. Sandy isn't paying proper attention, driving aimlessly until she finds herself at the outskirts of the city. Even though she had planned to earlier, Sandy doesn't make her way out to the reserve. She doesn't make it to the ceremony. She is too badly shaken by this meeting with Blue, and the bombshell that Heidi is pregnant. She swallows tears, feeling nothing but pain. Exiting city limits, the memory of Blue driving away in his patrol car races to the forefront of her thoughts. It spurs a moment of terror, reliving the night James drove her out of town and Blue offered no help.

An hour of driving goes by and her breathing is still erratic. By the second hour she has finished an entire pack of smokes. It is only in the third hour that Sandy realizes she's listened to the same tape over and over again. She's always liked the song, "Riders on the Storm" by the Doors. But now it brings with it a negative association. She pops the tape out of the deck and throws it out the window. She watches through the rear-view mirror as the cassette bounces off the pavement. Smashed. Ruined. It reminds Sandy of her relationship with Blue. She decides to make her way back to the city.

The sun is just setting and the sky has turned a glorious shade of pink. "Red sky at night," she mutters to herself just before lighting up one last emergency cigarette she'd tucked away in the glove box. As she reaches over to grab it, Sandy catches a glimpse of herself in the mirror and it frightens her. There are black streaks around her eyes and down her cheeks. Her eyes are swollen and red like she's been beaten up. Sandy needs strength. Direction. *I should call Joe. I should head out to his place. They are expecting me.* But she decides against it, heading home instead.

Once there, she lights a few candles that smell of cinnamon, enjoying the softness of their flickering light. The telephone rings. Sandy decides to let the machine pick it up. The voice on the other end makes her tremble one more time: "Hi Sandy. It's Blue. Listen, I don't know if you're home, but seeing you again today made me realize I don't want to lose you from my life. I can't. We need to talk. Please, call me when you get this message. I love you, my sweet angel." He hangs up.

Hearing Blue say those words is torture. Then, like an idiot, she decides to listen to the slurring of other bad spirits calling. She's been protected from them since meeting Joe and Amos and Kyle. Sandy hasn't touched alcohol in weeks. Tonight though, she figures, who gives a shit? She opens the cupboard. Still standing there to greet her are three old acquaintances. Merlot. Zinfandel. Smirnoff. Waiting for her return.

REDEMPTION

I t is the next morning as Sandy wakes up on her couch. Her eyes are sticky and she notices that the candles burned down and must have gone out on their own. It frightens her to know that if anything were set aflame at night, she wouldn't have known. She passed out. Sandy envisions a newspaper headline: "Native reporter dies in house fire." *If that did happen, who would even care?* But she's feeling sorry for herself. One of the people who cares is sleeping in the other room.

Upon hearing Sandy stir on the couch, Ellen emerges from the bedroom. When Sandy failed to show up at the ceremony, Ellen panicked and went to check her apartment with the key Sandy had given her. She arrived to find her friend passed out, so Ellen decided to put out the candles and spend the night.

"Make you some tea, my friend?" Ellen knows not to ask what's upset her. When she is able, Sandy will tell her.

"Sure." Sandy starts to cry and forces herself off the couch. A terrible dizziness strikes and Sandy knows it's best for her to head straight for the bathroom. After getting rid of the toxic waste by forcing a gag reflex and throwing up, Sandy checks herself in the mirror. She barely recognizes her reflection. Her face is puffy, her hair dishevelled. Sandy starts to cry again, out of self-pity. This is not the life she wants.

She knows that insecurity and anger demolish the spirit. They are powerful but ugly and destructive emotions. She hears a knock at the bathroom door, interrupting her malaise. "Sweetie, I have your tea."

Sandy opens the door. "Oh, Elly, what's wrong with me?" She takes a sip of tea and tells Ellen that a long, hot shower is in order.

As the water cleanses her body, she is honest with herself for the first time. At least the alcohol has shamed her into that. Sandy realizes that right from the start, things have not been right with Blue. It's always been a challenge. Some disruptive force has always been present and shows up to cause problems just as the two seem to connect. Why?

There's always been something urging her to leave Blue, emotionally, but she never fully listened. A torrent of tears blends in with droplets from the shower. She watches with a heavy heart as a whirlpool forms before the water makes its way down the drain.

After her shower, she goes to the answering machine and pops out the audiocassette, putting it in her special place. It is a wooden box that contains her memories of Blue. There are movie ticket stubs, photos and receipts from restaurants. She wants to keep his words now too. "I love you, my sweet angel." It might be the last time she hears him say that.

Sandy calls Joe. He answers, "Sandy, good to hear your voice. Where did you go last night?"

STRENGTH AND HONOUR

Ellen thinks it's a good idea for Sandy to visit Joe, but she insists on driving. There may still be alcohol in Sandy's system. Before heading out of town, Sandy insists on stopping off at a French bakery that is on the way. Over these past weeks, she's introduced Joe to a pastry called *tuiles*, a sweet flat bread coated in soft artificial sweetener that resembles icing sugar. Joe has developed a taste for them, saying they remind him of fancy bannock. She decides to pick up a box. Ellen chooses to bring a colourful fruit torte. Sandy orders the desserts and picks up two black coffees to go, mostly out of habit.

When the ladies arrive at Joe's they are greeted by the hearty smell of an ever-present pot of moose stew, along with his smile. "I was hoping you'd bring those," Joe says as Sandy hands him the box of tuiles. As they sit, eating the stew and then the pastry, Joe talks to Sandy about kindness. He makes it clear that kindness can never be extended to another unless that's how you treat yourself first. He makes the same point about forgiveness and honesty. Joe calls them "strong and beautiful gifts from Creator. That's how we build."

He places no blame on her lack of judgment the night before. He tells Sandy not to worry, the naming ceremony can be rescheduled. "Nothing is black and white. You can ask for guidance, but the decision is always yours, Sandy. In your heart, you know what's right. So you make a decision. And whatever that decision is, it is right—because it's your decision. I want to make the point, though, that while it is nice to be in love with someone, it's better to be in love with life."

It's hard for her to tell Joe what she has done. It makes her think of being in a church confessional, but worse. She tells him everything. Joe remains silent until she is finished talking.

"We all make mistakes," he says. "You know when people ask me how old I am, I tell them that I was born twenty-five years ago. That's when I quit drinking. So I guess I'm only twenty-five. I know what you're feeling, my girl. I drank right up until I was forty-five. It wasn't until I stopped that I found out who I really am."

Joe talks about how everyone handles stress and problems differently. "Sometimes we make the right choices. Sometimes we don't. Sometimes we think that drowning our problems in alcohol might work. It never does. I'm just glad you didn't wait until you're forty-five before making the choice to call me." He tells her it is our scars that define who we are. She prays that her scars aren't so deep that they prevent her from building on what she's recently come to know. Confusion is the roadblock at her crossroads. If she truly wants to grow, embracing Aboriginal teachings and traditions, she'll have to leave parts of her past behind. She already knows which parts, and prays for the resolve to do what is necessary.

Joe reads her thoughts. Before she leaves, he gives Sandy some herbs wrapped in cloth. He tells her to put them under her pillow. "It will help you to sleep, my girl. As for your decision, I will talk to the others. They will know how to help." Joe always offers lessons within lessons. He hands Sandy an eagle feather. "I know you long to dance, to make it a part of your life. Wear this in your hair as an expression of the strength and pride you carry." He points with his lips toward the wooden box that sits near the old wood-burning stove. Draped over the top is a colourful Pendleton blanket, a gift that someone has given to Joe. The box is where Joe keeps his medicines and other important items. "My pipe is in there."

"I know that," she says.

"I never told you how I got my pipe." Joe tells Sandy a story about how when he was a student of culture, a Gifted One took him under his direction. "It took a long time and plenty of patience, paying attention, watching and listening. But mostly, I needed to understand why we do what we do and why it is important. That Old One gave me my first pipe and explained the responsibility that comes with it."

Joe seems to lighten as a smile surfaces, remembering that moment as though it happened yesterday. The thought nourishes his spirit, the way memories should, making him appear as though he is a young man again. "He gave me another gift that day too." Joe pauses. "He said, 'You cannot smoke this pipe if you are going to pray in English.' The pipe comes with ancient knowledge that only understands the Old Language. He told me to learn to speak Dakota so the Spirits will understand." Joe explains that he then devoted the following winter to learning. "I'd walk for miles, repeating the words again and again. I sought the counsel of Elders. I listened. I learned. By springtime, I was ready to smoke." Joe's eyes glisten with pride. There is no need for further explanation.

Sandy understands that if she is to dance with the feather he offers, she first has to learn to speak Cree. Her own language. Her identity. "Thank you, Father, kinaskomitin. Kisakihitin." She wipes a tear from her eye, hugging the Old Man for sharing his teaching. She takes the feather from his hand, holding it high in the air for the spirits to see. The roar of Mugwah sounds from afar and gives her hope. She says a prayer.

EPILOGUE:
BEARSKIN ROBE WOMAN—MASKWAYANAKOHP-ISKWIW (OCTOBER, 2015)

Thirty years have passed as though they were thirty days. The dark times Sandy travelled through have been replaced by light and admiration. She's found strength and direction over the years, having mostly left the chaos of Blue behind—except for the memories. Her hands are old now but not frail, reaching for a mug of mint tea, wihkaskwapoy. She doesn't buy the leaves from the store anymore. The wild spearmint grows in abundance in the marshy area just down the road from her farmhouse.

Beside her mug today sits Sandy's wooden box of memories. She'd forgotten all about it. It was stored at the bottom of an old cardboard box filled with video tapes in the crawlspace under her garage. Sandy needed the old tapes for tonight. The industry hasn't used video tape in years and it's been that long since she even remembers packing that little wooden box as a reminder. A lot has changed since she started that collection. If it wasn't for the wisdom she found back then, in making mistakes, who knows where she may have ended up?

Sandy's hair is silver in colour now, the same colour that Joe's was when they first met. She glances in the mirror, brushing a few loose strands back behind her ear. It is important for her to be able to prominently display one of the many gifts that she's been given. All these years, Sandy has taken great care of the beaded/quilled earrings she received from the Spirit World, from her Cree mother, at her first powwow. She wears them only on the most special of occasions. Today is one of them.

A feast is being held in her honour tonight. Her own Aboriginal community and the film and television industry are the hosts, with the purpose being to bestow a Lifetime Achievement Award timed with Sandy's retirement. After a number of years in TV news, she had turned her focus to making films. Instead of just reporting on what other people were saying and doing, she found that by producing films she could speak up too. She found her own way of telling her people's stories properly and fully: with reverence and without stereotype.

As she opens the wooden box now, it makes her think about the many times she's given thanks for having met Blue years ago. If she hadn't, who knows? She would likely have never moved. She may have ended up following her initial dream, her first idea of success, which was to pursue her television career. Maybe Sandy would be working in Toronto, or in a US market; she'd been offered the opportunity on more than one occasion. Maybe she'd be lost in a haze of alcohol and unanswered questions, like several people she knows who followed that path. Maybe she'd be sad about this particular day, thinking that retirement from a profession marks the end. But that's not how she sees it; it is the start of something else.

Sandy has been moving toward becoming an Elder for several years now, and her teachers are some of the best. The most influential teacher in her life has continued to be Joe. "No, if it hadn't been for meeting Blue, I probably would never have changed my life at all," Sandy says directly to Joe, whom she feels is with her in spirit. She smiles at the thought that maybe he and Baba are sharing a joke over tea in Heaven.

Kyle is retired now as well. But Kyle has taken up still photography as a hobby: pictures of the land. He excels at it and is excited about his next exhibit happening at a prestigious downtown gallery. Of course Kyle will be sitting at the head table at tonight's celebration, beside Sandy, where he's been since they met. She refers to him as her best friend and still introduces him as her brother, though he is more like a brother-in-law now. Kyle and Ellen married. Sandy is godmother to their three children. She offers a prayer of thanks for Kyle. It is he, the monias, who started her on her journey. Kyle introduced Sandy to Amos. Amos introduced Sandy to Joe. Joe introduced Sandy to herself. Sandy loves that Old Man and misses him dearly.

Joe had a traditional funeral a decade ago. No sadness, just everyone in the community coming together to visit, drum, eat and celebrate life. For four days they gathered around the Sacred Fire that symbolized Joe's life. It is what Joe wanted. He went out with grace and dignity, the same way she always knew him. She still feels him around sometimes. His presence and spirit are strong. And when she does see him—in her dreams—Joe is wearing the moccasins Sandy beaded for him, specifically for his journey to the Spirit World. It's a teaching from Joe: when a person dies, make sure to bead a pair of moccasins for use in the afterlife.

Sandy closes the wooden box. It's time to make her way into the city. Her friends will be waiting at the feast. She grabs her speaking notes from the kitchen table and goes outside, climbing into a newer version of her old Jeep. A huddle of deer watch from a butte beside the road, prompting her to think of Blue again. She knows he's been married and divorced, twice. But in recent years she knew little if anything about Blue. He never went to community feasts, powwows or other gatherings of Aboriginal people, though she secretly always kept an eye out for him. It makes her sad to imagine that after all those years he still hadn't shed his cloak of shame. Carried it with him for a lifetime. He never embraced the community he was born into nor the teachings, as she has. They lived separate lives.

Still, Sandy could never fully let go of Blue. A small part of his memory just wouldn't leave. That's what prompted her into penning him a note a couple of years ago. She had seen an article in the newspaper about him receiving a long-time service award. She wished to congratulate him. But the letter came back unopened. Watching the family of deer scampering toward an open field, she remembers the sad reason he never got to read it.

She can still hear the faint knock at her screen door, opening it to find Constable Johnson standing there. Now retired, he looked the same as he did the day she and Blue made their way to Banff, just older with a few wrinkles and greying hair. Johnson had personally made the trip out to Sandy's farm to deliver the unopened letter along with some bad news. He started by handing over a shoebox that was at the back of Blue's locker.

"Seems over the years, Blue collected newspaper articles about your awards and other achievements," Johnson commented. Sandy took the box and found a dog-eared photo. The colour had faded on this Sulphur Mountain memory but the precious recollection was preserved nonetheless. Then Johnson handed Sandy a more recent newspaper clipping. It was Blue's obituary.

Sandy felt faint and was forced to take a seat on the wicker chair beside the door. "When did this happen?"

Johnson did his best to explain. "It was last month," he said. "I was surprised you didn't show up at his funeral." He told her the date of the accident. She calculated that it was the same week she had been out of the country, on holiday in Greece. Johnson described further. "The crash was just down the road from here." He talked about how Blue had made the trip to her farm many times. "He needed to see you again, so he'd make the drive out to your farmhouse. When he returned to the station, I'd ask him how it went. He always said 'Never made it.' He wasn't quite sure what to say to you, Sandy. He didn't know how you would react. He didn't know if you'd still accept him." Johnson explained that Blue finally faced many of his demons, having gone through the twelve-step program at Alcoholics Anonymous.

"He could just never face you."

To this day Sandy isn't sure how to feel when she remembers hearing the details on how Blue died. She could see it happening in her mind's eye and it has replayed many times in her dreams. On his last trip out to see Sandy, Blue swerved and lost control of his vehicle. He landed upside down in one of the many sloughs that dot the prairie landscape. The electric windows of his truck seized. Blue was trapped and drowned in shallow water. He was trying to avoid hitting a deer that stood in the middle of the road, a magnificent creature with a full set of antlers. "At least," Johnson told her, "that is how a witness described it."

A deer. Sandy remembers Joe's words in describing the teaching behind the Deer Spirit. *The deer, with its gentility and love, has the ability to guide those who are afraid—back to Sacred Mountain, the place where teachings and life begins.* It makes her wonder if maybe that was the day Blue's learning began, by finally returning to Sacred Mountain. She wonders if Joe has become Blue's teacher too. She hopes so. Sandy said a prayer on the day she found out about Blue. She offers another prayer of thanks today.

Gratitude—for too many things to count.

Special thanks to:

My ever-supportive husband Lyle W. Daniels
My baby bears—Jackson, Nahanni and Daniel

Thanks for friendship, love, support and encouragement from:

Richard Van Camp, Kenneth T. Williams, Annelies Poole,
Marie Powell, Mary Lee Morin, Terry & Charlotte Grosz,
Richard Wagamese, Janice Lentowicz, Brenda Montgrand,
Gertie Montgrand, Mae Desnomie, Mike & Emily Meguinis,
Mike Jr. & Violet Meguinis, Tom Cranebear,
Vincent Yellow Old Woman, Carol Todd, Oliver Munar, Dave Rae,
Kathy Daley, Brenda Pander-Stowe, Joely BigEagle-Kequahtooway,
Marc Proulx, Bev Jackson, Tiffany Thiem-Pennell, Marilyn Robak,
Terri Boldt, Heather Avery, Mike Linder, Jamie Hubbs,
Terry & Barb Parker, Jeff & Kathleen Coleclough,
Joan Halberg-Mayer, Davis Daniels, Don & Lynne Copeman,
the Erasmus family and all my friends in Yellowknife and in
Regina Beach, Bruce Spence, Oliver Bird, Garry Courchene,
Dave Pratt, Jamie Goulet, Mae-Louise Campbell, Wanda Wuttunee,
Wendy Prince-Moore

Canada Council for the Arts, the NWT Arts Council,
Saskatchewan Writers' Guild,
Saskatchewan Aboriginal Writers Collective

Carol Daniels is a journalist who became Canada's first Aboriginal woman to anchor a national newscast when she joined CBC Newsworld in 1989. Her work has since earned several awards, including the 2009 National Aboriginal Achievement Award. Her poetry and short fiction have been included in several anthologies. This is her first novel. Find out more at www.caroldaniels.ca.